WRONG WAY HOME

Criminal Delights: Taken

K.A. MERIKAN

Editing by No Stone Unturned

https://www.facebook.com/NoStoneUnturnedEditingServices/

Cover design by

Natasha Snow

http://natashasnow.com/

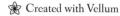 Created with Vellum

– ONE WRONG TURN. ONE RIGHT MAN. –

Colin. Rule-follower. Future doctor. Witness to murder. Captive.

    Taron. Survivalist. Mute. Murderer. Captor.

Like every other weekend, **Colin** is on his way home from university, but he's taunted by the notion that he **never takes risks in life and always follows the beaten path**. On impulse, he decides to take a different route. Just this one time. What he doesn't realize is that it's the last time he has a choice.

    He ends up taking **a detour into the darkest pit of horror, abducted** by a silent, imposing **man with a blood-stained axe**. But what seems like his worst nightmare might just prove to be a path to the kind of freedom Colin never knew existed.

Taron has lived alone for years. **His land, his rules**. He'd given up on company long ago. After all, attachment is a liability. He deals with his problems on his own, but the night he needs to dispose of an enemy, he ends up with a witness to his crime.

The last thing Taron needs is a nuisance of a captive. Colin doesn't deserve death for setting foot on Taron's land, but keeping him isn't optimal either. It's only when he finds out the city boy is gay that an altogether different option arises. One that isn't *right,* yet tempts him every time Colin's pretty eyes glare at him from the cage.

～～～

"When Taron looped the heavy metal collar around the slender neck and closed the padlock, his body throbbed with the excitement of knowing he owned this boy.
Was it wrong? Yes, yes it was.
Was it so, so good? Definitely."

Themes: prepping, alternative lifestyles, disability, crime, loneliness, enemies to lovers, forced proximity, fish out of water, opposites attract, abduction, Stockholm syndrome, family issues

Genre: Dark, thriller M/M romance

Erotic content: Scorching hot, emotional, explicit scenes

Length: ~ 70,000 words (Standalone)

This book is part of CRIMINAL DELIGHTS. Each novel can be read as a standalone and contains a dark M/M romance.

Warning: These books are for adult readers who enjoy stories where lines between right and wrong get blurry. High heat, twisted and tantalizing, these are not for the fainthearted.

PREFACE

This book features scenes where some of the characters use American Sign Language (ASL), which is a distinct language that has its own syntax and isn't just another way to speak English. Words and their modifiers can be expressed with hands but also body language, intensity of movement, and facial expressions. However, for the ease of reading and clarity reasons, ASL sentences will be translated into English and shown in <...>.

CHAPTER ONE

C olin wasn't really into cancer. Well, nobody was, except perhaps those freaks who found the topic fascinating and prolonged the lecture with a never-ending flood of questions. He sank deeper into the uncomfortable seat and looked at the clock again.

He understood that this was an important subject for any future doctor, but while he'd learned to cram like a pro, and he would memorize all there was to know by the time the next exam rolled around, he'd much rather have been dealing with something more immediate. Injuries, burns, broken bones were much more up his street. More hands-on. Practical.

If he absolutely had to make medicine his career, perhaps he should have gone on to become an emergency responder.

Or perhaps not, since that job required even better people skills. And his parents wouldn't have paid for it when he *"could be a doctor"*. And very soon, once Colin completed his bachelor's course, he would be off to medical school.

His future mental health was doomed.

When the class ended, he was so relieved he just sat there and enjoyed resting his brain instead of running for the door like usual.

"Hey, Colin! You coming for drinks with us? Thank God it's Friday, am I right?" Megan approached him out of nowhere, and he flinched as if she were an alligator snapping at his feet. It wasn't as if he didn't like her, and it was nice of her to be so persistent in inviting him even though he always said 'no'. Maybe she fancied him. Was that an option? Colin had never come out, but he wasn't pretending to be straight either.

A group of Megan's friends lingered in the aisle between the rows of seats, staring their way with so little discretion it remained unclear whether they were clueless or if it was their intention to make him notice.

He cleared his throat and took half a step back, scratching his neck. "I'd love to," he lied. But before Megan's smiling mouth could reveal the two rows of pristinely white teeth, he said what he always did. "But not this week. I have to revise, and then there's some work I need to help my parents with at home."

Megan threw back her long hair. "You sure that can't wait a few hours?" She glanced toward her friends. "Mikey's coming..."

Like that was supposed to entice Colin somehow—*oh*. She wasn't hitting on him. She was trying to set him up.

But what she didn't know was that he'd already hooked up with Mikey, and the guy was just like his name suggested—way too nice for Colin's liking. Besides, he and Mikey were too alike physically. Both tall, with long limbs, and while Colin had nothing against his own shape, that wasn't what he preferred in his men. If he had a choice, he'd always go for the square-jawed, broad-shouldered type with a mean mouth and even meaner hands. Unless he didn't have much choice while in a rut. That's how mistakes like Mikey happened in the world of online sex-dating.

He swept his wavy blond hair back, feeling like bacteria under the microscope. "I don't understand. I barely know him."

Megan flushed. "Oh. I thought you were friends."

Had Mikey been running his mouth to his bestie? Unbearable. Why couldn't people just mind their own business? Then again, how would he make connections if he didn't go out with his peers very often? He was almost done with his pre-med course and barely knew the people he lived and studied with. He'd considered joining a hiking group to make some friends, but that had been ages ago, and he'd never gone through with it because his father had said it was a worthless pursuit that would take up too much of his time.

Sometimes, Colin fantasized about taking two weeks off, finding another gay guy who liked to hike and traveling together with no strings attached. It would have been the most relaxing time since Colin's childhood had ended with the death of his grandparents. For now though, between the exams and papers that needed handing in, the part-time jobs, and his parents' stink eye, he couldn't bring himself to push for such a long time off-grid.

He offered Megan a polite smile. "I mean, we talked a couple of times," he told her, though the truth of the matter was that by talking he meant Mikey's dick filling his ass and Mikey's chattering while Colin cleaned himself and came up with an excuse to leave the guy's dorm room.

Megan rolled her eyes. "Never mind, then. I'm sure

you've got more important stuff to do. You know, it doesn't hurt to let your hair down every once in a while."

He took a deep breath, clenching his teeth to keep in what he really thought. If he ever got to the point where he had to become a teacher to young doctors, he would no longer mince his words. Well, at least not as much as he was now. Maybe then he could at last *let his hair down*, like Megan suggested.

He smiled at her, because there was no point in making enemies. He didn't feel like many people harbored warm feelings for him anyway. Then again, he didn't come here to make friends, and had never felt that he fit in with the other students.

Sometimes, he felt like there was no one at all he fit in with.

"Maybe next time. Thank you for inviting me. I'll see you on Tuesday," he said, and walked toward the exit, trying hard to avoid meeting anyone's eyes. He put on his headphones and was about to switch on the music when Megan's voice reached his ears, muted by the rubber and foam but clear nonetheless. "Jesus Christ! I swear I've never met anyone so predictable. No idea what Mikey sees in him."

Megan wasn't a mean person. She was the type of girl who would never say anything negative to your face, so she likely believed Colin couldn't hear her, but that didn't change the fact that she *was* talking about him behind his back. For the briefest moment, the heat of anger rapidly boiling under Colin's skin told him to turn back and reveal that the true nature she hid behind her good-girl act has been exposed. But Megan was well-liked while Colin was not, so he suppressed the urge to confront her over this and left the lecture room, heading straight for his car.

He was quick to select a calming pop playlist on his player, but the soft voice of the singer aggravated Colin even further. Why was he putting up with this? He was never outright mean to anyone, and yet his refusal to attend parties and lose valuable time on getting wasted was enough to make him a social pariah. Wasn't it enough that he followed the expected career path? That he had good grades and didn't take a year off after college, instead going into pre-med right away? Expectations were never ending, and he couldn't even be himself with hook ups, who, half the time, wanted dumb small talk over beer after the sex.

Some days, he wished he could just disappear as one big 'fuck you' to everyone, but guilt ate him up whenever he thought about how much money his parents spent on his studies, and how it would have disappointed them. There was no other way. He had to see it through.

Those thoughts returned every week when he was about to head home, to spend two days under constant stress and scrutiny. His parents insisted on them all eating together, and an hour or two of 'family time' on Saturday, which made him itch for the privacy of his single-occupancy dorm room, and for the books that gave him no joy, but at least offered benefits in the long run.

But despite all this, he got into the car and headed out from campus every week without fail.

The drive home would take three hours, and the pop music wasn't cutting it anymore. If he wanted to achieve any peace of mind tonight, it was time for the big guns, so he put on the latest audiobook he got in a bid to become a better person. *Meditation: Your Guide to Success.*

The foreword was the usual boring babble about the pace of modern life being a challenge to brains that were not equipped to deal with such large amounts of data. The narrator, likely the author itself, considering the issues with his pronunciation, then went on to explain it with a convoluted take on evolutionary theory.

It seemed like a load of bullshit, but as Colin listened, the theory made a lot more sense. At times, it was like listening about himself—overstimulated by sounds, images, and the number of people striving for his attention, when all he really needed was food, shelter, basic comforts, and perhaps a couple of people to satisfy his social needs once in a while. Following a script in life meant that bits of one's day were already planned out and that freed up mental capacity to navigate everything else. How did the others have the mental capacity for parties and active socializing?

The empty road he knew so well was yet another beaten path he never ventured away from. The darkness around him was comforting in some ways—just the night sky above and the knowledge that in a few hours, after going through Father's interrogation and an uncomfortable dinner, he would lie in a warm bed.

"So we get used to our ways and don't question them anymore. Work, home, sleep. Rinse, repeat," the voice went on. "But is that what we truly need? Does that tap into our primal instincts? We become robots, slaves to society."

Maybe this audiobook wasn't the best choice after all, since the author seemed to be going off on a personal rant, and his message angered Colin rather than provided relief. It was just like Megan had said. Colin *was* predictable and always followed the path laid out for him. He got good grades, he was studying to become a doctor, and he didn't even want to rock the boat by coming out to his parents.

He couldn't bear to disappoint them, no matter how much he resented the drill they had put him through since he was a little kid.

How pathetic was that?

The narrator went on, his voice a bit too shrill to be pleasant, but at this point, his words were the only break from the reality of the same trees and the same hills in the background. Colin drove down this road twice every week, and while he was glad to know where he was headed, the long drive provided no challenge whatsoever. He was bored.

The audiobook made him feel as if there was someone else in the car, entertaining him with the kind of one-sided conversation that didn't require his active participation.

"So try to look into your mind, or your heart if that's what you prefer, and change things up a bit. It doesn't have to be anything earth-shattering when you're only starting out. Meditate, eat a different kind of breakfast, wear a bright color, take a different way home."

And just as the voice in the speakers said that, the headlights of Colin's car revealed a fork in the road ahead, and Colin's heart beat that bit faster. He always chose the most efficient route, going right toward the highway that would take him straight home. The traffic sign suggested the other would take him to a small town that he'd never been to, but which also had a connection to the highway. If he chose to go the roundabout way, he'd lose what? Thirty minutes?

"Change things up a bit," repeated the narrator, and Colin made a rapid turn, changing direction to follow the advice. Because why the hell not? Nobody would know about this silliness anyway. Still, his heart beat as fast as if he were about to suck his first cock.

No big deal. No big deal at all.

And yet somehow it felt as if the door to the world behind him closed, and if he peeked into the rear view mirror, he would have encountered nothingness. So he didn't look back, for fear he'd still change his mind, and drove on toward the town ahead. A small detour was all this was.

His guts twisted with worry, as if this tiny change was about to start an avalanche, and he tried to calm down, because this was not a reasonable reaction. This was only a detour. He would be back on the highway soon enough, but the fact that straying off the usual route caused such anxiety was proof that he should have done it a long time ago. He wasn't scared of the dark, of the emptiness around him, or some imaginary axe murderer. His subconscious was throwing mundane fears at him of losing the connection on his phone and ending up lost because of it.

And if he did get lost, would that be so bad? He'd spend the night in the car and find his way home tomorrow. Nothing all that terrifying, since April was quite warm this year.

His phone came alive—first with vibrations, then with the aria Colin used for his mom's calls. He swallowed the dryness in his throat, briefly considering not picking up for once, but those thoughts only lasted for two seconds before he grabbed the cell and put it against his ear.

"Hi, Mom."

"Hi, Colin. Are you going to make it tonight? Dad's been asking, and he's got a late night shift at the hospital, so I just wanted to make sure you're already on your way?"

A car emerged from behind the trees ahead, the bright glow of its headlights stabbing Colin's eyes, but he kept on course, trying to follow the shadows on the right side of the road as a guideline. Seconds later, the other car disappeared from sight, once again leaving Colin alone on the country road, passing trees that stretched their tangled arms above the asphalt.

He swallowed, and the sense of adventure that had tickled his mind just seconds ago was bleeding out of him fast. This had been a mistake. He could swear the grooves in the tree bark formed faces, and each and every one of those had a mocking expression.

"Oh, when is he leaving?"

"In two hours, give or take. He insists that you eat dinner with us before he goes."

Shit. Shit. Fucking shit.

"Uh-huh, I should make it," Colin said, squinting at a shadow on the side of the road. He did not have the spare time to take the long way, nor would he be on time if he made a U-turn at this point. His only chance was to take a shortcut to his usual route, and the narrow road leading into the woods might just be it.

He didn't remember how this place looked on the map, but the distance between the two semi-parallel roads couldn't be that great. If he could traverse the woodland, he should be back on the right path in no time.

As he neared the narrow track leading between dense bushes, Colin slowed down until his car came to a halt. The asphalt ended here, but in the glow of the headlights, Colin spotted tyre marks, which meant that the dirt road would surely take him *somewhere*.

"When do you think you'll be there? I need to put the casserole into the oven on time," Mom said, coming up with yet another deadline.

Colin chewed on his lip, glancing at a rusty sign partially obscured by thick leaves. It read, *Do not enter. Private road.*

Just fucking great.

He put the car in reverse and backed away until the glow revealed more of the uneven road with pebbles scattered in the grayish dirt. Narrow and spooky, it might have led to a witch's house. But since it might just take him where he needed to be, he had to count on luck.

"Give me an hour and a half," he said, and headed into the tunnel of greenery. The moment his hind wheels slid off the asphalt, there was no way back.

This was just another shortcut to keeping everyone happy. No one would find out about this dumb venture. Neither his parents, who he'd keep in the dark like he kept them in the dark about his sexuality, nor the owner of the road. He probably didn't care either way, and if Colin stumbled upon someone's cabin, he'd just say he was lost. What was the big deal anyway?

He couldn't see far in the dense woods, even with the high-beam headlights on, but the road was clear enough, so he drove on with growing confidence. Just because the area looked as if he'd entered an episode of *The X-Files* didn't mean there was actually any danger other than a deer passing in front of his car. To soothe his nerves further and ease the sweat coming out of his palms, Colin itched to turn on the pop playlist again, but decided the audiobook would be more of a distraction.

The greenery around him seemed to thicken more, with long fern stems reaching out of the darkness like phantom fingers, and the farther away he was from the asphalt, the more plants invaded the single-track road. Colin took a deep breath and followed it with a slow exhale. He needed to be clear-headed about this thing. So what that there could be anything hiding in those woods? For all he knew, Satan himself could be tracking his car, and there was no way of knowing until it was too late.

But this was not a horror movie. Perhaps he'd conditioned himself to fear the dark because people had such free access to light nowadays? Nothing to worry about. He just needed to breathe slowly to trigger a biofeedback response and trick his mind into feeling relaxed.

There was plenty of research on that kind of stuff. Problem was, all of said research has been conducted in peaceful environments, not in the middle of nowhere, West Virginia, in a car filled with the sound of dirt crunching under the wheels and the scratching of branches against metal.

Research was definitely too far from real life to be relevant, goddamnit!

Colin groaned when faced with a huge red sign with the picture of a shotgun and *Private Property* written in bold letters below.

So there had been one at the start of this road, but it hadn't been as adrenaline-inducing. What use was that warning now when the track was way too narrow to turn around. And since he'd been driving for at least fifteen minutes, there was no way he could make it back on reverse —not on a road invaded by plants, not in the dark.

Jesus fuck. All he could do was continue and hope he didn't end up with bullet holes in his rear window. If worse came to worst, he would turn back where we was told to by the owner and be late for dinner, even if that meant having Dad rant at him about it all weekend.

A scream tore through the soothing voice coming from the speakers, and Colin jumped in his seat, looking around in panic, but he was quick to scold himself. It had to have been a fox. Their voices were weird like that sometimes. He turned the player off just in case, to be more aware of his surroundings, but the silence only made him focus on the tune of his rapidly beating heart.

Maybe driving back in reverse was still an option?

There was no traffic here, no other cars he'd be a problem for, no matter how slow he went.

Colin glanced into the rear view mirror, biting his lip. His mind was playing tricks on him, because the red glow of his stop lights suggested shapes crawling on the road behind the car. His vehicle seemed to be the only source of light for miles.

The sudden sound of feet crunching sticks and dried leaves tore his eyes away from the rear view mirror. Before Colin could as much as scream, two open palms banged on the side window, leaving red streaks on the glass. The man's face was a horrific mask, with one eye so swollen Colin couldn't even tell if it was still there. Blood shone all over him and darkened his blue shirt, but as he moved to stand right in front of the vehicle and banged his fists on the hood, Colin remained frozen, staring ahead while his brain told him this was just one of those dumb pranks that catapulted cruel jokesters to internet stardom.

"Open the car!" the man cried, his eyes darting wildly to where he'd just came from. His chest worked rapidly, fueling his large body with the power to bang his hands against the steel once again. "Are you deaf? He's coming! We don't have time!"

The next thump finally tore Colin out of his stupor, and he opened his door, unlocking his car and stalking outside on wobbly legs. He could sense it now—the familiar odor of fresh blood, of damp leaves, of ferns. But even as he took a step toward the injured man, he felt that he'd made the gravest mistake of his life, and instead of retreating—was diving further into the swamp. Then again, he was a future doctor. He couldn't just leave.

"I—what?"

"I don't have time to explain! Get in the car!" The man

tried to push past Colin, but he was limping, and groaned in pain.

"What? But—" Colin's mind got hung up on the thought that the guy's blood would soak into the seats. He did have some plastic sheets in the trunk, but getting them out seemed like a trivial thing to consider in this situation, so he stood there, unable to make up his mind as the intruder packed his body into the driver's seat Colin had just vacated.

Should Colin... fight him for the car?

The multitude of decisions formed a thorny collar, which tightened around his throat with each heartbeat, and left him so confused he didn't understand why his unexpected passenger frantically glanced between the trees.

A panting figure darted out of the darkness. He went straight for the man in the car, shoving Colin into the bushes. Branchlets scratched his exposed skin, but his flesh was numbed by the adrenaline pumping through his veins. The assailant wore black, but while tall, broad, and muscular like a grizzly, it wasn't claws that shone in the glow of the headlights, but a huge axe.

Colin should have never turned onto this road. He'd entered a horror movie set, and there would be no way out.

The predator went after his victim as if he wanted to tear all muscles from his bones. With the door still open, the bloodied man stomped on the gas pedal, reversing so hastily the car flashed in front of Colin's eyes before it hit a tree with a dull crunch of metal.

The man darted to the passenger door, trying to crawl over the gearshift, but the axe-wielding demon grabbed his leg and yanked him out of the car in one swift move, as if he were pulling on a cat's tail. The victim rolled over and dashed toward the front of the vehicle in a desperate bid to run off, but there was no escape from the angry forest ghost, and what happened next would be forever burned at the back of Colin's eyelids.

At a speed that shouldn't have been attainable by a human being, the predator caught up with his prey and, in the cold light streaming from the headlights of Colin's car, swung the axe behind his back before bringing it down on the helpless man. The last cry, cut short when the blade split the victim's skull as if it were a pomegranate, didn't even sound human. Just like that, in a moment of primal fear, a person had become an animal.

Time and time again, the murder replayed in Colin's mind—the axe going down and biting into the head so deeply the skull cracked with a nasty crack and teeth spilled onto the road.

Colin sensed a sticky dampness on his face, and when he realized what it was, food rose in his gullet. But the need to run forced down the nausea when the dirt-stained face of the stranger turned his way, terrifying like a ritual mask that hailed imminent death.

The bearded beast heaved over his prey while Colin sat on the edge of the road, paralyzed by the hope of all of this just going away if he remained still enough. Was this how a deer felt after seeing her sister mauled to death by a wolf? Frozen and hoping that one kill was enough? He wasn't sure if it was the sound of his breathing that gave him away, or the crack of a branch under his ass, or just the fact that the axeman had seen him stumble off the road, but when the blade eased out of the skull, further bloodlust was aimed straight at him.

He sensed it in his bones. It was run or be mauled, so he darted into the path and ran so fast his brain could barely catch up with the movement of his body. His joints were stiff yet efficient, as if there was a puppeteer somewhere above forcing Colin's muscles to work way beyond their normal capacity. He flew into the darkness, urged by the panting of the predator chasing him.

In the split second before Colin's eyes became all but useless so far away from the car, it occurred to him that one should never *ever* run from a bear. But there was no room for any more decisions when his toes hit something, and the force he'd amassed through his speed sent him face-first into the dirt. Pebbles scraped his knees and bare hands, but he was unable to break his fall and hit the side of his face so hard his brain mushed from the shaking.

The sand tasted of kale.

He held his breath, keeping still as if he were one of the pebbles on the road. Maybe in this darkness, he stood a chance. The axeman's footsteps did slow. Was this wild man able to sniff out Colin's fear? The notion was ridiculous, but nothing about the world was logical anymore.

A beam from a flashlight shattered Colin's hope. It blinded him for half a second, and he squeezed into a ball, unable to choose between running and begging for his life.

"I... I didn't see your face. Just let me go. I won't tell anyone," he whimpered, too stunned to move from the dip in the ground that now felt like a safe haven.

All he got in answer was a grunt, as if the man was a real beast. They both knew Colin was lying. He'd seen the man's face and would never forget it. A bushy black beard was its most prominent feature, and its wild, unkempt strands were like a warning that the stranger was feral. From the dark eyes, to the long tangled hair that partially obscured them, the axeman's appearance screamed that he was not to be approached under any circumstances.

Still, he was human. He had to be. So how was Colin to act? Show weakness and submission, or fight tooth and nail?

Colin's entire body shook under the weight of the man's sharp stare, even though he could feel it rather than see. The upcoming doom was inevitable, and he still couldn't decide whether he should beg or run.

"I... I'm so sorry. I shouldn't have used this road, I know, but I got lost. I didn't want to invade anyone's privacy," he sobbed, struggling for air while his throat clenched, as if the invisible collar was not only still there but also growing tighter.

The man stepped closer, letting out a low snarl. Was he planning where to strike with the axe? Would he torture Colin first? Chop off his legs? Maybe trying to run would have been Colin's best bet after all?

"I'm s—" his words turned into a yelp when the stranger sank to his knees and spun Colin around, twisting both of his arms back.

Fear held Colin rigid, with his cheek pressed against gravel, but the man paid him little attention, efficiently tying his wrists with rope.

So he wasn't to die just yet. There was still a chance, though the little flame of hope in Colin's heart dwindled when the man grabbed his ankles and tied them loosely to the wrists.

What the fuck was to happen to him?

"Please, my parents are waiting for me at home. They will be so angry if I'm late," he babbled, with sweat beading on his forehead.

The axeman paid little attention to Colin's pleading, and picked him up without effort. The heat of the man's body came as a shock. He had to be burning up under the sweater, because he was like a furnace. Was he that excited about his kill? Or about his new prey?

Colin's mouth kept working, but none of his wheezing apologies would alter his fate once it was sealed. The bear had him now, and once he was no longer sated from his last kill, Colin would be there to satisfy his bloodlust. The man was on his own turf and didn't even bother to gag Colin, because he knew no one would hear Colin's screams. The world was a mess of black and white around him, his senses aware of nothing but the smell of blood and male sweat.

So the man was human after all.

By the time the stranger pushed Colin into the passenger seat and, out of all things, buckled the seatbelt around him, the raw fear was losing its impact, and Colin went numb from the shock. He was able to breathe semi-normally again and watched the axeman circle the car in the bright white light. The stranger really was a giant, and when he hauled up the remains of his victim next, it was with very little effort.

The bloodstained body was limp, easy to reimagine as a mannequin to use on some movie set. Maybe there still was a chance that this was some sick prank?

Colin licked his lips, but the metallic taste left no doubts. Real blood.

When the axeman opened the back door and threw the body onto the seat, something in Colin snapped. His scream didn't even sound like his own voice, and no logic informed the way he writhed in the bindings. The seatbelt wasn't for his protection, but yet another way to keep him bound.

He couldn't breathe.

This couldn't be happening to him.

The victim's head was missing a huge chunk of flesh and bone.

The murderer slammed the back door and got behind the wheel. Instead of starting the car, he slapped Colin with his meaty hand so hard the back of his head hit the seat. Colin stopped wailing in an instant, but still let out a muffled sob.

The man huffed as if this was all inconvenient for *him*, and put his finger against his lips in a universal sign for 'stay quiet'. With the way his dark eyes pierced through Colin and kept him pinned to the seat, it looked more like a threat. If the body on the backseat was anything to go by, it wasn't empty one either.

After a moment of tense silence, the man started the motor, and the narrator's came through the speakers again, his lies making Colin's entire body itch.

The phone he'd left on the dashboard buzzed, creating a vibration that resonated in his bones and made him sob again. He wouldn't be home in time for dinner. He might never be home again.

The man grabbed the cell and turned it off, before glaring Colin's way and snapping it in two as if it were a twig.

There was no such thing as harmlessly switching things up.

He'd taken the wrong way home.

CHAPTER TWO

Colin let out a quiet sob as the grizzly bear of a human being drove his car deeper into the woods. He was no frail thing, but next to this guy, he felt like a twig about to be snapped. He'd done everything in his power to remember the route, but the fact that his captor hadn't bothered blindfolding him didn't bode well. Where were the superheroes now? Colin has seen too many movies where problems were solved by people made of steel and energy, but in real life, he needed to be his own savior.

Colin tried to keep a clear head, so that he wouldn't miss the right moment to strike, because the farther he got down this rabbit hole, the harder it would be to dig himself out.

After endless minutes—Colin's chaotic brain could no longer be trusted with measuring anything—the car entered a clearing, and the headlights revealed a large log cabin and several smaller structures. There was no one about, and only a single light proved that someone lived in this isolated place. As terrified as Colin was, nothing in sight seemed outright menacing, as if this was just a facade, a front of normal life designed to obscure dozens of graves behind the house.

The bearded man left the car, and then hauled Colin out as well, dragging him along with such ease that the inability to do anything scrambled Colin's brain.

Were the tall oaks really whispering that he should run if he ever wanted to see his family again? Or was he hallucinating from fear as the man carried him like a bundle of wood for the fireplace? His heels dragged over three wooden steps, and once the axeman entered the roofed porch, he kicked the door open.

A single bulb produced very little light, but it was bright enough to show the large spots of dried blood on a wooden table close to the entrance. A set of hunting knives lay by a sink, ready to use on victims while they were still fresh. Colin couldn't even assess the rest of the interior, too terrified by what he saw.

"No. No, no, please! I am *so* sorry. I'll go and never bother you again, I swear," he screamed out, backing away the moment something darted close by, tapping against the wooden floor.

The axeman growled, holding Colin close with arms like the roots of an ancient tree, but his grip loosened somewhat when a large gray cat emerged from the shadows and pushed between Colin's feet with a loud meow. The surreal nature of this moment made Colin look around with more awareness, and now that he knew what to search for, he was spotting cats everywhere around the room.

Oh, God, this explains everything. This guy was hunting to feed his cat pack. This would not be the way for Colin to go. No way in hell!

Something buzzed in the corner where little light reached, and a black cat dashed from there with a loud hiss, knocking something to the floor. The device fell, and a voice came on with a creaking noise, sounding like one of those CB radios for truckers.

"Taron? You there? All okay? It's been a slow day on my side, but I've tested the new Faraday cage—"

The axeman dropped Colin and flung himself at the device, turning it off with one quick move. Maybe it would have been safest to wait. Maybe this stranger didn't wish Colin dead and would just cut his hands and tongue off to prevent him from revealing this location to anyone ever, but fear did weird things to people.

Death had never seemed close enough to fear, but now that it approached so fast Colin could smell it, his rational brain shut off, allowing its primitive side to take over. He grabbed a clean knife out of the block and stepped toward Taron, hunched down to prevent the rope tying all his limbs together from cutting the floor from under his feet. His captor gave a low sigh, and for a terrifying moment, Colin thought he'd be caught in the act. So he attacked first, spinning his body to gain momentum, and just when he spotted one dark eye peeking at him over Taron's arm, the knife went in.

It was so easy. Like pushing into butter.

Breathless and shocked that this stunt worked, Colin stepped away, staring at the thick handle sticking out of Taron's unprotected side. The man gasped, but held on to the knife, watching Colin in disbelief, but this wasn't the time to assess each other. Taron would stay back to take care of his wound, or die, which at this point wasn't even a moral problem for Colin.

A loud meow tore through the sudden silence, but Colin wasn't about to wait to see if the pets ate their owner alive. He darted for the door, awkwardly tangled in the ropes and in constant fear of falling when they pulled at him.

The faint light from inside the house guided him from the porch, but when he faced his car, parked in the middle of the clearing as if Taron didn't expect any guests ever, he was at loss. How was he to drive if his hands were tied back? He was so fucking stupid. With all those knives laid out in the sink, he should have just used one to free himself. His other option was to make a run for it, but he didn't know where he was, and there were no guarantees Taron wouldn't chase him down once he patched himself up.

Colin would rather try to make his way back on foot than risk being caught. Maybe in an hour he could stop and rub the rope against a tree until it gave? For now he was stuck moving like a dangerous prisoner.

He didn't get far from the house before hearing the door slam open again, and the heavy footsteps that would be a permanent fixture in his nightmares followed.

Colin didn't have the time to assess the threat. He bolted.

But his tied limbs betrayed him after just a couple of steps, and he stumbled over his own feet, falling into the grass.

No.

Not fucking fair.

"Let me go," he shouted when Taron's freakishly huge hands pushed at his flesh and pulled him up like a ragdoll. He lost ground under his legs and landed on his captor's shoulders, swung over like a piece of meat.

He already dreaded the punishment that would surely come, but at least the fucker now moved as if he were making his way through a swamp, with the knife still sticking out of his side. Colin wriggled in a bid to irritate

Taron's wound, but it was no use. The mountain of a man carried him back into the house and slammed him against the blood-stained table. The cats watched as if they were bloodthirsty spectators of a lawless game, but Taron didn't waste time, and went into the other room as soon as he locked the exit.

The creak of rusty hinges moving had Colin's blood curdle.

A nasty little voice at the back of his head told him to make a run for it again, but what was the point? He'd be lying on his face within minutes, if not earlier. Perhaps cooperation would prove the lesser of two evils?

"Look, I'm sorry. I was just scared," he said in a shamefully high pitch, and one of the many cats lounging around him meowed in response.

What. The. Actual. Fuck.

And why wouldn't Taron answer? Was Colin just meat to be dealt with? Not worth the words?

When Taron stepped back in, Colin could see him in more detail, and while the blood wasn't obvious on his dark green sweater, there was a sheen to his face, and he walked slower, approaching Colin with hard eyes. The blood on his hands was a testament of the acts he was capable of.

Taron grabbed Colin by the front of his T-shirt and yanked him off the table, so perhaps he was now too weak to carry Colin. But with no means of resisting, Colin followed his captor to a simple bedroom. Light came from behind the bed, but as they approached, Colin froze when he saw an open trapdoor in the floor where the glow originated.

He only moved, following a strong shove to his back. Panic was an ice-cold presence inside him, and he glanced at Taron, feeling his teeth clatter. "Wait. You will need help with that wound, right? I'm a doctor."

Taron's lips curled, but he didn't look away, calculating. It seemed like progress until Taron shoved at Colin's back, pointing at the steep concrete stairs leading under the floor.

Swallowing air, Colin wouldn't let his gaze stray from Taron, terrified that if he went a step farther, no one would ever see him again. "Please, my parents need me."

But Taron was merciless. He pushed Colin hard enough to cause a fall, but instead of letting him break his neck, he grabbed Colin by the back of the collar and word-lessly urged him to descend on his own.

Any choices Colin might have had earlier were now gone, and he moved down the stairs, wary of the threat of falling while in bondage. The stairs were narrow and the steps lacking the width to accommodate the entire length of his feet, but in the end he entered a sparsely lit interior containing shelving units full of dried goods, jams, cans, and even a collection of magazines stacked by a worn armchair.

And a cage.

A cage large enough to accommodate a crouching man.

Taron urged Colin on with a shove. Had he lived here on his own long enough to forget how to communicate with other human beings?

Colin licked his lips and stumbled toward the seat rather than the cage. Who the fuck kept something like this in their house? But before his mind could produce a scenario in which something like this made any sense, his gaze swiped over a magazines stacked in the chair, and he found himself as close to fainting as when he'd seen a cadaver for the first time.

Two men faced one another in the photo, fondling each other's cocks while glancing at the viewer. Gay porn.

Gay porn.

Cage.

Dead guy in the woods.

He was in the hands of a serial predator!

When he turned to face Taron, the man let out a snarl worthy of a wolf and shoved Colin at the open cage. Colin couldn't even blink anymore, too afraid to lose Taron from his sight for even a second.

No. This wouldn't be his fate! He did not waste his life studying only to die before he got to live!

He charged at Taron with his mind blank, but it was like hitting a brick wall with no weaknesses, despite a crack in the plaster. Taron hauled Colin off the floor, where he'd slid to following the collision, and hurled him into the cage. Colin's head hit one of the bars, and the tremor it caused made him bite his tongue. The tang of blood filled his mouth when he looked at the metal ceiling of his prison, but with Taron kicking at him, there was no chance at winning this fight. As soon as all of Colin was inside, the door shut, and the clunk of a large padlock closing might as well have been a death sentence.

Taron gasped for air and slid down the wall, holding his side around where the knife stuck out of it. At least seeing him in pain gave Colin a degree of satisfaction.

They stared at one another through the thick bars in complete silence.

CHAPTER THREE

Taron couldn't believe this shit.

There was a boy in his bunker. Nothing about tonight had gone according to plan. What he'd wanted was a quiet evening—check the traps around the perimeter of his property and chop some wood, since even in late spring, the nights were cool.

Instead, he found himself with a dead body, two stolen cars, a knife in his flesh, and a boy locked up in his bunker.

Fuck.

The boy crawled farther inside the cage before curling his legs to his chest. He wasn't a teen—his narrow, angular features were too sharp for a man under twenty, but the huge eyes staring Taron's way as if he were a grizzly bear seemed deceptively innocent.

His city-boy looks wouldn't fool Taron again.

They stared at each other while Taron took his time to calm down after the unexpected attack. Little fucker claimed to be a doctor. Like hell. It was yet another lie to try to stab the knife deeper. Taron should lock the bunker so that if he bled out the boy would just starve to death for what he'd done.

Then again, wouldn't Taron have done the same in his place? It wasn't the guy's fault that he'd happened to be in the wrong place at the wrong time. Still, Taron had no patience for intruders.

Even if they claimed they were sorry.

If he hadn't acknowledged his mistake, the boy would had been dead already, but Taron's mom had taught him to respect an apology.

The boy took a shaky breath, his body becoming tenser, as if he were hesitating, but then he stretched and kneeled inside the cage. He wore the kind of tight jeans that would constrict his movements and sneakers that would soak through in the woods within seconds. When he crawled that bit forward, like a dog mistrusting its new owner, the light caught the color of the soft curls on his head. They were a dusky gold, just a few shades lighter than the eyes below. Pretty, even if the whole face was intriguing rather than handsome in the most obvious sense.

The boy's nose was narrow but large, like a sail that could steer his entire head off-course in the presence of strong wind, and his lips thin yet wide, almost too big for the breadth of his face. It was only fitting that so were his teeth —white and even but strangely overgrown.

"Hello. My name's Colin," the boy said, curling his fingers around one of the steel bars.

Taron couldn't help a snort coming out of his lips despite the movement reminding him of the knife lodged in his side.

I see what you're trying to do, he would have said if he cared to strain his damaged vocal cords. Colin was trying to gain sympathy for his plight. Pretty smart for a city rat.

Colin swallowed. He had a long, slim neck, and his Adam's apple bobbed when he was afraid. "And you are Taron, right?"

Taron let out a long sigh. He always chose to pretend that he was both mute *and* deaf. That way, it was easy to find out what people's real thoughts were. So he just watched Colin's lips move and hoped he'd get the hint. What the fuck was he supposed to do with this guy? City-boy had witnessed Peter McGraw's demise, and he would tell the police all about it as soon as he was out, no matter what he claimed right now.

Taron rose. If Colin pierced any vital organs, things could go south real fast once the blade no longer plugged damaged vessels. Removing the knife out felt like flipping a coin, only the two sides were life or death. Would have been just Taron's luck to die like this, even before shit hit the fan.

Colin licked his lips. They were pretty, a nice rosy color, his tongue a bit darker, though Taron wasn't sure if he should let his thoughts wander that way.

"I could help you with the wound. I'm sure it's all a misunderstanding."

The hole in Peter McGraw's head had not been a misunderstanding. Motherfucker had it a long time coming. The stabbing wasn't a misunderstanding either. Colin, *understandably*, wanted to run, and he'd do anything to achieve that.

No can do, boy.

Colin rested his head against the bars and shifted to sit cross-legged by the bars. His body language was growing more confident now that he no longer felt death was just a second away. "I know what you think, but what would you have done in my place? I was scared. But I'm also a medical professional, and it's my duty to keep people alive." He looked up, meeting Taron's gaze. "It was a blind stab, but it's awfully close to your arteries. If you try to deal with this on your own, you're at risk of bleeding out. I'm sure you don't want that."

Taron hated people talking to him as if he was stupid. He had a first aid kit, and he damn well knew how to treat injuries. To make his point, he pulled out the box containing everything he needed. He considered having some whiskey first, but liquor would make his fingers shaky. The pain was bearable for now, but he could really use some numbing after the procedure.

Medical professional, my ass.

Colin's fingers slid down the bars, and he barely kept his wide lips from twisting. *Yeah, boy, your plan's not going to work.*

"What's your plan if you don't want my help?"

Taron raised his eyebrows and forced a smile despite the pain. He shook the first aid box and walked up to the armchair, because he needed to sit down for this bullshit. Bleeding out all over his jerkoff chair with a pretty boy watching wouldn't be such an awful way to go.

Taron spared Colin another glance. He really did look fine. Taron made a point of pushing the magazines to the floor with nonchalance. Sure, he was embarrassed about Colin seeing them, but there was no point denying their existence now.

Colin flinched, but then his mouth widened in a smile. "I don't think my girlfriend would be happy if I read that."

Taron let out a low groan. Of course. Straight. Just his luck. A straight mouth to feed. It would still be interesting to see if Colin tried to buy his favor with sexual services. Taron shouldn't have been thinking about fucking the boy, with a knife in his side, but he couldn't help himself when he saw that handsome smile. It had been a while.

He took out a pair of scissors from the first aid kit and cut through the fabric around the wound. It was a damn shame, because the sweater had served him for the past few years, and he hated shopping for clothes. He was a big guy, and it could be hard to find his size second hand. He sure wasn't about to learn knitting. Though maybe Colin would like to if he got bored enough.

It wasn't like he was going anywhere.

Colin sighed in frustration. "Are you really going to just sit there and pretend I'm not here?"

Taron didn't have time for this bullshit and removed the sweater as soon as he untangled the knife from the fabric. Maybe he could still get the garment fixed. He glared at Colin as soon as he saw the blade lodged in his flesh. At least it wasn't all the way in.

Colin stilled, his eyes lingering on Taron for that bit too long. Was he afraid to be the captive of a gay man or was he not as straight as he'd claimed?

"What do you want me to do, huh? Are you an exhibitionist, or something?"

Did Colin have a death wish? Because he was sure as hell pissing off a wounded grizzly. Taron only had so much patience.

It was sink or swim. He had the bandage ready, the surgical spirit was on hand, and now he'd find out whether life or death was his destiny. He just wished Missi was there to comfort him with her soft meow.

The searing pain of pulling the knife out blinded him for half a second, but at least it took his mind off tonight's horrific events. Thank fuck Colin had grabbed a smooth kitchen knife, not the serrated one Taron used for hunting.

Pleasant things.

Taron had to think about pleasant things.

Too bad for Colin that he was the most obvious thing Taron could focus on to distract himself, and the images of Colin on his hands and knees, accepting Taron's cock, flooded Taron's brain with dopamine. Colin was tall, with long arms and legs, but not thin. Taron had felt some muscle through the clothes, which he appreciated, even though they were the type city boys grew in the gym, not doing actual work.

He tried to focus on imaginary Colin's sweater exposing his hipbone when he slowly but steadily pulled on the handle. It hurt like a motherfucker, and when blood dripped down Taron's exposed side, Colin's eyes were ready to pop out of their sockets. It was in his interest that Taron stayed alive after all.

"Christ, be careful!"

He gave Colin a cocky grin, as if he were invincible even though he would have probably screamed if he could. Instead, a nasty gurgle left his lips when he removed an inch of the blade.

Pleasant things.

Colin splayed naked on the floor, arching his ass up for cock. Whining, breathless with need that only Taron could soothe.

In one quick move Taron dislodged the knife, threw it to the floor, and pressed gauze against the wound when it drizzled blood all over.

"Disinfect it! Do you even have thread for this wound? I should take you to the hospital," Colin yelled, clutching at the bars that would become his tomb if Taron died.

But it wouldn't be so bad. As nasty as the bleeding was, it wasn't rapid. No major arteries have been cut. Taron had suffered through interacting with people to take a first aid course for this exact reason. So that he could deal with shit himself. Once the world went down, it would be each man for himself, and he would be ready.

He clenched his teeth during the disinfecting, and Colin's ongoing narration of the process wasn't helping. That guy was way too loud for his own good, and Taron would have gladly shut him up with his dick.

"What if you faint? It's not easy to put stitches into your own skin. Believe me, I tried!"

Taron shook his head and gave the knife a meaningful glare, to which Colin responded with a snarl.

"I'm talking to you!"

But Taron chose to ignore him and went on with the work at hand. It wasn't the first time he'd needed to do this, though the fucker could have chosen a more convenient place to reach. The needle biting into Taron's flesh burned and nauseated him every time the tissue was disturbed, but the faster he worked, the sooner it would be over, so he forced down his instincts and just got on with the job.

By the time it was done, Colin seemed as tired as him.

Which was annoying, because he only had a couple of bruises bothering him, and perhaps his tongue dried from all the chattering. Taron took a deep, painful breath and grabbed the whiskey bottle as soon as he was done. He poured a plastic cup of it for Colin and put it by the cage. His pretty face did serve as pleasure fodder to help Taron get through the sewing, so he deserved to relax a little.

Colin accepted the cup but gave it a suspicious glance instead of taking a swig right away. He dipped his tongue in once he saw Taron drink straight from the bottle, and when the sharp liquor was down his throat, he leaned forward and let his face rest against the bars. "I mean, I'm sure that guy did something to deserve what happened to him."

It was just Colin's way to endear himself further after the stabbing fiasco, but Taron appreciated the acknowledgement nevertheless, because Peter McGraw had done something inexcusable and deserved what he'd got. Taron took another gulp from the bottle.

He nodded at Colin, wondering just how much the boy would try to *endear* himself. He'd mentioned a girlfriend, but desperate times called for desperate measures. Taron wouldn't force himself on Colin, but if, and only *if*, Colin attempted to seduce him, Taron wouldn't be opposed to fucking his brains out, regardless whether the advances were sincere or not. Would Colin do it, though?

Taron hoped he would. Life got lonely in the woods from time to time, and there was only so much sexual satisfaction to be had with guys selling their favors in the area. It wasn't his style to make things overly complicated or form attachments with people, but if Colin was to stay, the two of them would feel the need to scratch an itch at some point.

So far though, all Colin had to offer were words, so many of them in fact that Taron's head was starting to hurt. How would he even go about fucking Colin? Would he keep the boy tied for safety?

"Look, how about we start with a clean slate, huh? Tell me about yourself. Do you live here, or is this like a holiday home?"

Taron rolled his eyes and had more of the delicious, pain-numbing whiskey. He gestured with his fingers, inviting Colin closer, and slid his hand over his crotch. It wasn't subtle, but would get the point across. He could imagine himself sliding his fingers into the blond hair and keeping Colin still as he came in the guy's ass.

The earlier smile froze on Colin's mouth, and he leaned back, hunching over in the face of the proposal. "It's uh... a compliment, but no. M-my girlfriend? Remember?'

Taron groaned. As if this night hadn't been bad enough. What a fucking mess. He had no idea what to do with Colin. No use for him, couldn't let him go, didn't want to kill him.

He got up and left without sparing Colin another glance.

CHAPTER FOUR

On the first day, Taron came to the cellar only once. Without even sparing Colin a glance, he cut him free of the rope and left him with a bucket to use as toilet, a large chunk of beef, a can of tuna, along with soup and a whole plateful of dry crackers. They were the type that could chip one's teeth, so Colin ended up soaking them in the hot, creamy vegetable soup until they were edible. The flavor of the crackers was unexpectedly familiar, evoking vivid memories of the ache in his gums that accompanied chewing. It brought back the scent of burning wood, leaves, and roasted marshmallows.

The happiest summer of Colin's life had been spent building camp furniture, learning the basics of survival, first aid, the names of trees and birds. He'd been a scout for less than a year before his parents decided he shouldn't waste his time on lessons he would likely never use in his adult life. His *real life*, as they called it.

Well, his real life right now was limited to a cage that didn't even accommodate the length of his body, so he sure could use some survival tricks.

Despite fear and resentment, Colin never rejected food, because he needed the strength if he wanted to get out of there. Boredom made his mind spin through hundreds of options for escape, imagining specifics, like the best angle to stab Taron again, if only Colin got his hands on the blood-stained knife that had been left across the room.

But as hours passed in silence, with no sign of life in the cabin above, Colin no longer felt homicidal. If Taron bled out, he'd be stuck here. Underground. With no way out.

Worry was replaced by a simmering anger. What good would it do him now that he followed the rules, went to med school, or didn't party? If he had stayed, went out with his classmates, messed around with Mikey, he wouldn't be in a dungeon in the middle of the woods, wishing a murderer wasn't actually dead.

In the dark, with just a tiny flashlight provided by his captor, Colin lost track of time. It could have been an hour, four or an entire day, but by the time he heard footsteps on the stairs again, his mouth was so dry his tongue had stuck to his palate. This time, the meal provided was heartier and tastier, but Colin could have lived without food as long as he knew Taron wasn't dead yet. That there was still chance for him to escape.

Taron refused to answer any of Colin's questions, and his silence once more left Colin terrified for his future. Something broke in Colin when Taron left again, and he cried for so long that in the end, he fell asleep from exhaustion. His father had taught him not to cry, but he wasn't here to see. Nor was he here to save him. No one would come, because he'd foolishly decided to 'shake things up a bit' and take a wrong turn home.

He wasn't certain of anything anymore. Was he getting only a single meal per day? Without windows, and with his

Fitbit dead, it was hard to say how much time was passing between the visits. He wasn't used to this kind of mental state. Usually, each day was packed, and any time off he got from studying had a purpose. He'd lived in a rush, always trying to fit as much as he could into his schedule, so he never realized just how endless hours could be.

Passing time made demons crawl out of the corners and sink their fangs into Colin by telling him of the horrible ways in which he could die. How Taron would dismember him and eat him. How the food he was getting was actually human meat. How this was the end of the road for him, and he would never again leave this cage.

In the dark, every sound turned into a threat, until his imagination produced shapes that did not exist, and made them creep up on Colin whenever he shut his eyes.

Colin hadn't lost hope, but it wasn't easy to cling to it either.

But on his third visit, Taron brought books and left the light on for Colin.

As usual, he didn't stay to talk, but the books were such a revelation for Colin's under-stimulated brain that he latched onto them and kept them in the cage in case Taron changed his mind and wanted to take them away.

World War Z.

Swan Song.

The Iliad.

The Complete Guide to Edible Plants.

A curious selection of books, not concise enough to make up Taron's psychological profile. It didn't help that Colin didn't even know if they were all Taron's favorites, or if he'd just offered him unwanted gifts he'd had lying around the house. Or if he'd actually brought the ones he hated, so he wouldn't be upset if Colin destroyed them.

Colin read them all, and it was only halfway through *The Iliad* that he realized he couldn't remember the last time he'd devoured a book in one sitting. And the last time he'd read a fiction book without having to ditch it for audio during drives and gym sessions? Two years ago when the campus had been snowed in, and he'd had an excuse not to go home early for Christmas. Fortunately, watching a movie took a bit less time, so a few times a year he treated himself to a sit-down at a cinema. Would he even live to see that upcoming *Avengers* movie?

The Girl in the Last Train Car by Anasstasiya Lucas had been stuck in his backpack for four months, because he always told himself he'd read it whenever he had the time, so he wanted to have it on hand. Yet between chores, his part-time job, and studying, he'd never found a spare moment.

Two days later, Taron offered him more books, and Colin reluctantly allowed him to take two from the pile of read ones in exchange for the new material. The silence was still uncomfortable, and the confined space—unbearable, but Colin no longer felt that his life was under threat. In this kind of scenario, he'd half expected torture of some sorts. Instead, he was served fresh food, and his captor even provided him with two pillows and a blanket. Granted, the bottom of the cage was still too hard to be considered comfortable, and his muscles ached from the forced inertia, but he tried to do as much exercise as the tiny space allowed.

About a week into captivity, even Taron's silence, while annoying, no longer felt menacing. And by the time Colin finished all the new books, he realized that he missed the sun and fresh air way more than any person in his life. It was a strange discovery, but at times, when he was busy rereading favorite passages, or napped without having to worry about his schedule, the captivity felt more like a forced vacation. His most basic needs were met, and for once he didn't have to think about conventions, listen to nagging or walk on tiptoes to avoid triggering his father's anger. For once, he could simply *be*, and as time passed, his interest turned to the only person to offer him human interaction.

That freak had thirteen cats, all named after American rivers, but Colin was yet to become their food. Rio, a muscular tomcat with just one eye and tawny fur, ventured into the underground room first. Then came Missi, a young female with red fur and a belly full of kittens, named after the Mississippi, and spotted siblings, Yukon and Pecos. Out of all the cats, those four were the friendliest, though it was Rio who'd first snuck into the cage and slept alongside Colin.

Colin had never heard Taron speak to them or call them, but they had collars with names, so Taron had taken ownership of them. The cats would sneak in whenever Taron came down to give Colin food, and then Taron would gently carry them all out, unless they were inside the cage.

Colin was surprised that the food Taron brought him was no prison slop but nice, if simple, warm meals consisting of meat and vegetables with either rice, potatoes or beans. In the monotony of his new life, playing a guessing game of what the next dish would be was *almost* exciting.

The cats provided a lot of Colin's entertainment, since Colin was a fast reader, and since he wasn't allowed outside, time became a straight line.

The sound of Taron's footsteps made Colin sit up and move closer to the bars of his tiny prison. The height of the cage wouldn't allow him to stand, but a week in, he was almost used to finding comfort in the confines of the bars.

Taron's intentions were still a mystery, because since the obscene proposal on day one, Taron hadn't attempted to molest or otherwise hurt Colin. Sure, he wasn't exactly providing him with much comfort, but he seemed as displeased with the situation as Colin was. Was there some feature Taron chose his victims for that Colin didn't have, or had he been left alive because the kill had been the result of a conflict?

The fact that Colin had witnessed the murder put them in a conundrum that neither knew how to solve. "Jeez, I thought you'd never come down."

As usual, Taron was followed by an avalanche of cats, and his brisk steps told Colin his wound was healing well. Rio slid in through the bars, meowing with the insistence of a civil defense siren and demanding attention. Colin pulled him into his lap, staring at Taron's somber expression. Sometimes, he wondered whether Taron's insistence on never acknowledging Colin with a word was his way of distancing himself from a man he would have to eventually dispose of.

Colin's throat ached with sudden worry, and the furry creature in his arms was the only consolation. His heart beat faster every time Taron came down there, both at the joy of having company, and in fear that maybe this was the day Taron felt ready for his next kill.

He'd been thinking a lot about his future there, and frightened thoughts kept directing him to the pile of porn mags by the armchair. Maybe he should try to make himself useful after all, if nothing else worked? It wasn't as if Taron was hideous, but the fact that Taron had to dispose of the waste bucket for Colin killed any sexual tension that might have ensued otherwise.

It was humiliating, yet Colin was ready to grasp at straws if there was the slightest chance of gaining ground in this war.

With his insides shivering, Colin pressed his cheek against the bar and caught Taron's thick, hairy forearm when the man scooted down to place the warm meal by the cage. It had to be nice outside, since Taron was wearing a T-shirt. Plain brown, with a pair of camo pants and heavy boots.

He looked up at Colin, but the firmness of his muscles and the warmth of skin that had been in the sun for most of the day were so distracting Colin didn't answer the unspoken question at first.

"Uh, I'm bored. Is it warm outside? You're tanned," Colin said, still holding onto the first human he'd touched in approximately a week.

Taron nodded, making Colin's heart jitter. This was the first time his words had been acknowledged. If Colin's mind wasn't playing tricks on him, Taron's beard seemed a bit tidier too. Still dark and bushy, but less rough around the edges.

Colin licked his lips, knowing it would draw attention to his mouth. He could suck off Taron—no problem—if it got him a short walk outside. Now that he was positive the guy wasn't some serial pervert, seduction seemed like a valid option in negotiations. "I'm so bored I'd even read those porn mags," he said, keeping his tone light, semi-inno-cent, to keep Taron in the dark as to whether it was a joke or not. It was true though. He'd flicked through the ones he'd been able to reach, before returning them to the pile.

Even though Colin knew he was dealing with a

monster, his heart still skipped a beat when he felt Taron's attention focus on him. He'd had time to assess every single bit of Taron whenever he visited him, and Taron's hands were something that always drew Colin's interest. If only he could disassociate their size, the thickness of fingers, and the grooves that spoke of physical work from what he'd seen Taron do to his victim, he'd consider them hot.

Taron nudged the plate Colin's way, as if trying to entice an ill animal to eat.

Colin sighed, leaning against the bars with a disappointed expression. Could *that* work? After all, if Taron had the heart for his cats, why wouldn't he extend the same to his newest pet?

"Could you move the cage upstairs? I haven't seen the sun for days now. Please," he begged, squeezing Taron's forearm a bit more tightly, but didn't dare pet it even with a fingertip.

Colin shouldn't have been here in the first place, and they both knew it. If only Colin had stuck to his beaten path, he wouldn't have to fear for his life, clean himself with a damp sponge, and pee in a bucket.

Missi rubbed her head against Taron's knee, seeing none of her master's actions as wrong. She reminded Colin of what he didn't want to become - a being so comfortable she didn't even know she was owned.

Taron scooted down and petted her head.

"Why won't you talk to me? I have a lot to say, and I'm sure you miss people sometimes," Colin tried.

Taron's dark green gaze darted from Missi, and focused on Colin instead, making him shiver for no reason other but the intensity of the wild man's gaze. He pulled his arm out of the grip, but before Colin could mourn another lost chance, he closed his hand on Colin's fingers. If he did that much, he might as well state his intentions out loud and save Colin the guesswork.

His palm was rough and so warm Colin felt the heat transfer to him, triggering a tingle in his balls. This had been his intention in the first place, but having Taron finally respond to the gentle seduction had Colin shaken to the core. After so many days in this awful cellar, the only person around wanted to interact with him at last!

So maybe Taron wasn't a good guy, but Colin couldn't blame him for not wanting to spend the rest of his life in prison when he so clearly was a man of the outdoors. In a twisted way, it was a choice he respected, no matter how it ended up affecting him.

Without looking away, he gently moved his digits, petting the palm of Taron's hand. "You must be lonely here. How long has it been?"

The long huff coming from Taron's wide nose reminded Colin of the sounds made by aroused bulls, and he wasn't sure if that comparison excited or frightened him. Should he wave the red cloth in front of the beast? What if Taron decided fucking was Colin's only purpose and kept him as a sex slave? Would that be his life? He'd wasted so much time preparing for med school, and now it was to be in vain?

Missi went tense, the fur on her back bristling as she glanced toward the stairs. Before Colin could make a guess about what was going on, Taron stood and put his thick index finger across his lips in a universal order for silence.

A shudder went down Colin's spine even before his ears caught the buzzing that got louder with each passing moment. A car.

Taron rushed upstairs followed by most of the cats that had come down with him, except for Rio who decided Colin's thigh needed kneading.

The thud of boots was followed by the familiar bang of the trapdoor, but this time, the sound wasn't completely muted, as if Taron decided he didn't have time to lock the cellar. Colin's skin tickled with trepidation, and he cupped his hands to his ear to amplify the sounds reaching to his ear from above. Rio was already purring, but Colin's focus was elsewhere—in the world of sunshine and people. And knocking.

An uninvited guest? Did Taron have family who knew about the cage? Or worse, what if Taron did have accomplices, and he'd invited them to meet the new caged pet?

And what if this was Colin's one chance to leave?

Though muted, the voices upstairs were clear enough.

"We know this is inconvenient, Hauff, but I've been told you were never great friends with Peter McGraw and so we want to check all the leads."

The sudden realization what was going on hit Colin like a truck, knocking his brain off its well-known tracks and into the ditch. *Peter McGraw.* That had to be the poor dead guy's name. Now that he was gone, it was only natural that there was a search underway. And who undertook searches and spoke of leads other than the police?

It was as if he were allowed to breathe clean air again, and in that moment, his lungs felt powerful enough to break glass with the voice they could produce. If Colin could hear the conversation all the way down here, it surely worked both ways. All he needed to do was shout.

Over here!

Help!

I'm trapped!

This man is a murderer!

Every time he inhaled and opened his mouth, silence was the only sound he produced.

The flood of what-ifs choked him and rendered him mute. What if Taron killed the policemen? Then, Colin's fate would be sealed. He'd be considered a troublemaker to be disposed of. What if Taron fought the policemen and killed them, but got shot in the process? Colin would have starved before anyone found him.

Then again, what was the alternative? Waste his life away in a cage? He'd already gone through panic mode on what he assumed by the meal frequency had been day three.

"I told you he's deaf. Write down your questions, unless you speak sign language," the other new voice said.

Colin stilled, stunned to the core. He'd been so fucking stupid. Why hadn't he assumed as much after Taron ignored him for such a long time? Isolation was fucking with his mind already.

This new information meant that while Taron couldn't hear him, the policemen would. He could alert them to his presence with risk reduced.

And yet he couldn't bring himself to scream, aware that Taron was the kind of guy who'd rather die than be imprisoned. By opening his mouth, Colin would be signing his death sentence, and Taron wasn't a bad guy at the core. He fed Colin, and his cats loved him. There must have been a reason behind the murder that Colin simply didn't know.

There was something more at play as well, which he didn't like admitting to. Regardless of the miserable conditions, for the first time in his life Colin was free of the endless expectations. He didn't have to cram for exams on topics that didn't interest him, he didn't have to answer e-mails or deal with his parents. Was it fucked up to consider that a blessing? Probably. Maybe being stuck in a psycho murderer's basement was already getting to him?

While his mind worked tirelessly, toying with the two options—risking everything by calling out for help and remaining at Taron's mercy—the conversation above became a blur. Two voices. Two policemen versus Taron. *They* had the advantage in numbers, but *he* was on his own turf—a big, strong guy who could likely snap someone's neck with ease.

It was an impossible decision.

When the lock echoed through the house like lightning, Colin's heart filled with darkness, and his stomach with nausea.

He'd blown it.

He'd blown his one chance at rescue because he couldn't make up his mind.

He was like those people who got abducted as kids and never told anyone a thing, despite being allowed outside. Only he was an adult, and his captivity had lasted a week at most.

How was he such a pathetic human being?

The orgy of self-pity quieted, retreating into the back of his mind when the trapdoor lifted, revealing Taron's shadow on the stairs.

His steps were slow and deliberate, as if meant to taunt Colin about his uselessness.

CHAPTER FIVE

Taron wasn't sure what to think. He'd been sweating bullets around the cops, coming up with a million explanations for Colin's presence when none made sense, yet the boy had stayed silent as asked.

By the time Taron entered his bunker, and Colin's pretty face came into view, the tension between them was so ripe it could've caused the room to explode any second. The rigidness in Colin's muscles was visible from afar. He sat cross-legged with his cheekbones pressed to the bars, and his knuckles resting on the bare floor. For a brief moment, Colin wouldn't look his way, as if he were catatonic, but in the end the two chestnut eyes turned his way.

Taron stood in front of the cage and pondered the wide eyes. How should he reward his pet?

Colin's chest went up and down, laboriously pumping air, but just as Taron was about to conclude that fear had gotten the boy's tongue, the graceful hands lifted and moved to form signs.

Words.

Taron was too stunned to believe it at first, but the gestures were too precise, too deliberate to be accidental.

Collin knew sign language.

<I didn't call out to them. I didn't betray you!> Colin told him without opening his mouth, his wide eyes desperate and his nostrils wide from rapid breathing.

Taron licked his lips, light-headed from this discovery and unable to pick himself up just yet. How well did Colin know sign language?

<Why?> Taron signed, keeping up the charade, just to test him, but his heart was pounding. He'd so far considered Colin handsome, worth fucking, but more like a classy piece of furniture or an artwork than a person.

Colin's face twitched, expressing a whole range of emotions—from joy to grief—within just a second. <I was worried that they would hurt you. I don't want that,> he signed, rapidly shaking his head before grabbing the bars and clutching them, as if he believed he could somehow bend steel.

Taron nodded. Very proficient.

All of a sudden, Taron wanted to know more. Did Colin have a deaf sibling? Parent? But there were more pressing questions at hand. He frowned.

<Why?>

Colin gave a high-pitched groan that might have as well come from a fox captured with snares. <I will not betray you,> He signed, staring into Taron's eyes in a desperate plea for help. <I just want to see the sun. I want to take a bath. A real one, not with a sponge. I want to breathe fresh air. Please, please, let me out!>

Taron leaned against the cage and looked at Colin from above. This past week had been tough on both of them. Colin was surely fearing for his life, and Taron found him difficult to ignore, no matter how hard he tried to pretend Colin was just a feral bobcat he kept downstairs.

<I can lip read.> Taron lied, to keep more of his cards. <I can't let you go, but you did well.>

Colin flinched as if Taron had struck him, and as he hugged the bars in front of him, his face twisted into a grimace of pain. "You want me to rot here," he whispered, shaking his head.

Taron groaned. <I want you to not be here. But you are. So we have to deal with that.> His life had been fine without a little fly buzzing in his bunker all day long. No one was even supposed to know about this place, so that Taron's future safety wasn't compromised when shit hit the fan. Still, he was too curious not to ask his next question. <How come you know sign language?>

Colin licked his lips, watching Taron as if it were an intrusive question, but once a moment passed, he spoke. "I'm gay."

Heat slapped Taron's face, and he wouldn't even blink, but that was exactly what Colin wanted. This was a game they could both play. Colin lying about being gay, Taron pretending to believe him. They would fuck, and once that urge was sated, all would be good in the world again.

<And all gay people know sign language?>

Colin snorted and leaned against the bars. "No. But it's why I learned the sign language. I had a crush on this guy who worked with deaf people, and I volunteered to be around him." He then signed, <It didn't work out.>

Taron couldn't remember the last time he'd had such an in depth conversation with anyone. It must have been years. Even his signing felt rusty. <What about your girlfriend?> he teased, cocking his head.

Colin rolled his eyes. "I lied, okay?" When Taron didn't react, Colin raised his hands in frustration and groaned. "You have a fucking cage in your cellar and I saw you kill a guy! What would you have done in my place, seeing all those porn mags?"

Taron gave that some thought. Was it possible that the boy *wasn't* lying? It seemed too good to be true, but had Taron really snatched himself an ASL-speaking pretty boy who was *also* gay? He wasn't sure if it was a fucked up gift from God or irony, because with how they met, Colin would never be his.

Taron tapped the bars. <I'd have offered a blowjob. And then bit the guy's dick off.>

Colin scowled. "Jesus Christ, what's wrong with you?"

Taron let out a soundless laugh. He hadn't been this amused by a human being in ages. <You do what you gotta do.>

Colin spread his arms as much as the cage allowed. "He would have left you to starve. What's the point? For petty revenge?"

<If you haven't figured that out yet, I'm a vengeful guy.> Taron wanted to make sure he put this point across before voicing his offer. <I can't let you go, but since you've been so good, I will let you see the sun. How about that?>

The expression of absolute joy on Colin's face made him look younger, for a brief moment, almost childlike. He reached out to Taron, as if he really wanted to take his hand and Taron was happy to grant that wish to the soft fingers. "Please. And may I take a shower?"

<I can arrange that,> he signed after a while, because he found it hard to let go of the fingers.

Colin smiled, and either he was that good of an actor, or

the promise truly made him joyful. "You will not regret this. I promise to stay put."

<You better.>

Taron walked over to the chest of gear he'd bought at a junkyard but hadn't yet gotten the chance to sort through. He had just the thing to make the whole endeavor easier. He grabbed the thick metal collar and attached a chain to it.

He did not miss the sudden intake of breath from the cage. "Please don't tell me you're a pervert after all," Colin asked, the moment Taron turned around.

<Just need to make sure you don't go anywhere.> Taron rolled his eyes but approached the cage, wary of items Colin could use as weapons. But since there was nothing sharp around, Colin could hardly do much damage with those delicate hands.

Colin snorted. "The cat collars have padding. What about this one?" he asked, shifting so that Taron could open the cage. He was cooperating, and his long limbs were even more of a temptation now that Taron knew his touch wouldn't be as unwanted as he used to believe.

He could have this boy if he played his cards right. Would it be fucked-up? Probably. But he'd stopped playing by the rules of society long ago.

<I'll get it padded for next time.>

He couldn't believe Colin had the capacity to joke in his position. He even presented his wrists when Taron grabbed more rope, and let Taron tie them together without complaint. There were no attempts to bolt once the door of the cage was opened for the first time in a week either, and Colin even asked for permission to stand. The relief on his face when he finally got to stretch his body made Taron feel a tiny bit guilty over keeping him in the small space.

<No screaming, or I'll gag you, understood?>

Colin actually smiled as he stepped closer, his eyes only slightly lower than Taron's own, even though the difference in body shape made him seem so small in comparison. "I promise."

When Taron looped the metal collar around the slender neck and closed the padlock, his balls became heavy with the excitement of knowing that he did in fact own this boy.

Was it wrong? Yes. Yes it was.

Was it so, so good? Definitely.

CHAPTER SIX

The collar felt oppressive, and when it locked, forming a loose ring around his neck, he wondered whether this was its original purpose. There was still a chance that Taron had been trying to put Colin's worries to sleep all this time and would only reveal his true face now, but the prospect of leaving the cellar was too exciting to think too much about that. His joints ached, and so did his muscles after days in confinement, but it was the type of pain similar to the burn following an intense jog.

He hadn't been this close to Taron since the abduction, so standing right in front of that wall of muscle felt both intimidating and exciting. A promise hung in the air, and while Colin was afraid of what it might entail, he would just go with the flow for now.

"Thank you," he said, briefly rubbing the backs of his bound hands down Taron's broad chest. The clothes his captor wore were always on the baggy side, but Colin had seen him half-naked, and the image of the massive pecs covered by black hairs, and biceps as thick as Colin's thighs was a prominent feature of Colin's daydreams. He couldn't help it when the sole person around was such a rough, hunky guy. Had they met on Grindr, Colin would have asked for a dick pic.

Taron took a deep breath, looking down at Colin's hands. The communication they'd established was exhilarating after days of being ignored, and Colin couldn't help the rush it created in his body. Only now was he realizing how alone he'd felt. He'd actually had whole conversations with cats. And now his abductor was ready to communicate.

Taron gave him a nod, but when he adjusted the oversized collar, as if to check if it fit properly, he rubbed his fingers against Colin's neck. Sneaky.

Colin would have said he liked it, if the situation wasn't so fucked up. Though he guessed the fact that Taron felt the need to steal touch rather than force it was a good sign.

He congratulated himself. The decision he'd made—or rather the one that resulted from his indecision—had been correct. He was getting under Taron's skin. Today, Taron would let him roam under supervision, which was *something*, but Colin was up for the long game. Step by step, he would break all of Taron's barriers until it was safe enough to steal his car and run.

Colin would be smart about this, not like all the reckless people in movies who tried to run too early and got killed in the process.

Taron led him up the stairs, and cats followed in such a herd that Colin had to watch where he put his feet. But then daylight hit his face, and he choked up, looking through the window above, at tree tops and the blue sky dotted with small clouds.

Considering that there was a cell in the basement, the bedroom was painfully average. A large cozy bed with a knitted throw on top, and a wood burner by the wall with an empty cup on top. That was it. The room could be a perfect place for a weekend retreat, and once Colin's feet touched the floor upstairs, he was in too much of a shock to speak. He saw rabbits frolicking in an enclosure outside. So this was the source of the delicate meat he'd eaten in two stews this week. His relief that he wasn't eating bits of Peter McGraw's flesh was beyond immense.

The sun already had an orange tint, and the way it played in the leaves of the tall trees was so beautiful that for a moment Colin was too choked up to speak. The kitchen table, which had looked so dreadful the night Colin had seen it for the first time was now home to a chopped onion and some fresh tomatoes, so red Colin's eyes hurt from the intensity of color after the days without sunlight.

As soon as Taron spotted Brazos on the table nibbling at the cut vegetable, he dropped the chain to Colin's collar and snatched the black cat off the table top. It meowed in complaint, but Taron wouldn't let Brazos go until he spat out the bit of onion he'd taken into his mouth.

Once it was over, Taron stroked the confused cat's head. It was as if he'd forgotten about Colin's existence, and only realized he had a man to guard when their eyes met. Taron coughed and let the cat down.

<Toxic to cats.>

Colin bent down to pet Brazos as well, pulling his bound hands all the way to the end of his tail. "Silly boy."

He then straightened and approached Taron in slow steps. He hadn't tried to force himself on Colin yet, and loved cats. Those were promising signs. "Maybe cover that chopping board and show me your place?"

Taron put the onion in a box but shook his head with a

frown. <Shower only.> He grabbed the chain attached to the collar and led the way to the door.

Colin scowled, making sure the expression of sadness was clear in its meaning. "Why not?" he asked and tugged on the belt loop of Taron's jeans. If he couldn't get to this guy through his brain, he would do it through his *other brain*, because Taron had made it clear he was interested.

<Because it's none of your business to snoop in my house.> The chain to the collar rattled in Taron's hands as he signed.

What else was he hiding if Colin wasn't allowed to see more?

The continuous distrust was a blow to Colin's plan, but he could work with it. He was finally in a position to negotiate. "I thought that it would also be my house now. You know, since you don't want me to leave."

Bingo. Taron slowed his pace, watching Colin's face intently for any words. <Maybe tomorrow.>

So maybe Colin was an idiot with less brain than he'd believed he had, but despite the collar and a week in a cage, he was grateful that Taron had allowed him out. He wouldn't be dying any time soon, and it didn't seem as if Taron wanted to torture him either. He was wild, not used to company, yet wanted a male presence enough to cave to Colin's wishes.

Colin sighed, trying to make the hunching of his shoulders pronounced. "Fine. Do you have any other plans for later, then?" he asked, clinging to the conversation for dear life. He'd finally established real connection and would exploit it in any way he could.

But when Taron opened the door and led Colin into the porch, the beauty of the clearing and the forest around it took Colin's breath away. Pine-scented air entered his nose, wiping away the events of the previous week. He kicked off his sneakers before jumping into the grass.

It was cool to the touch and tickled his soles in a way so familiar he couldn't help but smile. Even the pull of the chain couldn't bother him.

Taron hesitated but followed Colin with wariness, as if he were walking his cat for the first time, and wasn't sure where it would jump off to. They both stilled when something moved at the edge of the clearing, but it was only a deer, and it quickly disappeared between the trees.

A collection of simple sheds dotted the area around Taron's home, and on their way to wherever they were heading, they passed a chicken coop, the rabbit enclosure and a large patch of vegetable garden. Colin's car was nowhere to be seen, which wasn't a surprise, but just thinking about it brought back unpleasant memories of the man who held Colin's life in hands covered with blood.

Taron looked back at Colin and signed. <I've got work to do.>

Hope sparked in Colin's heart. "Maybe I could help? At this rate, I'm gonna lose all muscle," he said, hoping to appeal to Taron's interest in the male form as they circled the house and left the produce garden behind, heading toward a thatch of younger trees.

Taron cocked his head. <I will think about it.> In the daylight, it was hard to deny how ruggedly handsome he was, even if Colin knew the guy owned an axe he'd smashed into a man's skull. His green eyes wouldn't look away from Colin, and the bulging muscles on his hairy forearm promised no mercy if Colin were to run. But that was fine, because he didn't plan to flee. Not yet.

The sunlight revealed first wrinkles around Taron's eyes, and his skin looked slightly sun-parched, but that only enforced the image of a lone trapper who did not care what others thought of his appearance. And that beard? It was a bush, even though it smelled clean, and Colin could just about imagine it tickling his thighs during a blowjob. He'd never been with a bearded guy.

They stopped, and just as Colin was about to speak again, words died on his lips, because Taron grabbed the rope attached to Colin's wrists and tied it to a branch above them, forcing Colin's arms up.

Colin stiffened, trying to pull his wrists closer to his body. "What are you doing?"

Taron looped the rope around the branch several times. <Shower,> he signed as soon as his hands were free and pushed up Colin's T-shirt all too eagerly.

Colin was so freaked out he only spoke once Taron pulled his dirty T-shirt all the way to the bound wrists. "Um... are we waiting for rain?"

Taron shook his head and matter-of-factly opened Colin's jeans, as if he were undressing a doll. Colin got to his toes in the grass, and shuddered, fearful of what was to happen. "T-talk to me, okay? What's going on?"

Taron stilled with his meaty hands on Colin's zipper. He took a deep breath and nodded toward a green hose in the tall grass that Colin hadn't noticed before. It was attached to a crude tap sticking out of the ground.

Colin swallowed. He'd rather use the contraption himself, but he didn't want to push too much on the first day of real progress, so he eventually nodded and met Taron's gaze, shifting against his hand. "I'm just a bit scared."

Taron took that bait in an instant. <I'll make it nice.>

Colin wondered if Taron meant 'nice' for himself, because the big hands were right back on him, tugging down both his jeans and underwear, and leaving Colin painfully naked to Taron's hungry gaze.

The moment the clothes were off, his thoughts wandered to places that made zero sense in his current situation. He hadn't had the chance to groom in the past two weeks, and his pubic hair was already growing out into that awkward length between bare and neatly trimmed. What would Taron think about his body now that he saw it in its entirety? Would he judge the signs that Colin wasn't getting enough exercise recently? Without a mirror, Colin could not see the effects his new routine had on him, and there was no scale to check his weight either. Would Taron even like what he saw?

Colin swallowed the thickness in his throat. His thoughts were a whirlwind of images of violence and thoughts about Taron's big, sexy hands rubbing him all over. His mind couldn't settle on one version of reality, so he just stared at them, struggling to come up with something that could tip the scales to his advantage. "I trust you then."

Taron didn't sign in answer, but the way he watched Colin as he threw the jeans to the grass seemed to say, *you've got no other choice.* When he stepped back to remove his own T-shirt, alarm bells went off in Colin's head, and once again he was caught in the conundrum between shamelessly ogling the strong, hairy torso on show and feeling like a deer strung up for skinning.

He thought he'd already made up his mind about sleeping with Taron to earn his trust and gain privileges, but now he was no longer sure. It was like going through his first time all over again. "Are you showering too?"

Taron didn't seem to be bothered by his nakedness, and Colin took his time assessing the dressing on Taron's side before his attention inevitably drifted to the meat of Taron's strong body. It was an illicit pleasure to enjoy the beauty of his captor, but Colin had to admit that his memory of Taron sitting topless in the armchair that first night, hadn't given him justice. That night, Taron had sat in the armchair sweaty, bleeding, but he managed to grind his teeth and closed a gash in his own body as if he did that every day.

<No, but I'll get wet anyway,> Taron signed and untied his heavy combat boots.

Would he take off the jeans too?

Colin breathed in the scent of pines, but the longer he was naked, the colder he felt, and his skin was rapidly erupting in goosebumps. He'd be warmer with Taron's body pressed to his own. "You have a point," he said, trying to smile despite all the worries worming their way deep into his brain.

Taron smirked and flicked Colin's puckered nipple, only reminding Colin that he was a captive, and Taron could do whatever he liked with his body. At least some consolation came in the form of Taron taking his jeans off. The simple black underwear revealed a decently sized package, but since that wasn't being unwrapped, Colin stared at the thick thighs that seemed to be made of pure muscle dusted with dark hair.

Taron could choke people with those if he wanted to, and Colin imagined himself lying horizontally, and those thighs tensing on either side of his head while Taron's dick...

He swallowed a gulp of air, realizing he was being watched. Caught with his hand in the cookie jar! At least he was too cold for his dick to react to Taron's closeness, because otherwise his body would have betrayed him long ago.

Taron grabbed the hose and pointed it at Colin mercilessly before switching on the flow.

Colin clenched his eyes, tensed up and curled his toes, only to be hit by a shower of warm water. It splashed off his chest and drizzled down his cock, his legs, his hips. The caressing fingers of the warm liquid tickled his flesh, washing off all the sweat and dirt that short sponge baths of the past week couldn't. He drew in a sharp breath when Taron lifted the hose, so the water dampened Colin's hair before streaming down his neck.

Taron's fingers sliding against his side was such a shock to the system Colin's eyelids flew open despite water blurring the view. Taron was right in front of him, and he reached up, stretching his towering body to attach the hose to the branch above. In doing so, he brought his firm chest close to Colin, so close that the scents of the forest disappeared in the background, giving way to the earthy aroma of male sweat. Only then Colin noticed that there was another loop of rope there, so Taron must have used this spot for the purpose before.

Had he kept others? His mind whispered, but he was distracted by Taron's body hair tickling his skin and Colin shuddered, at a loss as to whether he wanted to back away or push forward.

"Do you usually do double showers?" he asked, nodding toward the other piece of rope.

Taron squinted at him with a frown and cocked his head, suggesting he didn't understand the question. As the warm water showered down on them, Colin was realizing just how much pleasure there was in this simple act of washing. Relief flooded his veins and purged him of all the little discomforts and fears. Violence was not coming, so he might as well relax and enjoy it while it lasts.

"I missed this so much," he whimpered, shivering when the water tickled him behind the ear. The ground under his feet was already soaked, but it didn't matter, because he could just wash his feet later, anyway.

He gasped when both of Taron's hands joined in, overwhelming him with their confidence. Slippery yet not soft, Taron's fingers seemed to do much more exploration than was strictly needed for washing. A part of Colin was ashamed and appalled. Another secretly loved it.

Hesitation was his other name, but when he looked down, at the meaty man-bear paws spreading foam all over him, desire hatched and forced its way to freedom. He whimpered when Taron cupped both his pecs, his long fingers reaching all the way to Colin's collarbones. Tense as a string, Colin met Taron's gaze, burning in the face of the lust welling over in the green irises like warm honey.

Had this been Taron's plan all along? If only Colin could separate Taron the axeman murderer from Taron hot man of the land, this moment wouldn't have been so adrenaline-inducing. Like a predator biding his time, Taron watched Colin, sliding his hands up to Colin's hair and massaging it as if he weren't Taron but his good-natured twin brother.

When Taron pressed closer, seemingly to reach the back of Colin's head, his stiff cock was only separated from Colin's trembling thigh by thin cotton.

Colin frantically pressed his legs together, but his balls were already getting heavier, and his dick filled in response to the dominant presence right before him. Despite his doubts, he kept staring at Taron, looking for clues about his future, and for the raw desire boiling in that intense stare.

They'd had whole conversations without speaking, just watching each other, though Colin was sure none of them had been about consent. He was trapped, and all he could do was give in or perish. How would have Taron treated a 'no'? Would he actually stop? His dick was only getting harder against Colin's flesh. The firm touch trailed down Colin's shoulders, and without warning, Taron twisted Colin around, and proceeded to wash Colin's back. The spot where Taron's cock had pressed still throbbed with heat, and now that he couldn't watch Taron anymore, Colin was a ball of anxiety. He could sense the blaze of arousal coming off the bulky body right behind him, and as Taron's hands gravitated lower under the pretense of washing, his breathing became noisy and laborious.

There was nothing he could do to avoid this touch. He was an open carcass about to be eaten raw.

He was at the mercy of this wild man.

Any resolve to fight his own lust was lost when Taron reached around Colin and cupped his crotch in the soapy hand. Colin's balls slid between the skillful fingers, and he moaned so shamelessly he blessed the fact Taron couldn't hear it.

The slick foam amplified the power behind the touch, and by the time Colin leaned back, thoughtlessly rolling his entire body against Taron's powerful form, his dick was fully hard and so sensitive he couldn't hold in the sounds of his pleasure. He wasn't usually like this. His sex life was about some quick fun, but the addition of anxiety created an addictive cocktail that had him drunker with every swig.

"Fuck..."

He'd never experimented with bondage either, eager to call the shots and leave as soon as he was done, but when he pulled on the rope with his wrists and couldn't get out, his dick twitched in Taron's hand. Taron's low groan against the back of Colin's head was reminiscent of a hungry bear, and the tickle of Taron's wet beard rubbing his flesh only amplified every sensation.

Fuck, yet again. Turned out Colin really fucking liked beards.

Why hadn't he fucked a bearded guy before? There were tons of them around nowadays!

Colin half-expected to feel the cock on his skin again, but Taron wasn't hasty. He had his prey where he wanted, and he would take his time before he bit in.

When the big hand twisted around Colin's dick, the tug made Colin push his hips forward and once again rise to his toes, seeking more touch. With the soaking wet ground under his feet, the fresh air, and the sun on his skin, the water might as well have been summer rain. It made no sense, but despite the bonds, and with the strong arms of his abductor around him, he'd never felt more liberated. He'd been taken. No one could blame him for not doing his homework, not making it on time for dinner, or not attending parties. Or for giving into the lust of his awful, *evil* abductor.

Taron pressed his cock to Colin's tail bone, right above his ass. There was no more fabric between them, and that thick tool had only one reason to be where it was.

The bite to Colin's ear was more animalistic than his former lovers' nibbles, and he whimpered like a wounded deer. There was no need for Taron to hurt him, because he would give in without a fight just to end this agony.

He'd been hunted down, and now came the time for the predator's meal.

Colin rolled his ass, so turned on he didn't even think about moving until the piece of stiff meat moved up his spine in a promise that already had his hole feeling ripe.

What the fuck was wrong with him? He should've been terrified. Instead, his brain was overcome with the need for dick.

Taron reached his slippery fingers between Colin's buttocks without any other foreplay, but he didn't just shove them in, and toyed with the opening of Colin's hole instead. Everything seemed to be happening too fast, yet his body screamed for much more, much quicker. He'd be fucked raw. He knew it and couldn't find it in himself to resent the notion.

Even with the soap for lubricant, Taron's fingertips felt rough against the sensitive skin around Colin's hole, and he arched into the touch as arousal finally took over completely, chasing away the fear of being mauled. His hips danced as he went up and down, briefly squeezing his buttocks around the thick digits, but when hot breath moved against the bare skin of his neck, that was where his attention shifted, and he crooked his neck to expose the vulnerable flesh to the man who wanted to mark him as his.

The bite was brutal, and would leave marks, but it felt like a wordless demand for submission, not just something to cause him pain. As Taron chewed on Colin's neck, he pushed in two fingers, stretching Colin's ass and getting him ready for what now felt inevitable.

Colin let out a strangled scream, shocked by the ferocity of the intrusion. The penetration wasn't there to arouse him, it was to prepare him for the girth that Taron wanted to stuff into his hole. And that was one of the most exciting things imaginable. A strong, handsome man like Taron was so turned on by Colin that he couldn't wait. That he needed to take him already, without discussing limits or sweet talking a new guy into trying bondage, or worrying whether Colin had sufficiently prepared himself for anal. He just did whatever his instincts told him, and in this moment, it meant roughly pumping two fingers in and out and leaving a fist-sized hickey on Colin's neck.

Just as Colin was easing into it despite his body trembling like a leaf in the wind, Taron removed his fingers, leaving Colin's ass hollow, and his cock begging for more touch. He yelped, weightless for a second when Taron pulled on the rope with enough strength to lift Colin, but Colin's feet slapped back into the muddy grass when Taron untied the cord completely.

Would he take Colin home for a fuck? Did he want to do it face to face so that they could communicate more easily?

Colin was about to turn and lean in for a kiss when Taron grabbed his shoulders and pushed his foot against the back of Colin's knee, forcing him into the foamy puddle . The bound hands splashed into the muddy water next, and Colin found himself on all fours, breathing in a mixture of dirt, grass, and soap while Taron's big hand slid up his back, pressing him down in a gesture of dominance.

His brain was empty, and he couldn't even process what was happening to him when Taron's knee briefly touched his ass, and his body twitched, reacting to it as if hormones had replaced rational thoughts. He'd never considered himself submissive, yet here he was, spreading his legs like a bitch in heat.

Taron spat, which had to be extra lubrication, because seconds later, the tip of his cock prodded at Colin's tender hole. No man had ever treated him this way. Not just because it was rapey. Taron's confidence was so overpowering, Colin knew no other way but to give in. He had no brain left to ponder if it was an age thing, or what because Taron thrust the head of his cock in with a grunt that seemed to come from somewhere down his throat.

The bear sank his claws into Colin's flesh, his rough fingers digging into the meat on his hips and buttocks, keeping Colin in place when he tried to flee the inevitable stab of pain. He'd done sex with sparse lubrication before, but the burn of Taron's dick entering him was like nothing he'd ever experienced.

Letting out a choked scream, he sank lower, hanging his head over the foam floating in the puddle, and hiding his head in his arms. He was at Taron's mercy, and he wouldn't try to run, he wouldn't struggle. What was happening had been inevitable from the start, and even though his sphincter budged against the intrusion, the discomfort would eventually pass, with Taron emerging victorious from this wordless fight.

Taron's hands glided down, up, touching Colin every-where, even under the armpits, before one of them settled back on Colin's dick. Their knees sunk into mud and wet grass, the lukewarm water still flowed from above, and the thick cock was forcing its way inside as if Colin were a toy for his captor's amusement.

Taron's bulk made Colin slide face first into the mud, and he yelped, ending up with some of it in his mouth, but he knew what Taron was doing. Squeezing Colin's cock in his hand, and forcing him to lift his hips, Taron started fucking Colin's ass like it was his God-given right. Maybe it was.

Colin squealed again when the friction became too much, rubbing him dry until Taron suddenly pulled all the way out, leaving him aching and empty. For a shocking moment, Colin wasn't sure whether he wanted more or not, but Taron spat on his hole, and the cock was right back, this time slamming all the way in.

The water flowing between their bodies splashed all over, and the brutal thrusts created a concoction of pain and pleasure that left Colin stunned that he wasn't breaking apart yet. His ass was on fire, rubbed so raw he'd expected his dick to go soft instead of hardening even further in Taron's hand. Every time it became almost too much, Taron would stop to add more spit, but didn't even try to be gentler, and Colin didn't ask for it either. His hole was a pulsing inferno, and at this moment it existed solely to serve Taron's desires.

Colin moved to meet the thrusts, his skin jolting when liquid amplified the force of Taron's hips smashing against his ass until each thrust feel like a slap. The whole front of his body was dragged back and forth through the puddle, pushed down by Taron's substantial weight. There was softness to the pecs and stomach pressed to his back, unlike guys who worked their bodies at the gym, but the strength in Taron's arms enough to snap Colin's neck if he so wished.

With a groan of satisfaction, Taron buried himself in Colin balls deep, and when his thighs trembled, it became clear that he was coming. Colin could sense the faint tremors where Taron's balls rested next to his as their contents filled his ass. He'd never fucked anyone without a condom, so maybe it was just his imagination, but he could feel heat expanding deep inside him as he rolled his hips toward the slick, hot fist that offered him a chance at satisfaction.

When pleasure exploded out of him and into the puddle below, his scream was like the howl of a beast finally returned into the wild after years in a cage. The burn in his ass only made the orgasm more intense, and his hole squeezed around Taron's dick as if it wanted to milk the guy for everything he had. As if that gave Colin a tiny bit of ownership over his lover as well.

He'd always been the one to call the shots with sexual partners, even though he mostly bottomed. This was something else altogether. This was insanity with no seatbelts. He hated Taron for disrupting his life, for keeping him locked up, and yet he couldn't find a fault in the cock, which was still stiff inside of him. He itched to worship this glorious tool with his tongue and fall asleep with his head resting on one of those strong, hairy thighs.

When excitement was slowly replaced by fatigue, the physicality of the whole situation assaulted Colin's senses. He lay in slop, dirtier than he'd been before the wash, his ass burned as if Taron's dick had been covered with cayenne pepper, and when his captor finally pulled out, a streak of dampness followed his cock outside, rolling down the curve of Colin's buttock and down his balls.

He could barely breathe.

What the fuck had he done?

CHAPTER SEVEN

What was done was done. Taron hadn't intended to have sex with Colin, but if Colin was responsive, Taron wasn't about to deny his interest.

Colin's greedy hole still throbbed around Taron's cock, but it was time to part. He murmured his pleasure as much as his partially paralyzed voice cords allowed, and gave himself a moment longer in the hot, lovely body. Last time he had an ass this good—he couldn't remember having sex with a guy like Colin. Not just because Colin was built so well or handsome—even though he was—but also because he was so animalistic in the way he'd given in. He'd yielded as if his only purpose were to milk Taron's cock.

Colin's breathing came out ragged. Was he scared or still shaken up after the fuck? His shoulder blades moved closer, like two parts of a bridge coming together, and for the briefest moment Taron was tempted to walk his fingers across them. But such gestures of endearment did not belong in what this had been, so he just leaned closer one last time and breathed in the intense scent that hadn't been washed away by water yet.

Taron enjoyed making his partners lose it, even when they were hookers. It made his own pleasure that much more satisfying. Colin had fulfilled that dream beautifully. Maybe he was meant to end up here? If Taron had managed to tame Brazos, why not Colin? It wasn't as if the boy could ever leave.

He withdrew from the warm ass, already missing the heat of Colin's hole, but it was time to get moving. He got up and smiled at the sight of reddened ass cheeks and the slim body resting bonelessly in the mud. Maybe if Colin liked showers so much, Taron could tile this bit of ground under the tree so that he didn't get his feet muddy next time.

He rinsed himself, but then pulled Colin up by the ropes on his wrists to do the same for him. The entire front of the boy was covered in mud, and he was far more in need of a wash than Taron. Colin looked back as soon as he was on his feet, his face still colored by a beautiful flush. The quivering lips were plumper than usual, but Taron would rather if they stayed shut.

"H-hey. Untie me."

Taron shook his head. It was far too soon for that. He hooked the rope over the branch and stroked Colin's dirty hair. Yep, more washing was needed. That kind of reminded Taron of Brazos, too. The wretched creature had arrived at Taron's with its ear torn off, and with fur matted from dirt, but he'd come around after realizing Taron would be good to him.

The weak smile on Colin's lips became a stiff, fake grimace. "Come on... I'm not a poodle you're getting ready for a competition."

Taron backed off to quickly sign. <No, but you are *mine*.> He slapped his hand hard against his chest for extra emphasis.

Colin stiffened, like a rabbit that was too scared to bolt out of the way of a speeding car. But he wouldn't just let the vehicle roll over him. He was still untamed and wouldn't listen to his master. "No, I'm not. I'm my own person, so stop treating me like a cow you're washing before slaughter!"

Taron gave a deep sigh and gently washed the mud off Colin's handsome face. The bruise from last week was fading, and Taron hoped it would soon only be a memory. Once he was done with Colin's front, he turned him around and aimed the water at the shoulders. He couldn't remember the last time he wasted this much heated water, but it was worth it, even if Colin didn't appreciate it just yet.

"I'm talking to you!" Colin tried to face him, but Taron kept him in place, intent to be firm. A cat would never learn submission—it was not in its nature—but a human could understand what was expected of them just like a dog.

He chewed his lip when Colin's ass tensed right in front of his soft cock, almost as if Colin were trying to tempt him into another round. But Colin wouldn't stop struggling, and in the end Taron felt compelled to slap his ass hard enough to make it a lesson.

Colin shrieked, curling his shoulders and stilling at last. Hunched over and no longer physically resisting, he wheezed before exploding into a rant that was clearly not meant for Taron's ears, since Colin wasn't looking back.

"Selfish fuck! You're not the fucking king of the universe. I have a future ahead of me, and what? Am I to be a living sex doll? Can't believe this is happening to me. I should have never listened to that goddamn audiobook. I should have just stayed on my route and gotten mediocre cock every week. So you fuck like some forest sex god. Big fucking deal if you're such a douchebag. A big dick isn't everything!"

Taron snorted. He couldn't help it. So Colin liked a big dick. He hadn't been lying about being gay just to appease Taron. He'd figured that much out from Colin's glances and just how quick Colin's cock had shot up at the touch, but this was something else. Colin had *really* liked the sex. Satisfied, Taron slipped his fingers to Colin's ass with a happy groan.

Colin glanced over his shoulder, arching into the touch regardless of the angry tirade. "What's so funny?"

Taron smirked and turned Colin around to watch his face. He should keep up the deception to hear more such juicy bits, but he was an impulsive man and couldn't pass on this one.

<You like a big dick?>

Colin's face went from confusion to utter horror, and the small, terrified sound that escaped his throat tickled Taron's pride. His captive went stiff as if his blood had been replaced with wax, and when Taron squeezed Colin's shoulders, the boy rapidly spun around, uttering a low sob.

Taron stilled. The fuck was he supposed to do with *that*? He'd dealt with Colin's tantrums when he'd been in the cage, but this was something else. He stood there for a while, unsure what to do, but when endless seconds passed, he turned off the water, and gathered Colin into his arms.

Taron wasn't a hugger, and even more so, he wasn't a cuddler, but he could think of no other way to soothe Colin.

Now that they were close, he could sense the boy's intense heartbeat and the pressure of Colin's chest expanding as he took deep, frantic breaths. "Y-you can hear... why didn't you tell me you can hear?"

Taron sighed and nuzzled Colin's ear. He wasn't letting go of the boy just to sign. Colin shuddered but eventually pushed into Taron's arms. "All I'm saying is... that I'm a human being. I know you might be used to only having the cats around, but I'm not a cat."

At least he wasn't crying anymore, because hearing him sob right after sex had been surprisingly unpleasant. Taron pulled away, but stroked Colin's hair for a while. <I know. Everyone has secrets.>

Colin watched him with shiny eyes and a set to his mouth. "You stole mine. And I'm really trying here. I'm trying to meet you halfway."

Taron ran his fingers through his hair in exasperation. <Your old life is over. You're never leaving. I can make it comfortable.>

Colin wouldn't look away, and his Adam's apple bobbed, but the raw fear that had been such a prominent presence in his pretty eyes when he first came here was no longer there. He was listening and calculating what he could negotiate. And Taron knew, because he would have done the same. "What do you intend with me in the long run? Why did you have this cage in the first place?"

<None of your business. You shouldn't have been on my property.>

Colin took a deep breath. "There's no need to get agitated. You know why I'm asking. I saw you kill a guy. Are you planning to get rid of me too, or did you kill him because he wasn't willing to put out?"

Taron let out a growl. Peter had deserved exactly what

he got. <I don't p-l-a-n to kill you.> He spelled out 'plan' just to be sure he was understood. He would do what was necessary, because he wouldn't be taken away from his land, from his life's work, and his cats just because Colin had decided to take a shortcut.

Taron wasn't a psycho, but he still chose to live outside of society and its rules. One day soon, the world built with modern technology would crumble, and Taron would be the guy who had the foresight and provisions to ensure survival. Tough luck for those who'd try to take it all from him, because Taron had a collection of guns and enough ammo to live through a siege. Not to mention the bunker where he could safely wait out the bad times.

Colin frowned. "Okay, that's something. What did he do though to deserve... that?"

Taron turned away and put on his underwear. He ignored the question in favor of pulling on the collar. Colin needed to understand he wasn't in charge. The sooner the better.

Colin let out a growl reminiscent of a frustrated chihuahua. "If I'm to stay here, you can't just ignore me."

Taron took his time to have a look at the marks he'd made with his teeth. <Test me.> He tugged on the chain attached to Colin's neck, intent on getting Colin's clothes later. They needed a thorough wash even more desperately than Colin's body had.

But Colin refused to leave and dug his heels into the muddy ground. "I'm not a cow."

Taron rolled his eyes. <Right now, you're being a donkey.>

Colin raised his chin, stubborn despite his nakedness. "I am a person, and you should treat me as such."

<Stop complaining and come.> Taron pulled on the

lead, but only managed to make Colin slide over the mud a couple of inches. <I've got nice food for dinner,> he tried, frustrated by the lack of cooperation.

Colin shook his head. "No. I'm not your pet. You can't satisfy me with treats."

<No treats then. Got it.> Taron growled and didn't try to drag him along anymore. He walked up to Colin, and as that chatty mouth was opening already, he grabbed Colin and threw him over his shoulder.

Despite his worries, Colin didn't struggle. He just wouldn't shut up.

"Oh, that's great. You're doing so well earning my respect right now. Because you know what? It's hard to respect someone who doesn't offer the same to you."

Taron slapped his ass. Not too hard, just to get his point across as he carried Colin back home. Fun time was up for both of them, because when Colin kicked, his toes hit Taron way too close to the crotch for his liking. "Put me the fuck down! Right now," he shouted, following it with a sudden jab to the spine with the bound hands.

So Taron did put Colin down. He dropped him to the grass unceremoniously. Being a nice piece of ass didn't mean the boy would be allowed this kind of behavior. He grabbed the collar and pulled Colin up a bit. <Stop it.>

"No. We just fucked, and I'm not allowing you to treat me like this. What the hell is wrong with you?" Colin asked, slapping Taron's hand. He was showing his teeth now, his chestnut eyes looking for weakness in Taron's resolve.

Which meant Taron had to remain stern. <Walk.> What did Colin think he was going to buy with sex? A boyfriend?

Colin stretched, staring back at him with defiance. "Where? I'm not going back to the cage."

Oh, so this was how it was gonna be? Taron grabbed the rope attached to Colin's wrists and dragged him over the grass. It would be unpleasant enough without actually causing permanent damage. Most of all, it would show Colin he didn't call the shots.

Colin yelped, but instead of getting up to avoid more discomfort, he delivered a precise kick into the back of Taron's knee, making him stumble. He was a wild animal that still refused to be tamed.

They weren't far from the house, and two cats had come to witness the fight from the porch, but Taron wouldn't risk getting more bruises while dragging Colin back down.

<I just want a shower. I want to see the sun. Please. You will not regret this.>

It took Colin a few seconds to understand Taron was mocking his words, but he sneered in response and kicked Taron's legs again. "I got molested instead, so there you go! You can't have it both ways!"

<Fine. No more touching. Just the cage.> Taron grabbed Colin's leg and kneeled down, tackling the boy to tie up his kicky feet as well. He was done with this bullshit. He'd had a good life here, all on his own, on his land, away from nosy fuckers, but people still had to meddle, and then complain when they got their noses snapped in the door.

He was almost done with the ankles when Colin punched him with his bound hands, hammering them against the back of his head. "No! Let me go!"

Taron's vision briefly went red, and he punched back without thinking. Colin's head dropped into the grass and he hid his face with his arms, shuddering as he kept in another scream.

Taron could only hope the struggle would now stop. He didn't want to hit Colin, but he wouldn't be a punching bag either. He picked up the unresisting boy and carried him back to the house. He'd lost enough time on this bullshit.

Colin stayed silent until they reached the house, but the moment Taron's boots thudded on the porch, Colin moaned and moved his fingers up his back. "Let me stay upstairs. I can't stand the fucking cage. *Could you?*"

With his hands occupied, Taron couldn't exactly answer, but he wasn't letting Colin stay upstairs after all that kicking. Plus, if the cops came back with a search warrant, there was a chance they'd miss the bunker entrance. If Colin was upstairs however, things could get messy. Earlier, Colin had proved he could stay quiet when needed, but he was growing volatile since the moment he'd sensed he had something to hold over Taron's head.

Taron headed straight for the bedroom, and this time, maybe for his own safety, Colin didn't wiggle like a rabid eel on the way into the bunker.

He remained completely still, like a dead body over Taron's shoulder, to be dumped into an unmarked grave deep in the woods. There was nothing erotic about Colin's nakedness now, and Taron wanted to lock him up as soon as possible to escape the discomfort.

Colin didn't even put up a fight when Taron pushed him into the cage, but no matter how much sense it made to keep him confined, it didn't sit right with Taron to leave him with nothing after they'd shared so much pleasure.

The atmosphere was somehow even denser than on that first night, and Taron sensed a physical discomfort deep in his chest when the boy refused to look at him, hunched behind the bars and wiping fresh blood from his nose. He got into Colin's line of vision so that he'd see the words meant for him.

<I will make it better.>

Colin swallowed and turned away from Taron, curling up in the corner of his tiny prison. "You can paint it with real gold, and it's still gonna be a cage."

CHAPTER EIGHT

This time, it was Colin who stayed silent, which was no easy feat, as he'd found out that biting his tongue when he wanted to speak was a constant battle. Colin wanted to give Taron a piece of his mind. Tell him to shove the new, comfortable mattress up his ass, to eat the Twix bars himself, and to take away the TV.

He was not a dog to be bought with treats and toys, especially when the swelling left on Colin's nose by Taron's fist was still painful.

Yet whenever Taron left, Colin ate the chocolate, watched television, and slept on the mattress. There was no point denying himself what little comfort was offered to him.

At least Taron wasn't raping him just because he could. That counted for something. His captor had even tried to engage Colin. Asked if Colin liked coconut, and what channel he wanted to watch. Colin stuck to his guns and ignored him. So he'd ended up with an Almond Joy bar and reruns of *Prison Break*, which felt very appropriate.

He'd gotten his clothes back as well, washed and fresh,

smelling of sunshine. Colin hadn't expected that. He'd assumed keeping him naked would have been Taron's prerogative.

But Colin wouldn't let Taron's bribes get to him. He was determined to find a way out. He considered ways he could use the springs in the mattress, the chocolate wrappers, or the button of his jeans in a bid for freedom, but he was no MacGyver, and he didn't know how to pick locks, so the sturdy padlock on the cage door could have been a cement wall.

As days passed following his single venture outside, his mood had been on the decline since his short walk, and the inability to help himself was proof that perhaps he wasn't as smart as he'd thought. That maybe he deserved all this suffering for breaking the rules that one time.

The yellow glow of the light bulb couldn't replace the sun, and energy was draining out of him with each hour spent underground. His ideas were getting increasingly colorless and lacking in finesse, as if the walls around him were sucking the life out of him, to leave behind a shell for Taron to play with.

And most shamefully of all, since the hard fuck in the mud, boredom put Colin in an erotic frenzy where he imagined Taron unlocking the cage and crawling in, to fill the available space with his bulk. To leave his seed in Colin again and rub him with fresh sweat that smelled like a real man.

And because Colin didn't want Taron to know he entertained such fantasies, he licked the traces of his own release each time, imagining it was his captor's. What Taron didn't know, couldn't hurt Colin.

He'd been considering jerking off for a few minutes now, because there wasn't anything much better left to do

once the TV got turned off. It only operated for an hour or
two a day, he'd read the books three times now, and there
were no cats to play with either. His decision-making was
cut short by the trap door opening above. Real light
dispersed the gloom of the cellar, and Colin didn't even care
that it wasn't shining straight at him. It was natural daylight,
so at least he knew what time it was.

Everything inside him itched to call out to Taron and
make an attempt at conversation, but then he remembered
how much it hurt when he'd been punched in the face, and
that he lived in a cage, not on an unusual bed, so he pulled
the blanket over himself, facing the wall instead.

Still, each heavy footstep echoed along his spine and
made his heart heavier, his throat tighter, until all he could
do was lie still, hoping the loneliness wouldn't triumph
over pride.

In the time he'd been down here, there had been no
other visitors, so unless Taron was going somewhere to meet
people, he had no friends. It wasn't all that surprising,
considering his attitude, but made Colin's situation even
more perilous. Why did Taron live here? Did he hate his
family? Did he *have* any family? Did he choose a remote
location to hunt for men who he'd keep for his pleasure?

The clack of a plate put down on the floor was by now
engraved inside Colin, but he pretended to remain ignorant
of its presence, waiting for the relief of the heavy footsteps
fading as Taron made his way up the stairs. But like many
times before, Taron lingered without trying to initiate
contact, and the distinct sense of being watched was like
tiny needles gradually pushing under the skin at the back of
Colin's neck.

Taron knocked on the floor to get his attention, but
Colin was having none of that and slid the blanket over his

head. He would only eat once Taron was gone. When he felt a gentle pull on the fabric, he cocooned himself inside of it, curling his knees to his chest for good measure. He didn't need Taron's presence. Or his dick.

If anything, Taron needed, *Colin* because he was a sad, friendless, sexless, murderous fuck.

"Co-lin..."

It took Colin a few seconds to realize that his mind wasn't playing tricks on him and that he had heard his name spoken in a deep, whisper-like grunt, which sounded like a call from another planet.

He wanted to ignore it, but the temptation was like a physical presence on his shoulder, and he found himself rolling to his stomach to glance at Taron behind the bars.

Taron sighed loudly, and presented Colin with a stack of books. On top of it lay *The Girl in the Last Train Car* by Anasstasiya Lucas. *His* book. Then Taron smiled at him and put that one on the floor, revealing the next book in the stack. *A Mirror Image*, also by Anasstasiya Lucas. The new book he'd been waiting for despite not even having read the previous one. It was a brand new shiny hardback too. How did Taron—?

Of course. He'd gone through Colin's bag.

More importantly though, the fucker *did* speak?

He swallowed, staring at the plate, which had a fancy-looking spiral made of carrot for decoration. What the hell did all this mean? "What are we celebrating? Captivity day 21?"

Taron groaned and sat on the floor behind the books and the plate, as if he knew he should keep his distance. With his heavy boots, biceps like boulders and the hunting knife at his belt, he didn't look any less menacing.

<I'm trying.>

"I can see. You even spoke right now."

<It's complicated.>

Colin crossed his arms. "I've got time."

They stared at each other for what felt like ages, but then Taron got up, grabbed a pen and a notebook, and started scribbling furiously once he sat back. Colin liked his food warm, so he reluctantly decided to eat in the meanwhile.

Once Taron was done, he ripped out the page and passed it to Colin.

I had surgery as a kid. Some nerves were damaged, so my vocal cords are partially paralyzed. It's unpleasant to make myself speak, and it sounds like I'm a swamp monster, but I can whisper if I have to.

Colin smiled at that last bit. Taron's voice did sound unusual, but it wasn't nearly as bad as he described. "I'm impressed. You're becoming more and more of a social butterfly," he said, chewing on the spiralized carrot.

Taron groaned. <I never planned on guests.>

Colin hesitated, but no matter how shitty the whole situation was, Taron was trying to start a dialogue, so he decided to once again ask one of his most pressing questions. "No? Then why do you have the cage?"

Taron punched the floor, making Colin jump and barely miss the roof of his prison with his head. He started signing, making sure Colin understood as he went along. <For intruders. When bad stuff happens one day, people will come to steal my shit. I don't want to kill them. But I might need to have a captive. Or if there is a

chemical attack, or Yellowstone blows, I could keep a goat here.>

Oookay. Colin enjoyed a bit of Science Fiction as much as the next guy, hence he'd been looking forward to the next big superhero flick, but perhaps Taron actually thought he *lived* in another reality?

"A chemical attack? Like... what? Why would anyone come after you? Is this about the dead guy?" Colin asked, eating the delicious stew. Taron might've been cray-cray, but he sure could cook.

<Yes, a chemical attack. You can keep your head in the sand, or you can face reality.>

Colin leaned closer and only spoke once he swallowed. "But that's what the army is for. I'm sure we're safer cooperating with people than hiding away in the woods."

Taron shook his head with a frown, and his signing became frantic. <We are on the verge of world war three. You believe this government will take care of you? Here, I've got power, water, food. I can survive. I am self-sufficient.>

Colin stared at the bowl, which was almost empty at this point. "I mean... I guess it is an interesting hobby. No one's going to hear any screams so far away from the nearest town, so I guess that's a plus."

Taron sat there with a disgruntled expression. <I only protect what's mine. You shouldn't be here, but I can't let you go, so here we are. If anything, when shit happens, you're safer here than in a city.>

Mine. Colin flushed when he remembered the context in which he'd last seen that sign. He was silent for several seconds, weighing his words, because as much as he wanted to punch Taron—if just verbally—such actions wouldn't be effective in the long run. "Do you intend to keep me like this forever, then? In a cage where I can't even stand straight?"

<I don't know,> Taron signed abruptly, but then got up. <I'll work out something better if you behave.>

Colin squeezed on the bars, and as he jolted forward, his plate slid off his lap with a clatter. A drive from deep within fought through the numbness that had overcome him, and as he caught Taron's gaze again, he spoke. "Why don't you just kill me? Who would want to live like this? And it's not like this is convenient for you either! I've seen you kill. Just do it already!"

It was a gamble, but Taron's behavior told him that his captor did not want to harm him, so he decided to stake everything on this lie.

Taron huffed. <You apologized. I've got to go. I've got work.>

Colin reached through the bars but screamed in frustration when he couldn't reach Taron. Every time he felt he had a grasp on this reality, every time when he felt he could change his inevitable future, Taron would crush his hopes into dust. He didn't even dare ask about the murder anymore. "Fuck!"

Taron pointed to the new book, but Colin shook his head, and the anger turned into anguish so explosive he'd chew at his flesh to get it out.

He wanted out.

He wanted out.

He *needed* out!

"Just get me some pills. There will be no mess," he whispered, shaking his head. He didn't actually want to kill himself, but given the chance and enough time in this enforced isolation, he just might. And when that happened, he wanted to have the means.

This gave Taron pause. With the backlight, his bearded face was obscured by shadows, and his stoic presence made Colin shiver with helpless anger. The man was built out of brick, and even after a stabbing, there he was—sturdy and alive like a thick tree trunk.

<No. You are staying, and you will earn your keep. If you're not fucking me, you will work with me. Understood? >

Colin's head shot up, and the promise of having something to do was like a breath of fresh air. He was not used to inactivity, and any task was preferable to lying in bed all day every day. What would it be? Would Taron lock him up with copper pots to polish? Would the task make sense or be a meaningless way to offer Colin something to do? He almost laughed at the idea that he'd be told to separate wheat from chaff. At this point, he didn't care much, as long *something* changed. "Understood."

Taron walked upstairs but left the trapdoor open as a promise that he was coming back soon.

Colin licked his lips, but when minutes passed, he cleaned up the mess he'd made with the fallen plate, but once this was done, he didn't want to start anything new, and even Anasstasiya Lucas's new book wasn't enough of a temptation to take his mind off the upcoming *change*. After two weeks—or God knew how long—of incarceration, he would at last have something productive to do other than verbally punching Taron, which wasn't nearly as satisfying as it sounded.

With a rattle of glass, Taron came down carrying a box of jars. He disappeared once more and this time brought a large bowl of small cucumbers, and lastly, a tray with garlic, salt, dill, and some kind of root vegetable cut into smaller pieces. He sat with all of that next to the cage, but warned

Colin not to even think of smashing the jars. It was crystal clear to Colin that the man who kept him here by force was also his sole way to freedom.

He started peeling the garlic, cutting up the dill and horseradish, with the knife that somehow seemed less of a threat now, as if it had been a man who'd turned out to be a scarecrow. In short instructions, Taron told Colin how to stuff the cucumbers into jars, how much salt to add, and how much water to pour.

Colin wasn't going to argue about being let out of the cage at this point. He reached through the bars and felt one of the raw cucumbers before smelling its earthy, fresh scent. "Do you grow those yourself?"

Taron nodded without looking up, focused on his work. It only then struck Colin that the pickled onions he'd had for one of his meals must had come from Taron's garden as well.

Colin sighed and prepared the first jar as he'd been told. It felt good to complete a task instead of giving himself unlimited leisure time. "When I was a kid, I would help my grandmom with her vegetable garden. She would make all those incredible jams and marmalades, and her own fruit juice," he said with a smile, remembering the little bench under the apple tree where he used to play on sunny days. That was before his life had become increasingly rigid once his parents had returned from working abroad and taken him back.

That must have piqued Taron's interest because he did glance his way every now and then. Did he have no other job? Was this what he did all day? Some of the books he'd brought Colin had a stamp of the local library, so he probably wasn't a big spender.

Maybe, just maybe, he appreciated the company, no matter what he'd said.

Colin went on, handing Taron the jars to put back into the box. "I used to like all this kind of stuff when I was younger. I would swim all day and I built my own tree house, which had the benefit of a nearly unlimited supply of fruit. This really feels a bit like a trip down memory lane."

Yet when he watched Taron's thick fingers work the knife on the horseradish, he could only wonder about the fate of Peter McGraw. Where had Taron hidden the body? Had he cut it up into little bits as well?

Had he ended up as fertilizer for the garden?

Would Taron grow impatient with him too?

CHAPTER NINE

E very day, Taron assigned Colin a different job, but
always one he was supposed to do in the cage. It
was depressing, but even with Taron not talking
much, having another human being with him down here
counted for something. Once, Taron even stayed to watch
some TV with Colin. He'd sat in the armchair that still had
stains from the blood which had soaked into it on the night
Taron brought him here, but he didn't seem bothered by the
rusty spots and even smirked when Colin commented on
the events on screen.

Still, the excitement and novelty of manual labor were
running out fast, leaving Collin frustrated with the inaction.
Each day was more or less the same, with Taron only
spending a couple of hours tops in the bunker. If Colin was
lucky, he'd have a cat with him, but the passing time was
starting to gradually freak him out. Days lost their rhythm,
and despite there being no daylight to disturb his mornings,
he kept waking up too early or laid motionless waiting for
sleep that just wouldn't come. He felt dirty again, and while
he was taking regular sponge baths and changing into fresh

clothes every day, he missed the opportunity to submerge in water, and when he did sleep, he dreamed about walking barefoot in damp grass.

Yet he was locked up underground, like a vampire during the Arctic summer.

Every day, the walls seemed that bit closer to the cage, and he wondered if this place would be his tomb.

Colin didn't have a perfect grip on time, but either Taron was taking longer than usual, or Colin was getting so anxious about his solitude. He couldn't tell the how long it had been anymore since Taron had last come down. The familiar screech of hinges was something he usually greeted with excitement, but today, he just sat there, tired even though he hadn't done much.

His brain ached from the constant ruminating, as if it were swelling inside his skull. The sight of the boots emerging from the trapdoor had such a visceral effect on him that, despite the frustration and anger, he still felt his heart speed up in anticipation.

He hated Taron, yet also yearned for his presence every single day, and the dichotomy was slowly driving him mad. "You're late."

Taron frowned at him and kicked the cage. He put down a McDonald's paper bag that seemed so out of place in his hands Colin's mind went blank at first. Taron had been away, not just working on his freaky off-grid fantasy homestead.

<That's demanding,> he signed. <Eat.>

Colin clenched his teeth, even though he craved a cheeseburger, regardless of how unhealthy they were. Enough was enough. "I'm not hungry."

<You complained I was late.> Taron huffed, tense as a bull about to charge, which in turn got Colin on pins and

needles. Taron's black beard was messier than usual, even if shorter, and his hair had been cut, but when he took a step to the side, Colin spotted something else. A dark bruise emerged from under Taron's facial hair and went all the way to his eye.

Some of Colin's anger evaporated, and he kneeled in the cage, looking through the bars, because if someone landed a punch on a man like Taron, they might have as well killed him, leaving Colin to die here.

Or perhaps Taron had killed his next victim and the bruise had been the last *fuck you* of a dead man.

"What happened to you?"

<I said, e-a-t.> Taron spelled out the last word, but abruptly took off his plaid shirt.

Colin hadn't seen Taron shirtless since that one-time-only fuck that kept haunting him, and he averted his eyes, focusing on the McDonald's bag instead. "I'm considering a hunger strike. Enough is enough. You don't let me out, you don't tell me anything, but somehow you can go to town all. You. Want," he growled, kicking one of the bars to make the metal thud."

Taron threw the shirt at the cage, then grabbed a small fabric bag off the shelf and flung that as well. <There's a hole. Sew it up.>

The itch to take the shirt, which was likely still warm from Taron's body heat was hard to deny, but Colin had a point to make, and he would never succeed if his resolve collapsed every time loneliness got the best of him. "Let me out of the cage."

<Bad attitude.> Taron snarled, but it was impossible to miss another dark bruise on his stomach. Colin swallowed, his gums itching to bruise him further, even if just his pride.

"Are you talking about yourself? It seems your next victim managed to fight you off."

<Shut up.>

"Why? Saying what I think is the only freedom I have."

<Unless I gag you.>

Colin snorted, but the scowl that twisted his face reached all the way to his heart. "You would have to unlock the cage then. Maybe you should try me. And feed me by force while

you're at it. Because, you know, you wouldn't want your new pet to die."

<You're not a pet. You're a pest.> Taron slammed his hands against the cage, breathing hard. Clearly the anger over whatever fight he'd had wasn't going away.

Colin flinched, but as the handsome face disappeared from view, Colin was faced with Taron's crotch and licked his lips. "I'm your pet rabbit. You keep me in a cage, and you feed me. If I'm really a pest, where's the poison? In the burgers?"

Taron hunkered down in front of the cage, his gaze hard. <Maybe.>

Colin was hit by the sight of the dark hairs covering Taron's chest. The meaty pecs promised the warmth of another human being, and if only Taron hadn't been his captor, Colin would have gladly hugged him, even though he'd never thought of himself as affectionate.

His heart thudded as he leaned forward, raising his chin to expose his throat. "Or maybe you'd rather get rid of me with your own hands?"

There. He'd caught Taron's attention. Despite the baggy clothes he was wearing courtesy of his captor, Colin had no doubt he held appeal to Taron even the way he was now—ungroomed and inactive.

Unless Taron had visited a lover and let off some steam. Which was doubtful with a personality like his. Colin was Taron's only option.

That was it. His way out.

He could almost feel the flavor of another man's mouth on his when he pushed his face between the bars, staring into Taron's eyes as if they were the most fascinating thing in the universe. It was an act, but once the connection was established, and the tension rose in the silence, the dark green of those irises was like a window to all of Taron's secrets Colin was yet to unlock.

"Aren't you tempted to do that every time I annoy you?"

<Kill you?> Taron reached out, and when Colin didn't flinch, the thick fingers grabbed Colin's throat. They were hot, rough, and while they exerted pressure, they weren't choking him yet.

Fear crawled up Colin's back, but it just made his skin more sensitive. "What else would you do with me?"

Taron must have not wanted to let go of Colin's throat, because for the first time since once voicing Colin's name, he spoke. "You k-know what I'd do—with you." Just as Colin remembered. A barely-there raspy whisper interrupted by a choking grunt. For some unexplainable reason, this almost-mute man struggling to speak for him was like a shot of absinthe, and he shuddered, swallowing against the hand.

"How about we trade then?" he whispered, pulling up the large sweater Taron had given him to wear.

There was nothing sexier than seeing Taron's pupils widen. Colin had enjoyed so much sex in the past, and yet it felt disposable somehow—distracted. The way Taron's focus centered on Colin was already addictive. Sure, he still remembered that the trap door wasn't locked and allowed escape if he convinced Taron to open the cage, but he'd also grown to crave Taron's attention.

Deep in the woods, he wasn't one of many pretty faces on Grindr. He wasn't someone's Saturday boy, as forgettable as any other guy fucked that week. Taron was so hot for him his body could've burned Colin's fingertips.

"Hn?" Taron grunted.

Colin reached out for his other hand and brought it closer, shuddering when he rubbed his nose against the middle of the palm and smelled *skin*. No perfume necessary. That raw masculine scent was the epitome of sexy, and Colin was eager to lick its saltiness.

"You said I have to either work or fuck you, right?"

In a cage, in a bunker, in the middle of the forest, Nowhere, West Virginia, Colin had never felt more in control than when Taron's breath got shallow. Taron's hand was around Colin's throat, but Colin's was around Taron's balls without even touching them.

The man was *thirsty*.

Taron nodded.

Bingo.

Colin licked his way up Taron's index finger and then, without warning, sucked it in, only stopping once his lips tightened by the knuckle. The digit was thick, uneven on his tongue, and wonderfully heavy.

Never looking away from Taron, Colin withdrew and kissed the damp fingertip. "And I want fresh air. I need exercise. I'm sure we can work something out." Wasn't even a hard bargain to make. Despite being an evil murderer, Taron seemed to care for him in his own way, and was a stud Colin wouldn't mind fucking.

Taron reached to his back pocket and pulled out the small key. In a breathless moment, they watched one another as the padlock clicked open. The raw lust reflected in his gaze gave Colin more of a rush than the cocaine he'd once snorted during exams. It had an electric quality that tickled Colin's flesh, as if he were already being touched between his thighs. He decided to make it easy for Taron and pushed off his sweatpants.

"Show it to me," he demanded, realizing he hadn't even seen Taron's dick, even though he'd felt it for two days after the fuck.

Was Taron still convinced Colin was out for him and would stab him in the dick at the first opportunity, or was he so entranced that his brain had stopped working?

Despite Taron opening the cage, Colin's focus was on the massive man crawling into his space, not on the trap door. He missed attention, he missed human connection. Taron pawing at his thighs as if he was a bear who finally got his honey made Colin's cock swell.

The sole reason Taron pulled away once inside the cramped space was to open his own pants.

The cage was small even when Colin was the only person inside it, but Taron filled it so completely that if Colin's intention was to attempt an escape, he wouldn't have had the chance. The beast smelled nice tonight, with a hint of cologne, and Colin grabbed his beard with one hand, dragging him down for a kiss, but Taron dodged it, going for Colin's ear instead.

One of his hands was on Colin's bare ass, but the other was already sliding his own pants lower. The tickle of facial hair against Colin's neck made him shudder and curl his toes. Taron had to be at least thirty, and Colin would've been lying if he'd claimed Taron being older wasn't a turn on. He'd always played it safe with guys his age. He'd always played it safe, period.

Taron on the other hand was a force of nature, and one couldn't fight his tide forever. No matter how beautiful your gated community was, if a tornado rolled over it, you could do nothing but let nature take its course.

Colin was somewhat disappointed that Taron didn't want to kiss him, but the sharp teeth nipping at his sensitive neck already made him sweat.

And he still hadn't seen Taron's dick.

Breathless, he pushed the mass of wool up, forcing Taron to pull away, but getting naked brought Colin such relief that he smiled at Taron as soon as they saw one another again. But then his eyes were drawn lower, and his breath caught at the sight of that wonderful picture. Taron's cock was as big as Colin had suspected, with foreskin only showing the tip of the damp cockhead. He gave a shuddery gasp and rubbed Taron's muscled thigh before reaching his goal.

"Okay, wow."

Just thinking of that cock inside of him, forcing its way in, made his mouth go dry.

Taron let out a groan of satisfaction and pushed Colin back down.

Colin rocked his hips toward him and clutched at some of the dark hair on Taron's chest. "I wanna suck you dry."

Disappointment shuddered through Colin with a surprising force when Taron shook his head. He was reminded of their conversation about dick biting. So Taron didn't trust him enough to put his cock in Colin's mouth yet. Damn shame, because Colin would have given Taron the head of his life.

Taron ran his hand up Colin's side with adoration, but soon enough shifted to reach out through the bars, all the way under the armchair. Next to the porn mags, stood a bottle of lube Taron must have used for jerking off. It would now serve a much more important purpose.

Colin grunted, gently scratching Taron's pec to agitate him further. "Did you jerk off thinking about me?" he whispered and slid his other hand to his own growing dick.

Taron groaned in reply, but the enthusiasm in the sound meant it was a yes. Once the lube was inside the cage and within reach, he grabbed Colin's thighs and wrapped them around himself, rocking his hard cock against Colin's knuckles. Taron's groin was hairy, yet another feature Colin had rarely encountered with other lovers. Sure, some were trimmed not waxed, but the rawness of the man on top of him was an unexpected thrill.

He let his hands wander up and down the muscular body, marveling at its sturdiness. If the roof collapsed, perhaps Taron's steel-like frame could provide Colin with shelter. Denied the kiss on the lips, he pushed himself up and savored the taste of the shaven neck, still fragrant with some kind of aftershave. His legs were tight around Taron's hips, and even in the cage, where their bodies completely filled the space, he wanted to get even closer, craving that same human touch that he used to avoid when he was free.

"My side of the bargain," he whispered, looking between their bodies, where their cocks shared heat, resting on Colin's stomach.

Taron nodded, but then sat up so fast he hit his head on the cage's ceiling. Colin couldn't help a smirk of satisfaction. It had happened to him many times already. It was about time Taron felt the discomfort he so insistently punished Colin with. Taron grunted like a wolf that had had its prey taken, but grabbed Colin's hips and flipped him onto his stomach.

Colin purred into the sheets on top of the mattress. The

confined space didn't allow Taron to straighten up and keep his body heat to himself, and Colin tried to adjust his position, but Taron wouldn't let him do even that. Grabbing Colin's hips as if they belonged to an animal, Taron first pulled him to his knees and then kicked them open, leaving him so exposed Colin could sense cool air on his hole.

A drizzle of lube down his crack made him arch his spine, which turned into a gentle rocking motion when two fingers followed the damp trail. Taron breathed heavily just above Colin's ear, rubbing his cock against Colin's buttock like a beast about to rut. It was as scary as it was arousing. Would it hurt again? Colin almost wanted it to. He wanted to feel the reckless passion Taron had unleashed on him that first time, so different from the mundaneness of his past sexual experiences. He craved that kind of untamed lust to wash over him and cling to his skin, erasing the emptiness he'd felt all his life.

Colin uttered a growl and arched his back, pressing against the wide chest of his grizzly. The body hair was coarse enough to scratch his skin, and combined with the pace at which Taron fucked Colin's ass with his fingers, transported Colin somewhere else altogether. To a time before cell phones or cars, when all that mattered was food, shelter, and fucking.

When Taron pulled his fingers out, his lubed-up cock-head instantly replaced them, demanding entry. Now that Colin had seen it, he couldn't stop thinking about how thick it was, how rigid with the need to fuck him. Still, when the head pushed in, the inevitable discomfort made him rapidly inhale. He found Taron's forearm and held onto it, rolling his face over the pillow until his neck ached. When he opened his eyes, he could see Taron's wild face looming above, his wide arms tense, his chest full of air, his entire body ready to mercilessly fuck Colin whether he wanted it or not.

Colin dragged his teeth over his lips, his heels rubbing the backs of Taron's thighs as the thick girth eased inside him. The guttural moan that came from Taron really was like that of a bear when he pushed his cock all the way in. His pubes tickled Colin's ass, and for a moment Taron was just nestled inside, panting into Colin's nape. His beard smelled so good. Had he been to a barber?

But any and all of Colin's thoughts blurred the moment Taron grabbed his thigh while pulling out at such pace that for a horrible moment Colin thought the fuck was over. When the cock moved back in, like a piston pumping fuel into Colin's waiting body, air left his lungs, leaving him lightheaded and breathless. His balls were so heavy every movement made them ache, yet he needed the penetration so much he pushed back as soon as Taron retreated again, spearing himself with the hard dick. Stuck between reality and erotic dreams, he spat into his palm and started frantically jerking off. The sex had just started, and he was already high.

Taron ran his palm all the way from Colin's stomach to his pec, rubbing the nipple with the heel of his hand. His hips never stopped working, pinning Colin's ass time and time again. Colin had even once had a fling with a quarterback, but Taron would have towered over that guy. He wasn't just tall, which Colin was as well. The sheer size of his chest, his arms, the weight of his muscles, made Colin feel like there was no other way but to submit. It was only natural to let this big, strong guy take him and protect him from whatever disaster he believed in. Colin was fine with it as long as Taron continued.

He spread his thighs wide, letting Taron fuck him bare, ready to accept his cum.

His eyelids fluttered when Taron whispered in that nasty rasp that right now sounded like the strongest aphrodisiac.

"So f-fucking tight..."

A wave of heat flowed into Colin's chest, and as Taron withdrew his dick again, Colin purposefully clenched his ass around it while jerking off with increasing aggression. His orgasm was already building, and each shaky tone coming to him with the heat of Taron's breath, the tickle of his beard, were all combining into the mind-blowing wave that was coming.

"I'm gonna milk you so good," he babbled.

Taron stabbed his cock into Colin time after time, but when he started rubbing it rhythmically against the prostate, Colin was gone. He came, moaning without shame and grabbing Taron's steel-sturdy forearm.

Taron kept grunting against Colin's nape, increasing the speed of his thrusts until his balls slapped Colin's ass over and over. While Colin was still riding the wave of his pleasure, Taron bit his shoulder, making him whimper. Now, the thrusts were slow, harsh and deliberate. Taron was coming, pumping his seed inside and stirring it in for good measure. They wouldn't be making any babies, but Colin's instincts didn't seem to know it, nor did he care. For all he knew, he was a bitch that had just been mounted by a stud.

Colin shuddered all over, and he brought his numbed hand to his lips, once again cleaning it off his own juices. He felt so full. Completely taken. And while he knew his feelings might change once the excitement passed, in that moment there was no place he'd would've rather been than under Taron. In the cage. In the Bunker. In the woods, Nowhere, West Virginia.

He didn't bother to look for a weapon, strike while Taron wasn't attentive. He wanted to lay under the sturdy guy, enjoy the cock inside of him, think about the cum, and breathe in the scent of beard oil. After all the days spent alone, the skin-to-skin contact was all he craved.

He laughed, gently rubbing Taron's flesh with his thumb. "Okay, *now* I'm hungry."

Taron let out a grunty chuckle and reached out for the bag of fast food without even pulling out yet. Colin had pondered many times if Taron was trying to 'tame' him with all the treats, but maybe it was him who could domesticate Taron? He was a man with a lot of potential but wild even in his attempts at good behavior. With time and care, Colin could see great return for that investment. For now though, he opened the bag and fished out a cold fry. It still tasted like heaven.

"You don't have a habit of usually skipping condoms, do you?" he asked, looking over his shoulder. He should have worried about that earlier, but here in the woods, STDs didn't seem as real as they did in the outside world. Not to mention that the first time they'd had sex, using rubbers had been the least of Colin's problems. Still was, really.

Colin whimpered when Taron slid out of him but was relieved when Taron gave his ass an appreciative pat and shook his head.

They both lay on the mattress, cage wide open, trap door open. It was either a test, or Taron no longer believed Colin would just run off on him.

Either way, Colin didn't feel like moving yet. He rolled over to face Taron and put the food bag on his stomach. The post-coital laziness was a prominent presence in his muscles, and he offered Taron a silly smile, weirdly content with the stickiness and mild soreness left by the fuck. "Satisfied?"

The lazy grin was all he needed to know, but Taron still nodded. When he looked so good, with his cock sticking out of his pants, chest and face flushed, Colin almost forgot he was dealing with a murderer. But as much as Colin enjoyed this transaction, he still wanted his reward.

"So... how do you plan to pay me for this... job?" he asked, picking out a chicken nugget.

Taron's smile faded, and he started signing. <I've been working on something, I'll show you.> He crawled out, showing Colin the upper half of his ass. It was nice and muscular, but Colin didn't want to tempt fate by slapping it. One could never know with a macho guy like Taron.

Colin followed him out of the cage tentatively, half-expecting to be pushed back in, but nothing like that happened, and he stretched, until his back creaked. "Oh, damn, this feels so good!"

His nakedness must have been enough of a distraction, because Taron didn't even seem particularly attentive to Colin's movements.

Was this the moment to grab a weapon and strike?

If his blow was strong enough, lethal enough, he would be free. He glanced to the trap door under the pretense of looking around. It was open, and he could easily leave the house once he was up there. Even if he was to run naked, he wasn't bound. Taron didn't have a bunch of dogs to guard the premises.

But if Taron survived, the trust Colin had managed to build would never be restored. It would have been game over for him.

So Colin needed to bide his time for a better opportunity. After all, he'd only just gotten the chance to step out of the cage for the second time. There was no need to get hasty, since it wasn't like the sex was a chore.

<Wait here,> Taron signed, as if Colin had anywhere to go. Unless it was a signal not to follow Taron upstairs.

Rio poked his nose in and jogged down the stairs, but Taron grabbed him on the way and held him in his arms. The cat became a purring machine Colin could hear even from afar.

Colin smirked. "You look good from down here," he said, wanting to push his claws deeper into Taron's flesh, but he wasn't lying either. He was hoping for many, many chores like this one until he finally freed himself, once his stars aligned.

Taron glanced over his shoulder, but he was impossible to read. When he came back down after a couple of minutes, his pants were back in place, and he held something large in one hand.

Two cats followed him to the bunker, meowing as if they needed assistance. Had he come down to feed Colin before them? It was definitely a privilege. "Where is the red bow on that present?" Colin asked with a small smile, though he was feeling a little bit nervous.

Colin's stomach dropped at the sight of the collar with some kind of device attached, but he still took it in his hands when Taron passed it to him. <You won't like it. It's a shock collar. Best idea I've had so far. You will be able to come out of here with me.>

Colin felt somewhat deflated, but this was at least *something*. It meant Taron had been planning to give him more freedom. "Won't it suddenly shock me at night or something?"

<No. It's remotely operated and has a tracker. I will

shock you if you run. But if you kill me and walk off far enough, it will shock you still.>

Those weren't the nicest words to hear from a man you'd just fucked, but Colin wasn't in a normal situation either.

He reluctantly turned the heavy collar in his hands. "I wouldn't kill you. I literally still have enough spunk inside me I might be 5% you."

Taron let out that weird snort-grunt and ruffled Colin's hair.

CHAPTER TEN

Taron had been working on this collar for a while, but seeing it locked around Colin's slender neck still gave him shiver of satisfaction. He had no idea how things would go from now on, or how Colin would act once he was allowed outside, but people were unpredictable anyway, so Taron wanted to give this solution a shot.

It wasn't his intention to keep Colin in a cage underground forever, since it would have been unbearable in the long run. He could've just as well put a bullet in Colin's head and end his misery. But Colin hadn't complained about the work, the stories about his grandma's garden inspired confidence in Taron that Colin would adjust to the life around the homestead, and he was a great piece of ass, on top of that.

The sex had worked wonders to Colin's temperament too. When Taron had first come home after his visit to town, Colin had been spiteful and aggressive, but now his body language was relaxed, and he didn't protest the collar nor the rope attached to it.

As soon as they were outside, Colin insisted on removing his shoes and stepped into the yard naked, arguing that he'd still need to wash later, anyway. Taron would've been happy to arrange that, if he was allowed to watch.

Taron assumed Colin's excitement wasn't entirely sincere, but it was still nice to hear so many questions about his homestead. If this was to be Colin's home, Taron needed to give him a tour. He had mixed feelings about having to live with another man under his roof, but there was nothing to be done about it, and sex sweetened the deal.

And speaking of sex, Colin was walking so close their skin was in a near-permanent state of almost-touching. It was difficult to figure out someone whose tactics changed so much, but for now Taron decided to go with it and see what the guy's next step would be.

It was a warm afternoon, and he didn't feel like dressing, so there was odd tension in the air even though technically they weren't doing anything erotically-charged. Taron showed Colin the rabbits, and then his workshop, where he manufactured all the items needed around the house, including the collar.

<And this is Wyoming.> Taron pointed to the large black and brown rabbit hopping in the enclosure. He'd named her after his home state, but it felt strange to sign the word to Colin. The past he'd left in Wyoming wasn't something he wanted to think about.

Wyoming made a strange turn before chewing on the grass, and Colin smiled, watching the younger animals play. "I'm surprised you don't produce your own dairy." he said, smiling at Taron, as if the heavy collar on his neck was just an accessory.

Taron nodded with pride. <I've been thinking about it. Might buy some goats in the future.>

Colin rubbed his shoulder against Taron's arm. "Someone's happy with himself. You actually do this all alone?" he said, looking around the homestead Taron had been building over ten years.

Taron stood a bit closer, and his fingers briefly touched Colin's on the fence. <All my work. Built the house myself.>

Colin swallowed hard, letting his hand linger in the air. The sun created patterns on his bare chest—bright with the shadow of branches for pattern, and Taron took it in despite his best intentions. Was he falling into Colin's trap already?

"But you do get lonely," Colin said, focusing all of Taron's attention on his words. "There are some things you can't exactly be self-sufficient with."

<Too much work to be lonely.> Taron shrugged. It was a half-truth, because he did sometimes yearn for companionship. The problem was that he also loved the freedom of doing his own thing, on his property, however he pleased, without having to consult with anyone. Also, <people are a liability.> He'd learned that the hard way.

Colin sighed, staring back at Taron so intensely the touch of his fingertips on Taron's palm came as a complete surprise. His eyes were bright, intelligent, yet so seductive he would have made more cash doing *that* than healing people, if he'd been telling the truth about being a doctor in the first place.

"But you clearly enjoy having a partner. How did you deal with that so far?"

A *partner*? More like 'prisoner'. <Sex?>

Colin took a deep breath, the tip of his finger drawing a

line by Taron's elbow. "Yes."

How much should Taron even tell him? It wasn't like he was obliged to divulge the details of his uneventful sex life. He settled on, <rarely.>

Colin's teeth pulled over his lips. "Wouldn't it have been easier and safer to find yourself a boyfriend and live with him? I mean..." He chuckled and rubbed his face, hiding a growing smile. "There's so much sex available. How do you manage without it?"

Taron cocked his head. Did Colin have a lot of sex then? He'd intended to keep things as transactional as possible, but the burning question inside of him created a surprising flame he wouldn't be able to put out without asking. <Do you have a boyfriend?> Just the thought of that alone had Taron itching with such anger he didn't know what to do with himself.

Colin blinked, as if he hadn't expected that question. His face relaxed, and the light brown eyes glanced at the trees nearby. "I... I never had the time for boyfriends. I just hook up with people."

Taron leaned against the fence, wondering if he could stand having another mouth to feed around his house. Sometimes the cats seemed like too much hassle, and he didn't have the complication of fucking them. On the other hand, sometimes the itch got so bad, he couldn't help but seek out a guy, so maybe this kind of partnership was a good way to deal with the problem, both now and once shit hit the fan?

Colin's hand moved farther, eventually resting on Taron's bicep. "I was pushed to study all the time, and this whole internet dating thing seemed like a lifesaver. If I can't fuck once or twice a week, I get really agitated. Sometimes, it's almost like a pill that I need in order to function. Like caffeine."

Taron liked the sound of that so much he didn't even care if it was a lie or not. That was so hot. How would it be to have Colin around, though? Now that they'd fucked again, would Colin want to laze around all day in a hammock, or would he be up for helping around the homestead? If he could do some of the gardening, Taron's workload would become much smaller. He didn't like to hire people, because they always got too nosy, and communication was hard because most didn't know sign language. And Colin... he had to stay here anyway.

Taron stroked the fingers touching him without prompting. At least he knew that Colin did like to be fucked by him.

Colin smirked and tickled Taron's hand, gravitating closer until Taron could smell his hair. "It's weird, but now that my brain isn't so goddamn busy with cramming all the time, I actually want to spend time with people."

That instantly got Taron tense. <You can't go to the town.> *And you're not fucking anyone else.*

Colin didn't seem displeased and only moved closer, circling Taron's arm with his hands. "Well, in that case I'll just have to satisfy all my social needs with you. You think you can keep up?"

Taron shook his head, but smiled with relief. <Will you be able to keep up with gardening work?> When had he become so soft? The boy was doing something to him that he never expected to feel. He'd been perfectly happy falling asleep with a cat on his feet, and now he was considering moving his bed to the bunker. They could sleep together then, and if they got in the mood in the morning, falling into sex would be so easy.

Colin made a little jump and put his arms around Taron. His face radiated happiness that Taron hadn't seen on his handsome face before. "Yes! I'd love to keep up with the gardening work. And I'll gladly keep up with you, too," he said, dropping his voice to a whisper.

The flood of emotion was choking Taron and he couldn't bear to push Colin away, no matter how much he'd meant for this thing between them to stay strictly transactional. He'd kept a dam on his feelings for so long he'd forgotten they were there, just waiting for a crack in the concrete. Why the hell was he doing this to himself? There was no way Colin could ever grow fond of him.

<I know it's not ideal.>

Colin was silent for a while, but then his fingers danced across Taron's chest, making his heart reach a furious pace that Colin could surely have sensed. "Why didn't you want to kiss me?" he asked in the end.

Taron licked his lips, embarrassed by the truth, but something else became much more pressing.

Someone was driving toward the house.

CHAPTER ELEVEN

There was someone coming.

Just a few heartbeats ago, Colin and Taron had been negotiating the nature of their relationship, but the sudden invasion of their bubble offered Colin a variety of new, unexpected choices. Before he'd heard the approaching car, there had been a plan in his head, but now he was no longer certain of it. He didn't know what to do.

The decision was made for him—the story of his life.

Taron opened the door to the chicken coop and pushed Colin inside, spooking two birds sleeping on perches close to a couple nesting boxes. The straw dug into Colin's bare feet, and when the scent of wood and excrement filled his nose, he spun around, eager to go back outside. Taron stopped him with a hand pressed to Colin's chest and frowned. He whispered instead of signing, as if he were desperate for Colin to understand him without fail.

"You c-come out, all you gonna get is a cellmate, understood?"

"I know you're here, Hauff! Come out and show your

fucking face!" someone yelled from the other side of the house in a thick local accent.

"Who is that?" Colin whispered back, shocked by the angry tone in the stranger's voice, but Taron was already running, and the door of the coop shut halfway on its own, leaving a gap that allowed Colin to peek outside. His bare skin covered in gooseflesh, but he didn't retreat deeper into the small shed and stayed close to the door, listening in.

The man's voice was smothered in anger, so he couldn't have been a friend of Taron's. If he found out Colin was a prisoner here, would he choose to help? And if so, was he even capable of withstanding the power of Taron's muscles? Colin watched them move rigidly on Taron's back when the stranger came into view.

Colin's heart stopped beating, and he had to bite his tongue not to scream. It was the dead guy, Peter McGraw, only his skull was intact, and he came at Taron as if he had nothing to fear from him. What the fuck was going on? Colin had seen his head split open, he'd seen the blood and smelled the fear on him, so how could he possibly be alive?

He couldn't breathe, frozen in place as he watched McGraw shove Taron's chest hard, as if he were taking revenge for the kill weeks later. This couldn't be. It couldn't. People didn't recover from head wounds so fast, and Colin couldn't see a trace of scars or swelling either.

As if the murder had never happened.

Taron stood his ground, stepping into the guy's personal space.

McGraw's teeth glinted when he snarled, reminiscent of a dog about to strike. "I know it was you, no matter how many times you deny it!"

Taron spread his arms, and when McGraw mocked the

gesture, twisting his face as if he were imitating a chimpanzee, Colin's mouth fell open at the offensive behavior. And then he realized that Taron didn't have an easy time communicating with people who didn't sign. Sure, he could express his thoughts on paper, but one couldn't exactly diffuse a fight by writing 'Get off my property!' and showing it to a furious man.

So Taron pushed at McGraw's chest with one hand and pointed for him to leave with the other.

McGraw's face twisted, and he spat to the ground between them. "My brother *was* here! I can fucking smell him. What the fuck did you do to him?"

His brother.

Colin's heart skipped a beat when he realized this stranger wasn't a nightmare come to life. Twin? It now made sense why McGraw had a hunch who his brother's killer was, despite not witnessing the murder.

Colin's head pulsed, as if his cerebrospinal fluid was about to boil over. This was his chance. McGraw was a big guy. Surely, together—

McGraw pulled out a handgun, and Colin's guts twisted.

He didn't want Taron dead.

It made zero sense. Even though he could put himself in Taron's shoes, his own wellbeing should've been a priority. He needed to escape, even if Taron was to pay a heavy price for his actions. He knew this. He knew he shouldn't worry about Taron before himself, but his instincts kept him quiet even when one of the chickens unexpectedly rubbed her wing against his calf.

Taron held his hands up, his back tense.

McGraw waved the gun around like a madman and

spoke as if every single word needed to be spat out. "You're an outsider! You don't deserve to own this land!"

Rio emerged from behind the cabin, lured by the noise, and approached the unfamiliar man fearlessly, but Colin's attention was drawn back to the gun. He didn't know whether McGraw was drunk, high, or simply too furious to control his body, but his outstretched arm shook. If McGraw, in his rage, fired at Taron from so close, he'd kill him on the spot.

Colin's muscles were stiff as if they had calcified, but when something poked the back of his knee, he let out a strangled yelp. A quick look down confirmed it was only a chicken, but McGraw's attention was already on the henhouse, and Colin's guts twisted further.

"What else do you have here? Where's my brother, you fuck?"

But when McGraw stepped forward, Taron stood in his way, and shoved him again despite the gun pointed at his chest. Colin's blood curdled. If he wasn't here, Taron wouldn't be taking such risks

He was worried what McGraw would have done to him if he found him here—naked and with a collar around his neck. Taron might have taken him against his will, but he was also the guarantee of Colin's safety.

His gaze swiped over the coop to settle on the curious chicken, which was now pecking something off the floor. Without thinking, he picked the bird up and tossed it through the gap left by the door. Its loud clucking was like a battle cry, but when Colin stepped closer to see if the distraction has been effective, a bullet hit the wooden doorframe, sending splinters into the air. He froze, falling to his knees just in time to catch a glimpse of Taron smashing his fist into McGraw's jaw. He had the gun in hand and pointed it at McGraw without hesitation.

The guy stilled, his hands rising in submission. His skin was pale, with bright red spots. "I told my guys where I'm going. You pull that trigger, you're as good as dead. But before they string you up, they'll do the same to all your fucking cats!"

Taron growled so loudly even Colin could hear him and pointed to the car with the gun in a universal gesture of 'get the fuck out'. McGraw moved, unsuccessfully attempting to kick Rio on the way. Taron shot, and while Colin couldn't see it well, the metallic thud suggested he must have hit McGraw's car.

"You sonofabitch!" McGraw yelled, but with the firearm out of his hand, he had to follow orders, and climbed into the vehicle. "This isn't the end, Hauff!"

Colin was back by the door, tempted to run out of the coop, but for what? He could have tried to run while Taron was distracted, but his mind was way more preoccupied with the danger to the homestead.

It was only then that he remembered the shock collar around his neck and touched the lock at the front. Taron could be bluffing about its properties, but could Colin afford to risk it?

The car took off, with a crunch of gravel beneath its wheels. The timing of this random attack was odd. Was McGraw the person who Taron had a scuffle with earlier in town?

Colin burst out of the chicken house. The fresh air blew into his lungs, but he only felt at peace once he stood next to Taron and touched his warm skin. "He wanted to kill you," he whispered in disbelief.

"Fucking shitbag," Taron whispered, even though Colin

could hear the effort he needed to put into choking out the words. His chest was heaving, and yet Colin wasn't afraid of the gun in his hand.

"How does he know?" Colin demanded, curling his hands on the waistband of Taron's jeans.

Taron emptied the gun and put it away so he could sign. <He doesn't. He suspects it. We're not friends.> Even in sign language, it sounded like a euphemism.

Colin felt heat rush to his head, filling it as if it were a balloon about to float into the air. "You don't say," he uttered, hesitating, but in the end he put his arms around Taron and rested his cheek on his chest. He did it to communicate his distress to the man who he needed to consider as his protector for the time being, but the heat of the skin that still smelled like their sweat combined, and the tickle of body hair against his face made him melt into the sturdiness of Taron's body.

The regular thumping of his heart—slower and easier than Colin's own—brought unexpected relief, but then Taron cupped the back of Colin's head and stroked it, as if Colin really was a new kitten he needed to take care of. One Taron hadn't chosen to adopt, and yet had no other choice but to keep.

That was it. Colin had found Taron's weakness, and he *would* exploit it, both for the sake of his future escape, and in order to make his stay in Taron's home more bearable. The fact that Taron was an attractive man was a bonus, but being held like this still made his body react as if they weren't captor and abductee. It was just the feedback loop— an emotional reaction to a physical stimuli—but he chose not to talk himself out of letting warmth and touch fool him.

"But how does he know? What did Peter do that his brother thinks you might have killed him?"

When Taron pushed at Colin's shoulders, Colin felt bitter about the rejection at first, but then he realized Taron needed the distance to effectively communicate his thoughts.

<He killed my cat.>

Colin stared at him, at first unsure if he understood him right. "*Killed* it?"

Taron took a deep breath, and his signing became so erratic Colin had to focus to understand it all. <Killed him. Cut his head off, and was bringing it to me that night as a threat. I think he wanted to leave it somewhere, but I was out late, and tracked him down. I know it doesn't sound right. Killing a man over a cat, but you don't understand. Sacramento was my first cat. He found me here when I first bought the land. He was just a kitten, he was ill, and weak, and I nursed him to health, and he always followed me everywhere. I loved him! He was my family, and for that got treated like nothing. He suffered because of that mother-fucker.> To Colin's disbelief, Taron rubbed his reddened eyes with his hairy forearm. <I'd rather the cunt burned the place down. That cat did nothing to him. NOTHING. And if you don't protect what's yours, who will?>

Colin stepped away and shook his head, taken aback. "What a psycho..."

Taron sniffed, but his expression was carved in stone. <He was. So, no, I don't regret smashing his head. Fucking stain on society. I just regret he got away far enough to reach you, and now you're stuck here.>

Colin felt his heartbeat under the collar, tightening around his neck like an invisible rope and pulling him Taron's way. "That's awful. I'm so sorry about Sacramento. People like McGraw don't deserve a place in society. What kind of monster does such a thing to a defenseless animal?" he asked, placing his hand on Taron's back.

<You don't have to pretend. I know you think I'm a monster. It is what it is.> And yet in the bright spring sun, Taron's green eyes were nothing like those of a monster. His size spoke of strength, but Colin was slowly getting the idea that Taron didn't use his massive hands to strangle people, but to chop down trees.

He'd never wanted a captive. He only kept Colin here because he didn't want to spend his life behind bars, and he couldn't trust Colin to keep his mouth shut. Maybe that was the key? Maybe one day Taron would trust Colin enough to let him go?

Colin swallowed, staring at the tendons in Taron's neck trembling under his skin. "There are many people who don't deserve to be here. That's why everyone loves a vigilante. Out there, in the world, we like to pretend we live by some kind of high moral code, but at heart we all want revenge."

Taron took a deep raspy breath, and clenched and unclenched his fists. <Let's go see the rest of the homestead.>

Colin squeezed Taron's wrist and stepped into his personal space, his heart skipping a beat when the damp green of Taron's eyes flashed his way. "He deserved it. I understand why you did it. And I know why you don't want to let me go. It sucks that I can't just drive to the store or see a movie, but I understand why you're doing it."

Their eyes locked, making tension rise in Colin's body as if he were once again seeing a broken arm swell into an unnatural shape. Lightheaded, and unable to speak, he just stared back.

<I'm glad,> Taron communicated in the end, making some of the knots in Colin's chest unwind.

They stood motionless in the sun, Colin's body experiencing the after-sex soreness, and his heart still agitated by McGraw's intrusion. He wasn't sure where it would all lead, but he wanted to earn Taron's trust, even if he was to misuse it in the future.

"Why didn't you want to kiss me?" he asked when the silence stretched out a little too long.

Taron rubbed his face, messing up his beard, but answered. <I've never kissed anyone, so I'm not good at it. No point to.>

Colin's gaze was drawn to Taron's lips. The fact that they were so easily visible was yet more proof that the beard had been trimmed during Taron's visit in town. An intense color and smooth, they tempted Colin all the more now that he hadn't gotten a taste of them when he'd wanted to. "Are you really telling me no one wanted to kiss a beefcake like you?" he asked, pulling his fingers through the soft, fragrant beard.

Taron shook his head, but still smirked. <Flattery.>

Colin sucked on his bottom lip, drawn to the heat of Taron's body like a cat to a laser dot. "Maybe I could be your first then?"

Taron snorted. <It could be lousy. I like to fuck, but I don't look for boyfriends.>

Colin frowned, seconds from retreating.

He was offended. He really fucking was.

"Tough luck, because you said yourself I'm not going anywhere."

<So?>

"So it's awkward. We can't exactly fuck and then pretend the other doesn't exist for the rest of the semester, like I'd do out there. We're stuck here, and that means we need to make things run smoothly."

Taron cocked his head. <You want to play house?>

This time, Colin did step away. "What is that supposed to mean? It's only natural to maintain physical contact with the person you're fucking on the regular!"

Taron followed him and grabbed his hand. <Okay. I didn't think you'd want that.>

The way Taron leaned over him—sturdy like a brick wall—turned Colin's insides into hot vapor. "What did you think I'd want? Fuck and then not speak to each other for the rest of the day?"

Taron rubbed his thumb over Colin's wrist, and even though Colin thought he was pumped out for now, that small touch had excitement dripping to his cock.

<I don't know. Tell me.>

Colin swallowed, stuck in that weird state between lust and latent anger. Taron was too attractive. Why would a guy who chose to live like a hermit, with only animals for company, be this hot? It just wasn't fair. "Put your hands on my hips," he said in the end, meeting the green gaze.

Taron didn't hesitate to follow that instruction, but quickly deviated from it and slipped his fingers to Colin's ass. Colin took a sharp inhale, falling into Taron's arms. Once he was there, surrounded by the fragrant heat of his bare chest and arms, he couldn't be his usual eloquent self any longer. Swallowing the scent of Taron's flesh in big gulps, he moved his hands to the handsome face, caressing the tanned skin and gently pulling on the smooth beard. "Now open your lips and kiss me. Slowly."

Taron didn't close his eyes as he lowered his head so that his lips could meet Colin's. The beard tickled Colin's face, smooth and smelling of sandalwood. Did he visit the barber for Colin's sake, or was it a luxury he afforded himself from time to time? Colin guessed it was the former, and it tickled his ego, because Taron had gotten that done before ever knowing he'd get to fuck Colin again.

That thought made the kiss sweet. At first gentle, as if Colin were fragile porcelain, Taron kissed him with short pecks, only teasing his tongue into the mix once Colin opened his lips in invitation, scratching up Taron's sides.

It didn't feel at all like an unskilled kiss. A shy one, but not at all the saliva-dripping, biting, or tight-lipped messes Colin had experienced when he'd first started hooking up. What Taron didn't have experience with he clearly made up with theory, and while the kiss wasn't earth-shattering, it did cause a tremor in Colin's heart.

He murmured, melting into the embrace as the kiss went on, until his hands clutched Taron's shoulders, and their chests pressed together like two mismatched puzzle pieces that desperately needed to form a picture.

It even felt mutual when they both came up for air, as if they were already understanding each other's body language.

<And I can do that any time?> Taron asked, as if he hadn't put a shock collar on Collin's neck and hadn't dragged him here kicking and screaming.

Colin exhaled, nuzzling Taron's beard. "Sure. But what about the blowjob? Did you not want to go there for the same reason?" he asked, grinning at Taron, still drunk on the intense kiss.

Taron lowered his eyelids and shook his head. <I don't trust your teeth on my cock.>

Colin grunted, shaking his head to show his displeasure. "Fine. We'll deal with that later."

Taron kissed him again, as if he wanted to show that he

wasn't as worried about Colin's teeth on his tongue, and Colin could no longer be irritated. It was fine. So maybe the circumstances weren't ideal, and his parents were probably worried, but trying to make a run for it now would have been not only risky but also stupid. Taron, like any man, had weak points, and Colin would use them to gain his trust. And then, he could run.

After all, hadn't he secretly wished for a gap year?

CHAPTER TWELVE

The next two weeks were oddly normal. As normal as life could be for a man who was locked up underground every night and slept on a mattress inside a cage. As normal as life could be for a man who had a shock collar around his neck.

It was a weird kind of normal, but that's how it felt to Colin, and he didn't fight it.

Since Taron had first brought him to the windowless cellar, his body seemed to have undergone a reboot of sorts. Gone was the daily uneasiness and sleepless nights spent on tossing in the sheets while hours went by. Gone was the constant sense of fatigue and the need for coffee. Each morning, Colin would wake up well rested, just in time to see the trapdoor open and hear the soothing sound of Taron's boots on the wooden stairs.

Breakfast would await him upstairs, and while there was variety to lunch and dinner, the first meal of the day always included hearty scrambled eggs with a side of seasoned rabbit belly. He'd been apprehensive the first time he'd found out what the meat was, but by that time he already knew it was delicious, so he didn't fight his instincts, and allowed rabbit to become one of his favorite meats. Taron even made his own rabbit jerky for snacks.

After breakfast, they would both do their chores, which was still kind of exciting at this point. Colin fed the chickens and rabbits, cleaned their coops once a week, gathered the fresh eggs. In some ways he was a little kid in his grandmother's garden all over again.

Over a month ago, his life had gone off the rails, yet when he was outside, his skin absorbing the sunlight, when he smelled the woods and listened to the singing of birds, nothing felt out of place. It was like an odd dream where, instead of spending endless hours at a desk or listening to lectures, he was expected to do work that fed both him and Taron. When he'd been first allowed to roam without Taron's constant supervision, his brain had still been galloping as if it expected messages, questions, and new stimuli every moment of the day. But as days went by, he gradually became more peaceful, getting in tune with the beautiful spring deep in the woods. Almost like a mindfulness retreat.

For once in his life, he didn't have to constantly worry about an abstract future and the consequences of not listening to well-meaning people. He was grounded in the here and now, with a man whose quiet presence didn't make Colin annoyed or uneasy. Instead, Taron being around meant little touches, kisses, or random lunchtime jerk-off sessions.

They both had chores, things to do, but if anything, Colin was getting the long end of the stick. He tended to the garden under Taron's instruction, while Taron did most of the heavy lifting, the planning, the stocking up. He never seemed satisfied with what they had, instead finding minor things that could go wrong with his solar panels or prioritizing repairs of the ram pump, even though they had endless gallons of filtered rain water stored in barrels on the property. If anything, the amount they had already seemed excessive.

It was a peaceful life, one that eliminated all the background noise in favor of work that made him feel useful and deserving of time off in the afternoon. He couldn't remember the last time he'd allowed himself to let go so completely, but once work was done for the day, he and Taron did whatever they liked—reading, going for walks, or fucking—all with the comfort of not having to worry about not doing enough.

But while Colin enjoyed the easy silence, the books, and the time outdoors, one thing stood out more.

He and Taron worked very well together, and perhaps, had they met in different circumstances, Colin might have reconsidered his no-boyfriend policy.

Unlike most guys Colin had met hooking up, Taron had drive, a goal, and wasn't a self-absorbed douchebag always on the chase for the next shiny fling. He was a hard worker, had real-life skills, and his patient, steady demeanor never failed to endear him to Colin. But the other side of him, the one that emerged when their eyes met, causing sparks, had Colin throwing all rules out the window.

In his real life, he had never considered skipping condoms with anyone. It seemed like such a reckless thing to do, but in the deep woods, in the log cabin that smelled of char and herbs, STDs didn't seem as real. He longed for the raw heat of Taron's hands, for the scent of his cum, and for the passion glinting in his green gaze. If any other man had tried to mark him with hickeys, Colin wouldn't have allowed it, but Taron could leave as many bite marks as he wanted, and Colin relished in seeing them in the mirror every day.

No one would see them anyway, because since Tom McGraw had visited, they'd been undisturbed. Colin didn't even know how far off they were from civilization, because that first night was one big blur of horror. But that was all in the past, for Colin had other things to worry about.

The bright spring days came to an abrupt end. The weather went downhill fast, and the usual rustle of leaves whispering in the breeze was replaced by howling wind. Since Colin only had a few items of clothing, Taron offered him his own windbreaker, and the way the garment hung off Colin's form served as a reminder of just how much bigger Taron was. The sheer width of Taron's back, the strength of his arms were an aphrodisiac to Colin, and even now, covering the vegetable plot with tarp in the vicious rain, his mind briefly wandered to their morning cuddle.

The distant sound of thunder echoed across the sky as soon as Colin managed to attach the waxed cloth, and when Colin stood, assaulted by cold droplets hitting his unprotected face, he was ready to head back to the cabin and have a drink of warm cocoa.

He was surprised to see that Taron was still on the porch in this unholy weather. He had the radio in hand and communicated with someone by Morse code. It wasn't the first time Colin had seen him do this, since Taron did keep in touch with a network of gay men, who also lived off the grid. Colin wanted to call out to him when a piece of rope snapped, uncovering the patch of strawberries and tossing the loosened flap of the tarp at Colin.

Taron abandoned the radio and ran into the rain to help. Once they reattached the covering, Colin withstood the icy blow that pushed him toward the covered patches, and smiled at Taron from behind goggles that protected his eyes from sand and debris.

"Thank you," he shouted to be heard through the noise, even though they stood so close.

Taron just shook his head and, in the daddiest of dad moves, zipped Colin's jacket all the way up. Colin knew he should've scolded him, but the gesture was so endearing that he scrambled to his toes and gave him a kiss instead.

For the briefest moment, Colin stilled, entranced by the warmth of his partner's mouth, but the sudden crackling of the radio lured Taron back to the porch. A familiar voice, though distorted, called out from the speaker.

"It's really bad over here. You might have to deal with a supercell very soon, maybe a tornado. Stay put."

There was no use screaming into the receiver about being kidnapped even if Colin had wanted to, because it transmitted voice just one way. Colin had found out about it when Taron had been unbothered about Colin speaking to him when he'd communicated over the radio before.

<I've taken care of the rabbits and chickens. I've got almost all the cats in the house too, but I can't find Missi. Have you seen her?> Taron asked as soon as he tapped one of the radio buttons to finish the conversation.

Above them, the treetops were in constant movement, bending toward the ground at unnatural angles, but Colin could only shake his head. "Oh no. Does she have any favorite places around the woods?" he asked, closing his coat. Missi could give birth at any moment now, and she was the last cat that should've remained outside in this weather.

Taron pulled on the hood of his jacket when it got blown off. Considering the conditions, Colin was beginning to doubt if the vegetables he'd worked so hard on growing would survive the night. Taron and his radio buddies kept discussing upcoming disasters with so much excitement, they seemed to anticipate them with glee, but now he was starting to think that maybe there was method to their madness.

<I can't think of any. I'll just go look for her.>

A thump reminding Colin of a bomb going off had him jump closer to Taron, and he got a brief hug.

<A tree must have fallen. Go to the house.>

Colin took a deep breath and looked around, at the woods that became increasingly gray until the rain intensified, hitting him with its full force. "But... she can't stay out there. I can help you search for her. There's still time," Colin said, taking hold of Taron's hand. If the poor cat had her kittens in this weather, he had no doubts they would all die. There was nowhere to hide, and Missi, while wandering outdoors each day, was used to being fed and sleeping in comfort.

Taron's distress was loud and clear in the way he squeezed Colin's hand.

<Go North, along the river, and remember to not go past the abandoned car,> he said, offering Colin a metal whistle attached to a black lanyard. <If you find her, or if you're in trouble, call for me.>

Colin might have asked for this, but he was still surprised that Taron was willing to let him out of sight, for whatever reason, but the mention of the landmark reminded Colin of the shock collar around his neck. Not only was Taron able to shock him at any time, but the device also kept Colin within a certain perimeter around the property.

If it wasn't a bluff. If it was, Taron was too desperate to bring Missi home to think clearly. There was still a possibility that Colin could just leave. Taron was a smart guy, but for all Colin knew, he wasn't an inventor or a tech whizz. And if the threat of shock was real, then so be it. He was positive it wouldn't kill him, but at least he'd know his real situation. If push came to shove, he could blame leaving the perimeter on the weather and not much knowledge of the terrain.

Rebellious thoughts invaded his mind like mold overcoming the walls of a cold house in winter, and the collar that he barely noticed anymore, now stood out as a heavy presence under his jacket.

For all he knew, Taron could even be lying about the collar being fitted with a tracking device, and if that were real, would he risk his life and abandon his home to chase Colin in the upcoming storm? Either way, tonight Colin would find out. He could always lie that he'd lost his way in the torrential rain if Taron caught up to him.

If Taron was bluffing about the collar then Colin could follow the river into the nearest town. He would be free. If he survived this awful storm out in the wilderness, he could return to his normal life. To the comfortable desk, to the memory foam mattress and wedge pillow, to his audiobooks, his music, and his parents, who must have been worried sick since he'd been taken.

He nodded and put the whistle into the deep pocket of his borrowed coat, stepping away from Taron, but he wouldn't look away even though he had so much to hide. Droplets of water splashed off Taron's hulking form, obscuring his features until he didn't even seem human, but more like a woodland monster that stalked in the night if you ventured too far into the forest.

Colin shuddered and turned away without a word, marching off into the avalanche of rain. It was the middle of the day, but the dark clouds made it seem as if daylight was already dying. His feet carried him past the chicken coop, past the showering area and then along the path leading to the river, but his brain felt numb, as if it didn't yet comprehend that this might be the final day of his captivity. An invisible leash pulled on the collar around his neck every time he imagined Taron realizing Colin wasn't coming back.

Would he only care about his crime being exposed, or would Colin's betrayal hurt him, even if just a little bit? Colin didn't want to dwell on it, and wiped the cold water off his face. At least he had the goggles to shield his eyes. They were the only ones Taron owned, so giving them away to Colin left him without any.

Colin considered hanging them somewhere for Taron to find, but he ultimately decided against it. Whatever motives Taron had had for taking him in the first place shouldn't matter. He'd still been abducted and shouldn't feel responsibility toward the man guilty of causing his fear and suffering.

The forest was vaster than he could comprehend, and in this rain—with the wind carrying leaves, small branches and bending trees until they cried in pain—the landscape turned into a coffee spill, uneven and impossible to read. But he couldn't give up because of a bit of bad weather. The single road leading to civilisation was on the other side of the homestead, and if he tried to get there, he risked running into Taron, so the river was his best bet.

Colin sped up, knowing that if he wanted to cross the waters safely, he needed to do so before the storm became even worse. A sudden gust of wind shoved at his back so hard he had to grab a nearby tree for support, but when he was about to let go and run to the artery that would lead him away from captivity, the world creaked, and a branch fell only a few steps away, squashing the undergrowth beneath it.

Colin's knees softened. The piece of wood was thick and long like the arm of a giant, but even it had been unable to withstand the force of the tempest. Despite the downpour, he raised his chin until the drops started drizzling under his hood to dampen his dry flesh and clothes. They were icier than rain should have been in the spring, but Colin couldn't worry about something so trivial when he stared at the place where the branch had been brutally ripped from the trunk, leaving behind a ragged wound of wood and bark.

Had Colin been moving faster, this could have been the moment of his death. How ironic would it have been if he'd escaped abduction only to get himself killed by a falling tree?

He gave a barking laugh and tried to move despite his legs not wanting to cooperate and already growing roots in the damp ground. With wind so forceful, getting struck by another branch, or by lightning for that matter, was not out of the realm of possibilities. But this was his chance. His one chance to get his life back, and he needed to force down his fear.

Once he let go of the tree and moved farther down the uneven path, he no longer took his time thinking. Closer to the river, the trees and bushes weren't as dense, so when the damp moss gave under his weight like soaked sponge, he could practically smell the gasoline and asphalt already. But the moment Colin stepped out of the forest and saw the rapid stream, the real world stopped being an achievable reality.

The waters which, while brisk, had always been calm

enough to cross by walking over rocks sticking out over the surface, were now overflowing and spilled into the woods beyond the river banks. They were foaming, like a rabid dog guarding a gateway Colin needed to cross.

The rain kept slapping Colin's face with the hard droplets until his skin was numb, but he didn't hesitate and followed the stream in hope of finding a bridge, a place where something allowed him to make the crossing. Or perhaps he could just run along the bank until he saw a trace of human presence? All he needed was to keep focused on the ground under his feet and walk, walk, walk until he was out of those woods. The constant rapping of raindrops against his hood muted him to most other noises, and he could hardly see the world around him, so when he first sped up, a terrible thought invaded his brain and spread like wildfire.

This could be a test.

For all he knew, Taron might have been following him all this time, way more familiar with the terrain and adept at tracking. Just like that, Colin couldn't shake off the sense of being watched, and he made a rapid spin, seeking the familiar form in the gray-and-black woods. Seconds passed, and he broke into a run, speeding along the riverbank. His heart beat in his chest in warning, but like a horse in blinders, he could only see ahead.

If Taron had been following him, then he already knew of Colin's plans, so Colin might as well try to outrun the man who may, or may not be there.

The wind shoved him forward over and over again, as if the forest had had enough of him and wanted him to leave for the city, where he belonged. At a desk. In the sterile spaces of a hospital. In his room at his parents' home where he pretended to fall asleep early so that he wouldn't have to continue their endless, uncomfortable conversations, which always touched upon the same topics.

Out of nowhere, the collar around Colin's neck beeped, and he missed his step, stumbling into the mud. Fear clawed itself into his flesh as he waited for the stab of pain, but when it didn't come, Colin ignored the dirt soaking through his pants and sought the abandoned car Taron warned him not to pass. The downpour colored everything with a stormy tint, but far off, Colin noticed a flash of red, and when he looked on, he realized that it could be nothing but the vehicle.

He was still, trying to even out his breathing despite the insistent tune of the collar.

Beep. Beep. Beep.

A rhythm as steady and quick as his heart. A warning. Colin moved his legs despite his better judgement, stomach squeezed into a ball of anxiety. Now or never. He would find out if the shock was real, and if it was—if the pain was bearable.

His body was like a bag of cotton balls, but he trudged on, for once uncaring about the rain or the wind tugging him toward the rapid waters. His brain could focus only on one thing—the way the beeping sped up with each step he took. He hesitated when there were barely any breaks between the sounds left, but he would either suffer now or rot in the forest forever, so he took a tentative step and froze when the collar switched to a long, continuous signal.

There was a tingling around his neck, where the collar rested, but it was not pain. Just an itch of discomfort—something he could soon get rid of once he reached the nearest human settlement. When he took the time to think, he realized even the tingle came from his imagination.

He would be free. He would be free.

Even his gums throbbed from the exhilaration. If this wasn't some sick test with Taron actually trailing him, then he was free already.

Free of spending his nights in a cage, free of being stuck in the woods without Internet, free to pursue his degree... Free of Taron's hands. Free of the rabbit bacon. Free of waking up with a cat numbing his arm.

He was an idiot. The nice aspects of his time in captivity changed nothing when it came to the shock collar around his neck. If only he wanted to, he could get a cat, he could get a boyfriend, and even an allotment if he so fucking pleased. His parents didn't need to know about any of that. If anything, they should be glad he came back.

His heart was working overtime, as if it couldn't handle liberty anymore. Or was he just running too fast? Mud slowed him down, but he was quicker than the invisible swamp monster grabbing at his feet, and wouldn't be pulled back, even if the stormy rain was so much colder than an empty bed.

The moment his mind went that way, the warm breakfast in bed was all he could think about. And then the kissing, the hands caressing his thighs, his torso, his face as if nothing about him was disposable.

Colin hadn't even realized he'd stopped until he found himself looking back.

Why did he only think of the good times, not of being punched or slapped? Of crying himself to sleep, fearing for his life, or the lack of proper hygiene. If he went back now, when would he next have an opportunity like this?

Whenever, a little voice whispered.

Didn't he now know that the collar couldn't shock him? It only made sense to leave later, without a tornado approaching the area.

What if there wasn't another opportunity? Staying with Taron was not an extended vacation. He was being held captive, even if in moderate comfort. Held captive by a man who hadn't shown remorse after killing another person.

A high-pitched shriek tore through the wall of rain, pinching his heart awake again. He instinctively knew what it was, and he'd heard enough meowing in the last month to be sure. It shouldn't matter that he might have found what he'd been supposed to look for, and yet it did. It was in his best interest to keep on moving and leave Taron to deal with his missing cat, but the animal wasn't just a nameless being anymore. If it was Missi, then Colin knew her and the way she would sometimes lick droplets off newly watered plants in the garden. She'd come to him when he'd still been terrified of his cage, and in his head he'd already imagined the kittens she'd have.

Colin looked around. He would just make sure she was fine, maybe whistle, then run. Taron would surely take care of Missi first before even considering whether he should track his prisoner.

Colin glanced at the river flowing toward Taron's house and forced his numb legs to move. He knew he should ignore the cat and keep walking, yet there he was, inching closer to the water when he heard another desperate meow as if he were a puppet in someone else's hands.

The beeping was once again a slow sequence—a warning rather than the sign of doom, but Colin no longer cared the moment he saw a sliver of ginger fur across the stream, but it disappeared from sight before he managed to focus on where Missi was.

He wiped water off the goggles and eventually pulled them off, calling out for the cat, and then he saw the bright color of her coat again. Between the bulging roots of an old tree all too close to the water pouring beyond its usual borders, he saw her raise her head. But she wasn't the only thing that moved, and in that moment Colin knew that the worst had already happened. Missi must have given birth and wouldn't leave her young, even though the stormy water was putting them all at risk.

Colin's logic lost the battle against the emotional part of his brain, and he put the metal whistle in his mouth, blowing into it time and time again.

He could run another time. Tonight, Missi and her litter needed saving, and he wouldn't just selfishly leave them. Even if he didn't trust himself into the rapid stream of water, there was someone who might know what to do.

Dropping the whistle from his lips, he put his hands into a tube and screamed for Taron at the top of his lungs.

Missi kept calling out for help, just a couple of big steps away, and once again he approached the river, staring at the foam and the debris carried by its waves. Branches, leaves, even some trash flowed between him and the cats, but as the ancient tree that offered Missi and her young shelter bent toward the water, pushed by a harsh gust of wind, Colin screamed out and put his foot into the icy current.

Before he could make the decision to go on and try to brave the river despite his blood freezing, a whistle tore through the air, preceding the thunder that came right after.

So Colin blew the whistle again, laughing in relief when the wind carried an answer from up close. Taron didn't really need to whistle, he wasn't the one being searched for, but Colin imagined he wanted to assure Colin that help was on the way.

He never took his eyes off Missi, and the endless minutes of waiting passed all too slowly, but soon enough, Colin heard heavy footsteps, and the mountain of a man emerged from the wall of rain. Colin ran uphill, wanting to meet Taron halfway, but when trees above bent, as if the hand of a giant pushed them toward the ground, the blast of air tossed Colin into the mud. The cold that had previously soaked into his jeans was back with a vengeance, and with his hood knocked off, the torrent turned his hair into a soaking wet mop, but he scrambled to his feet, seeking Taron again as the light around them dimmed, as if it had been artificial all along.

<Okay?> Taron signed as soon as he was close enough, and pulled Colin into a surprising, if wet, hug. He wasn't expecting betrayal, backstabbing, or threats. All he cared about was if Colin was all right, and that fact was so touching that for a moment Colin felt bad about wanting to leave without saying goodbye.

He would flee. But not now.

When the thunder struck next, he shuddered against Taron's strong body, but the noise also reminded him why he was here in the first place. "She's there. I tried to get in, but the river's just too rapid," he shouted, pointing toward the tree that would inevitably have the ground washed out from under its roots. Within hours, it would drop into the river, becoming a coffin for Missi and the kittens.

Taron's attention turned to the water, and this time when Missi meowed, it seemed like she was talking to him in particular. He raised his arms, as if he wanted to say 'what have you done', but then started rapidly unzipping his jacket.

Colin stared at him, shaking from the cold. "Do you have rope or something? What can I do?" he asked, swallowing some of the rain.

Taron pointed to a fallen tree and together, they managed to move it closer to the water. It would provide something to grab onto, but without anything to secure it on, at least this end, Colin was fighting the stomach cramps that accompanied stress.

Still, he did as instructed and helped Taron push until the trunk was lodged by an underwater rock and reached close enough to the other shore for a cat to jump on. It was only when Taron kicked off his boots that Colin understood the madman was actually about to cross the river.

"No. You can't do that," he said, grabbing Taron's wrist. He searched the woods for something, anything they could use, but even when lightning turned the world bright again for a few moments, he saw nothing that could have worked.

Taron gave him a quick kiss, as if they were the most regular of couples, and he wasn't about to risk his life but climb a small tree to retrieve someone's pet. <If something happens to me, hunker down in the basement. You've got lots of supplies there. Wait long enough, and someone will come for you.>

Colin froze, still clutching at Taron's clothes even when they too were discarded. "No. Don't be stupid. We need a rope to secure you. Either of us could run home and get it," he said, following Taron when he entered the stream.

Taron made a gesture with his flat hand, stopping Colin from going any farther. <The water is rising too fast. Sit on the tree and hold it so I have something to grab.>

Taron stepped farther into the freezing stream, holding the jacket above his head with one hand, and Colin knew there would be no talking him out of it. All he could do was follow instructions, so he dropped into the mud with his knees and held on to the narrow trunk, desperate to keep it stable for Taron's use.

The current reminded Colin of wild rapids, but despite all the dark scenarios playing through his head, Taron emerged from the water victorious, and moved through the mud on his hands and knees. Relief overflowed Colin's chest, and he hugged the broken tree, yelling his support as he watched Taron pack all the cats into his jacket.

Lightning kept blasting in the distance, sending sparks and thunder rolling across the sky, but in the streams of rain, kneeling in the cold mud, Colin's focus was entirely absorbed by Taron entering the river again. In the surging waves, even his tall and broad form seemed like a dry twig, but he remained firm and withstood the current, his eyes focused on the foaming water. The bundle Taron carried above his head remained still, as if the cats were too fearful to present any signs of life, so he trudged on, undisturbed.

Something dark flashed in the corner of Colin's eye, but when he noticed the thick branch carried Taron's way, a shout of warning was all he could do. Taron stared back at him, but the piece of wood smashed into his side before he could try to avoid it. The scowl twisting his face spoke of agony, but the cats remained above his head, even when he lost footing and hit the trunk, Colin still tried to keep still. It moved under pressure but didn't dislodge itself, offering Taron much-needed support.

The moment Taron's bare feet stepped out of the water —so cold they looked gray—Colin rose and tugged him away from the river, his arms circling Taron's hips so securely he wasn't sure if he would be able to let go if he had to. The firm muscles that usually felt so warm had now turned into ice, and Colin helplessly rubbed at Taron's sides in the hope of making him that little bit warmer, despite the downpour and the wind that made the damp fabric of Taron's under-shirt stick to drenched skin.

"You did it! You have her," he whispered with disbelief, still shocked by what had just transpired.

Taron flinched away from the touch. He was soaked from top to bottom, and couldn't communicate well without his hands, but he still held on to the bundle of meows he'd risked his life for.

Colin shuddered when he spotted blood on his fingers and on Taron's top.

Without hesitation, he pulled up the garment, and in the sparse light saw the wound. It was a cut—ragged and bleeding, but it was not an immediate danger. Exhaling with relief, Colin kneeled and grabbed Taron's boots to help him put them on. Above him, everything was subject to the harsh wind, and even Taron stumbled, leaning on one of the trees as Colin pushed his icicle-like feet into the boots so that he could walk home without injuring himself any further. His brain was a chaotic mix of anger and protectiveness, but by the time he stood up and pulled Taron closer, he no longer held it against him that he was so stupidly brave when it came to the animals.

Getting home was all that counted now.

The soaked shoes were an obstacle too, but at least they provided protection from rocks and branches. The bundle in Taron's arms mewled, but he didn't loosen his hold on the cats for a second. Not to check the bleeding wound that had opened on his side, nor to wipe the blood from a cut over his eyebrow.

Colin didn't attempt to talk to Taron, watching the road for him instead, and guiding him along, toward the house which he'd so desperately tried to run from.

When thunder rolled above them again, following the bright lightning by mere seconds, Colin sighed with relief at the sight of their home. It was within reach now, and the memory of the slow, never-ending trek in constant discomfort dispersed in favor of absolute focus.

He encouraged Taron with a whisper and led the way, numb to the harrowing elements. When they rushed past the shed, he was ready to cry with joy, but when he finally opened the door to the cabin and pushed Taron into the safety of its wooden walls, relief was so great he forgot to close the door and just stood there, shocked when it slammed shut behind him. He was quick to lock the entrance with the padlock.

He'd never been so happy to have shelter. In just the short time he'd been outside, the weather had taken a turn for the worse, and Taron didn't even need to gesture toward the cellar. When Taron had taken the cats there, Colin had been secretly rolling his eyes, not sure why he was so afraid of a little rain, but now Colin appreciated the thought Taron had put into the preparations. So maybe it wasn't doomsday yet, but if the tornado hit the area and blew the house away, they'd be safe underground.

Colin reached the trapdoor in Taron's bedroom in no time and hauled it up, to the pitter-patter of paws. He scowled and grabbed Rio, who attempted to sneak past him. "Not now, boy," he said, glancing back at Taron and switching on the light downstairs.

Colin went down first, clearing the path of cats who wanted to climb back out. The last thing they needed was Taron falling down the stairs because one of his pets was overly eager to greet him. The whole operation was a convoluted process, since Taron wouldn't empty his arms, but eventually Colin ran back up and closed the hatch.

He didn't like the violent shivers shaking Taron one bit, and wanted to grab a blanket from his cage, but Taron called him over with a grunt instead, and placed the jacket full of kittens into Colin's arms.

He stilled, overwhelmed by the sensation of movement

in the bundle, but the spell was broken the moment Taron's teeth clattered so violently Colin wished to put a piece of wood between his jaws.

"Come on, you need to get off all those damp clothes," he said. He had no idea where to put Missi and her babies, but in the end chose an empty pet bed Taron had carried down here earlier. It rested on the roof of the cage, so when Colin placed the wet jacket right next to it, Missi would surely know what to do next.

Taron wasn't paying attention and instead fiddled with something in a large metal shelving unit. Was he searching for cat food, or about to have a pickled onion? Colin wanted to scold him for risking so much earlier, but words died on his lips when the whole thing, all the shelves, moved aside on hinges, revealing a round metal door reminiscent of a bank vault entry with all its locks and a complicated-looking mechanism on the inner side.

He wasn't sure anymore if he'd made the right choice when he hadn't run away. Whatever secrets the door hid, he wouldn't be able to unsee them.

CHAPTER THIRTEEN

Taron pulled open the vault door despite the pain nipping at his side. The fucking branch got him in the same area where Colin had stabbed him just last month. Talk about bad luck.

The cats were already familiar with what was behind the reinforced entrance, so they poured in first, eager to reinstate it as their territory. Missi and her kittens had experienced enough stress for a lifetime tonight, so Colin picked up the pet bed and carried them in.

He followed Taron in tentative steps, his brown eyes wide. The elongated room was furnished with rifle and gun holders, and ammo of all kinds was piled up in wholesale boxes. Taron even owned tools to produce his own projectiles, as well as knives, and other weapons that didn't rely on ammo supply. The weapons gathered in the armory could last many people years if need be, and while Taron hoped he wouldn't have to use them for anything besides hunting, it felt good to be prepared for any situation.

"Jesus Christ. What are you, preparing for? Another civil war?" Colin uttered.

Taron ushered Colin inside once he was sure all the kittens were safe and accounted for. Only then did he lock the vault with a code. At least that gave him a safety net in case Colin did want to run after all, and used Taron's weakness to do so.

<It's good to be prepared.> Taron looked around, not without pride. A lot of the stock gathered down here used to belong to Old McGraw, but Taron had added his share since.

Colin's attention was already on the other side of the armory, or rather on the door leading farther into the bunker. "Yeah, but this is... an insane amount. You're the only person here."

The fear of all these questions was a big part of why Taron hadn't wanted to show Colin the extent of his underground hideout. Beyond the armory were endless shelves of food storage, and Taron knew the contents of each. He grabbed an empty cardboard box from the top of the unit, then a blanket from a chest nearby and kneeled by a table to prepare a cozy spot for Missi and her young.

The earlier work and the stress the rescue had taken on his body were finally catching up with him to the point where he struggled to keep his eyes open. The wet clothes clung to his flesh, creating a barrier against warmth, so the shivers going through his flesh were getting more violent by the moment. The last thing he wanted was to explain himself, but he wouldn't be given the peace he so desperately needed. Not with Colin breathing down his neck.

"Did you build this yourself?" Colin asked, knocking on the steel wall.

Taron squinted when an old light bulb winked at him with white flashes. <It's complicated.>

He let Missi out into her private space along with the

tiny kittens, and finally took a deep breath of relief, but that only made the ache in his side more intense.

Colin helped him up, but his touch made the cold even worse, with freezing water drizzling out of the clothes. "Come on, let's go to the bed. I'll need to have a look at that wound," he said, stepping back toward the exit.

Taron shook his head and pointed to the door at the other end of the reinforced shipping container. They needed to pass the shelves full of soaps, cleaning products and essentials to get there, but despite Colin's impatient huffing, he followed Taron into the cool darkness of the next unit. It served as a junction where the bunker branched out in several directions, and when a bewildered Colin stopped walking the moment the light went on, Taron pulled on his hand and led him to the room to the far right.

The large fireplace was a prop, and so were the windows opening up to photographs of a forested landscape, but the living room in its entirety might as well have been set up in a regular house. Comfortable armchairs faced a coffee table, and wooden shelves held a collection of books that might prove useful after the upcoming catastrophe.

Colin walked inside in silence and stared into the eyes of Old McGraw's trophy deer head. He stood still, as if he expected the taxidermy to speak, only to suddenly look back at Taron with red blots on his cheeks. Tension snuck to his shoulders, making them square. "What is this?"

Taron leaned down to get his icicle-like shoes off but ended up falling to his knee when a jolt of pain seared along his body close to the new wound. <It's a safe place.>

Colin rubbed his face and turned to Taron with his whole body. His chest worked fast, just like when it did when he was about to cum. "There are actual pillows here.

And a rug made of a dead bear," he said, nudging the large fur under the coffee table.

Taron shrugged. <Old McGraw arranged all this. There was no point in redecorating.>

Colin raised his arms. "Who's *Old* McGraw? The dad of the cat haters?" he asked, while Rio lazily rubbed against Colin's calf.

<Uncle. I bought the land from him years ago. His nephews think it should have been their inheritance.> Which was the precise reason why they hated Taron so much.

Colin massaged his temples before letting his arms drop. "I was in a cage. *In a cage.* Why didn't you just lock me up here?"

Taron stared. The shivers and pain radiating all over his torso made thinking difficult. Couldn't he just lie in bed and bother with the question later? For someone who'd just been led into a complicated bunker system deep in the woods, Colin was way too preoccupied with why he hadn't been offered more *comfort.*

Taron growled. <I don't show this to people.>

Colin rolled his eyes and walked toward the next door as if the place belonged to him. Once he switched on the light there, revealing the large bed and a tub in the corner, his throat made a noise that reminded Taron of an angered hornet. "This is a goddamn condo. What the actual fuck?"

<You don't like it?>

Taron sighed at the muddy stains Colin was leaving on the floor, but at least it wasn't carpeted. Even if dated, the bunker suited Taron. He'd found it comfortingly homely during many long nights alone. He wasn't going to apologize for old taxidermy or furniture from a different era when it was *his* home.

Colin touched his head again before rapidly moving his hands away from it. "I couldn't sit up straight, and I had to shit in a bucket inside the place where I slept while all this was here? I can't fucking believe it!"

Taron lost it. He was too tired for this bullshit. He removed his soaking sweatshirt and dropped it into the tub. <I had no idea who you were or what to do with you, so no, I didn't trust you with any of this.>

Colin followed him, barking like a rabid Jack Russell Terrier. "What did you think I could do? Spray the furniture?"

Taron couldn't believe his attitude. <You stabbed me. Yes, I expected you to cause havoc.> He lifted his T-shirt and showed off his bruised side, with the healed stab wound, to prove his point.

Colin's lips twitched, and his face became tense, looking as if it was a battlefield between two expressions. "Let's get you out of all those clothes. Is there some kind of heater we can use?" he asked, pulling back the bedcovers, but his gaze landed on the second door in the room. "There's more?"

<Not now. There's a portable heater. I'll get it going.>

Colin grabbed the waistband of Taron's soaked pants and tugged them off, along with underwear. "You need to get warm. Now. I'll deal with the heater if you tell me where it is."

Taron resigned himself to the undignified circum-stances, but sitting on the bed provided so much comfort he couldn't refuse the offer. He pointed to the heater by the copper tub. At least Colin had shut up about the cage.

Once he sat his bare ass on the icy sheet, Collin tugged Taron's socks off his purplish feet, leaving him completely naked. He then tossed all the garments into the tub before pushing Taron down and pulling the bedding over him as if he were dealing with unwell people every day of the week. The covers were heavy—stuffed with down—but after weeks without any heating, they felt like a layer of snow on Taron's damp skin.

Before he could say anything, Colin put two of the cats on the bed.

Taron signed, <I'm not a baby.>

Colin let out a loud snort, and for the first time since they'd come down there, his expression brightened. "Don't talk back to your doctor. I am prescribing bedrest, heat, and cat compresses."

Doctor. At Colin's age, he was likely only studying to become one, if he hadn't been lying about it this whole time. But he lay back and watched Colin drag over the heater and turn it on. Left without a task, Taron could do nothing but shiver, even though the little aches all over his body remained a constant nuisance, but at least two more cats joined him in bed, purring.

But perhaps Colin did have *some* medical training, because once he got his hands on Taron's medicine stash, he seemed to know what he was doing. On the lookout for the right items, he didn't miss the use by dates on some of the medicines, and kept scolding Taron about it as he rummaged through the large wooden box.

"I can't believe this. If you really insist on stocking up on all this stuff, you need to make sure you have everything you need and that it's all usable. Once we're out of here, I'm gonna make you a list, because you're doing it wrong," he said with a scowl that Taron found oddly endearing.

Colin's anger came from a place of care. Could it be possible for him to understand or even embrace Taron's lifestyle?

Despite his rash behavior earlier, Colin made sure not

to press down on the aching flesh too firmly as he examined it in the light of the small bedside lamp. The stove had only been turned on, but Taron's own body heat and that of the cats were making the temperature more bearable. Taron couldn't remember the last time someone else had looked after him, and the mix of fear and glee that created, confused him to no end.

Colin had also removed his soaked clothes, but since it was still cold, he put on the first thing he could find—stripy pajamas that must have belonged to Old McGraw. They were comically huge on him. But even the hideous brown-on-brown-on-brown or the dated cut couldn't change the fact that Taron was under Colin's spell.

He was discreet about staring at Colin, but he didn't need to be too wary, not with the way his blond eyebrows drew together to form a little valley above his nose as he examined the injury.

"That whole thing, getting into the river to save them, it was brave but also stupid. You could have died."

<I know, but someone would have found you eventually, and there's more than enough food in the homestead.>

Colin groaned and pulled on surgical gloves. "You're such an idiot. That's not the point. I was worried sick that you'd drown, and that I'd have to save you, and then we'd have both fucking died!"

Taron had never before felt like a marshmallow thrown into a cup of cocoa, but that was exactly what he experienced hearing Colin's words and watching the slender fingers in gloves prepare the needle and thread.

Colin's care was much more than he could have wished for or expected. Where Taron had assumed he'd get a tit-for-tat sex arrangement, he'd gotten this strange kind of companionship. He didn't deserve so much affection after what he'd done to Colin, yet here they were, and Taron wouldn't let go of it. He was far too selfish, far too greedy for Colin's company to ever let him go. If someone had arrived at his house today, told Taron he would take Colin, and the police would never find out about what had happened, Taron would've told them to go to hell, and then would've shot the fucker for good measure.

Colin was his no matter how wrong it was. Even the nagging showed a degree of caring that Taron had learned not to expect from anyone.

Colin disinfected the wound with a spray that must have contained alcohol, since it stung like an eye rubbed with a salty finger, and briefly met Taron's eyes. "This will hurt. Do you have any anesthetics?"

Taron forced a smile. <I've got moonshine.>

Colin licked his lips, stilling with the curved needle. "Where?"

<First storage room. In jars. Box on the bottom right.> He'd actually love the drink to warm him up as well.

Colin stood up without a word and was gone—gloves, thread, needle, and all. At Taron's side, Rio rolled to his back, purring softly, completely unaware of his owner's distress. Maybe it was for the better. Taron sighed and took his time petting his battle-scarred companion.

Colin was back not long after, but when he opened the jar, instead of handing Taron the jar, he took a swig himself.

Taron snorted. <Good. That'll make you easy.>

Colin's lips twisted at the strong taste of the alcohol, but he stared at Taron from behind the jar. "You better watch your mouth, or my hand might stray from where it's supposed to go with that needle."

He had one more gulp before handing the container to Taron. It took effort to sit up for drinking, because his body had found comfort and was reluctant to let go, but the harsh flavor of alcohol flooding his insides with sparks was enough to do the trick.

<Now I know you'd be sorry if I died. I'm not scared.> Though he wasn't looking forward to the pain either.

Colin shook his head, touching the injured skin with one of his latex-covered fingers. His face was contemplative, with lips slightly parted as if there was something he wanted to say but didn't trust Taron with. But what came out was dismissive and surely not what Colin had been considering. "I'm a doctor. Of course I don't want you dead," he said and leaned down, pushing the needle through skin.

<Child prodigy?> Taron tried to distract himself with the conversation, but at least the moonshine warmed his insides.

Colin frowned at him. "Oh, you're so clever. So I might not be quite there yet, but I know enough to help people. I've got the best results in my year, and I've been volunteering a lot," he said in a biting tone, but there was no anger in the way he was stitching up the wound. If anything, he was painfully careful, making the whole process so much more comfortable than Taron's own effort would have been.

<Will you miss it? I could get hurt more often.> Taron signed, clenching his teeth at another needle stab. He hated that there was no way for them to be together if Colin were to go back to his old life. Mr. I-am-a-doctor wouldn't stay with Taron in the woods nor introduce him to his parents. What would he have even said? 'Oh, and by the way, this is my boyfriend who'd abducted me last month'?

Colin blinked but didn't look up. "Miss what?"

<Study.>

Colin let out a sigh and said nothing until he was done

with the stitches. He might have done more than was strictly necessary, but Taron wasn't about to scold him. The sound of gloves being peeled off his hands was so final Taron was starting to agonize that maybe he shouldn't have mentioned Colin's dream career, but Colin spoke once he finished dressing the wound.

"Studying is probably the only thing I'm good at, but there's just so much pressure and competition to have the best scores, to outdo everyone else in order to get into one of the top medical schools."

Was he suggesting he wouldn't miss the stress, or was it just something he claimed for Taron's benefit? Then again, he'd proven today just how willing to speak his mind he was.

<Is there anything you like here?> Taron winked. <Other than me.>

Colin snorted and pretended to knock on Taron's forehead. "I never said I liked you." But he let his hand linger against Taron's skin, and watched him in silence. His fingers moved back and forth before sliding to the side of Taron's face. Finally, Colin looked away. "I like the quiet. The scent of the woods. It's so peaceful. Like a digital detox. I can be out in the sun for the whole day without worrying if I'm not needed somewhere else. Without listening to someone telling me I've wasted so much time on stuff that doesn't matter. I like that when I tend to the garden, I know that everything I do there matters, because we're going to eat the food we grow."

<Will you miss helping people?> Taron slipped his hand to Colin's thigh and massaged it, yearning for closeness in a way he'd never understood before. He froze when Colin entwined their fingers and laughed.

"No. I don't like to be around many people. Small

groups, yes, but it's exhausting to be around them too much. I was always more interested in the science of it all than in the people themselves."

Taron gave his hand a short squeeze. <You're awful.>

Colin's mouth stretched into a boyish grin, and he picked up the jar of moonshine again. "So are you."

<Good fit?> Taron wordlessly asked for the jar once Colin had his sip.

Colin lowered it toward Taron's hand, only to take it out of his reach, giggling as if it were the funniest joke ever. "You know what's a good fit? This booze and me."

Taron shook his head and pulled Colin closer. <You're drunk already.>

The room was getting warmer by the minute, the alcohol pulsed through his veins, and the tornado that could now be ravaging his home above was forgotten. The one thing he needed was Colin next to him in bed, out of Old McGraw's ridiculous 1970s pajamas.

Colin took two more gulps before handing over the jar. He was leaning against Taron, intimately close, with a blurriness in his eyes that betrayed just how fast the moonshine had hit him.

"I'm still cold though."

Taron didn't care for the spirit anymore. He put it away on the nightstand and focused on the handsome young man who'd warm his bed much more efficiently than a whole herd of cats.

He invited Colin under the comforter and ignored any aches, in favor of unbuttoning Colin's pajama top. Colin watched him with a half-smile but stayed passive. "I see someone's been lying about his poor condition."

<I need you,> was all Taron could communicate without tearing his hands away from Colin for too long. But

in the quiet room, he realized they were close enough for Colin to hear him if he spoke. "I need you."

The light brown eyes glinted when Colin removed the pants that were far too big on him anyway. He was breathing through his mouth, completely focused on Taron.

"I suppose you do need a bed warmer after getting soaked," he said, pulling off the unbuttoned shirt.

Taron smiled and ran his hands up Colin's slim but sturdy shoulders. "I've literally saved kittens, Colin." He hated his voice. Barely a dull whisper, sometimes a stutter, hurting his throat with the effort, but using it meant his hands were free to roam.

Colin smirked and gently pushed Rio off the mattress. He moved under the comforter, his knee first nudging Taron's skin, then moving across his thighs. "I suppose that makes you a hero. You deserve a reward for your bravery," he whispered, straddling Taron, who didn't even care that meant his chest had been left uncovered. With all of Colin on show, Taron would be going up in flames fast anyway. This boy, who'd invaded the peaceful solitude of Taron's life was now his addiction, and Taron would fuck him even with a wound on his side and scratches on his face.

Colin's limbs were long, hips narrow, and he had the prettiest nipples Taron loved sucking on. His cock, not too thick, but long, was nature's perfection when it got swollen and dark. If Taron didn't have so much work around the homestead, he'd spend all day in bed with Colin, waiting for their cocks to harden so they could fuck again.

Colin exhaled, shifting on top of Taron until their balls and cocks touched, and he chewed on his lip, leaning forward to rest his elbows by Taron's shoulders. "I'm gonna take care of you, like a good doctor," he whispered so close his breath caressed Taron's skin.

<Please. I'm in *so* much pain.> Taron pulled on Colin's lip with his teeth, and let his hands roam up and down Colin's thighs as soon as he was done signing. His cock was already responding to Colin's closeness, hardening under the touch to signal just how much he wanted to fill that gorgeous body.

Colin's eyes shut, and the brief expression that passed over his face was the very definition of ecstasy. He rolled his hips, thrusting his dick against Taron's as they kissed again, limbs falling into place without either of them having to think about details.

If Colin's actions were just a ploy to distract Taron and shove a knife between his ribs, he didn't even care. He'd die a happy man.

Taron could sense the lean muscle playing under the softness that was Colin's skin, and he wondered if this boy would have spared him a glance if they met in different circumstances.

What could have been ceased to matter when Colin took Taron's breath away with a bite to his lips. Taron slid his hands over Colin's hips and to his ass, eager to plunge his dick into Colin and watch his face flush, hear him moan. This, Colin wasn't able to fake. He was a horny guy, and it was one of the things Taron loved about him.

But Taron's interest didn't only lay in the orgasms anymore. He craved the connection that sparked between them when they had sex. Before Colin, he'd hardly ever fucked the same guy twice. It had been quickies with random guys or with prostitutes, but with Colin he could take his time, knowing that his partner would still be in his arms once their sweat dried. Something he'd never known he wanted.

Colin was there with him every step of the way.

"What do you want?" he asked, obscenely licking the rim of Taron's mouth, already gasping. His hips kept stirring, pulling his balls and dick over Taron's skin, but before Taron could find the strength to answer, Colin took both their cocks in one hand and squeezed them together.

Taron's eyelids fluttered, and he considered asking for Colin to jerk them both off like that, but he craved more intensity tonight. Even weakened and aching, he needed to mark Colin as his again and again. The illogical need to pump Colin full of his seed was more pressing every time they fucked.

"R-ride me," Taron whispered, eyes locked with Colin's. His stunted voice cords already felt overused, but he wanted to communicate with his lover, be his world. "I want you on my cock."

Colin drew in a sharp breath and pumped their cocks, his gaze becoming more intense with each stroke. Taron could feel the hair that had grown back on Colin's previously shaved balls, the tightness of his muscles, the way he curled his toes by Taron's calves.

Colin wasn't the most beautiful man Taron had ever seen, but there had never been anyone so desirable, touchable, so real with him. The heat of their closeness couldn't be compared to anything he'd ever experienced.

"Oh yeah? I hope this won't be a rodeo," Colin said, brushing his fingers along Taron's side, as if to signal he wanted him to be careful.

"No. You can ride as long as you like." He exhaled deeply, rubbing his finger between Colin's spread buttocks.

Colin stretched over him like a cat and tilted his hips to rub his hole against the fingers. "Fuck, even your fingers are thick..."

Blood trickled from Taron's brain to his dick, and he

couldn't look away from Colin's face even as he pawed at the nightstand, trying to fish out lube from the drawer. Thank fuck he'd spent some nights here.

Colin pulled his teeth over his bottom lip, making it flush. "Somebody's desperate."

Taron let out a needy grunt, not even caring how he sounded. Yes. He was desperate. For once in his life he wanted someone close and couldn't talk himself out of it, so all else be damned—he would keep Colin.

He couldn't open the pot of lube with one hand, and he was getting frustrated, but the boy took the container out of his grip and did it for him with a mischievous smile on his lips. He offered it to Taron, for him to dip his fingers into, and it had to be one of the hottest things Taron had ever seen. Colin was inviting him into his body. He was willing, full of need, and even complimented Taron.

Colin's lips twitched, as if he knew exactly what kind of power he held over Taron, but he didn't mock him and just moved forward, rubbing his face against Taron's cheek while his tempting ass tilted up in invitation.

Taron screwed his fingers into the hole, and the moan Colin voiced into Taron's beard only spurred him on to make the prep quicker. His own cock was so hot between their bodies it might have been emitting steam.

"Yes," Colin uttered, arching so suddenly the tip of his cock slid down Taron's stomach, leaving a damp trace behind. He opened to the invasion with ease, spreading his legs and relaxing fast. It was so different from the first few times they fucked Taron almost felt bad about having cared so little about Colin's comfort back then. Tonight however, Colin was a pet longing for caresses and treats. His hole was hot and smooth as silk, but the moment Taron pushed the digits all the way to the knuckles, Colin stirred his hips, wanting their touch in a very particular spot.

Taron looked up, but Colin's eyes were closed, and he clutched at Taron's shoulders with a moan when Taron gently rubbed his prostate again and again. Few things got him as horny as seeing Colin give in to his animalistic instincts. He couldn't wait to bury his cock in that hot tightness and make Colin scream for more.

In moments like this, Colin lost his inhibitions, writhing and rolling over Taron in response to the caresses. His plump ass massaged Taron's digits, and at times it almost felt like they were getting sucked on. With three fingers in Colin's hole, everything became more intense. Colin gave a sharp cry and moved up and down, riding Taron's hand as if he wanted to get off that way. His breathing came in rapid gasps, but when his eyes cracked open, and the intensity of his gaze clashed with Taron's, something about the energy of this encounter changed.

Taron knew what to do without being asked. Pain in his side be damned, he pulled out his fingers, and instantly plugged the twitching hole with his cock. His mind was fogged with excitement, but he still didn't want to hurt Colin. When he hesitated, Colin pressed down, taking Taron's cock all the way to the base.

The moment Taron's balls aligned with Colin's hole, the boy shifted on top of him, to support most of his weight on the front of his feet. His eyes were open, but they seemed so out of focus Taron grabbed Colin's hips to steady him. In this position, he could see it all—the pink flush on Colin's lean chest, his golden body hair, and the gorgeous cock that at this point was so engorged it seemed it might burst at any moment.

Colin groaned and rested one hand on Taron's chest

before grabbing his cock to give it a steady pump. "I want your cum inside me."

It was the mirror image of Taron's own wishes, so he nodded with his lips parted and slid his hands across Colin's flushed stomach. The ache in his side became more irritating but he ignored it when Colin's body clamped down around his dick. He wanted to thrust with his hips and give Colin what he wanted, but Colin stopped him with a confident gesture. Their eyes met in a moment of meaningful silence, and Colin didn't even need to say it for Taron to understand. Colin didn't want Taron to hurt himself any further, and he would take the lead.

Never looking away, he moved his hips up and down. He started out slowly but built up the pace and milked Taron's cock with extra squeezes of his sphincter. When his face contorted in ecstasy, he was beauty personified, and if Taron had done art, he'd have wanted to sculpt him just the way he was in that moment.

There was something so naked in the way Colin gave in to pleasure when they were together that it suggested things Taron didn't want to project onto him. As good as the sex was, Colin was still an unwilling captive, getting his pleasure however he could in the absence of other people.

But oh, he was so magnificent in the way he wasn't ashamed or afraid of anything. Unlike any of Taron's other lovers, Colin was a hundred percent there with him. The head of Colin's cock emerged from his fist over and over as he furiously jerked off, moving his hand between the tip of his dick and balls, which slapped against it each time.

The red flush on his chest, neck, and face was getting darker, his breathing more shallow, but Colin kept watching Taron, his gaze just as hypnotic as the image of his tight ass swallowing Taron's cock whole. His eyes were so enticing

Taron almost missed seeing that beautiful cock spurt cum, but when he felt the droplets on his chest and chin, he looked down to admire the red cockhead dripping seed. Colin was barely catching his breath by the time he was done coming, but he never stopped riding Taron, going for it like a pro.

Just the sight of him so naked, so dirty, and yet so stunning, had Taron make those last few thrusts himself despite the pain in his side. He pushed his cock in as far as it would go, and let it nestle there with a groan when his balls tightened. When Colin tried to pull up in a daze, Taron tugged his hips back down. Pumping cum into Colin was his whole world, and he could hardly breathe when he thought about making Colin his on some primal level that defied sanity.

Warm hands rubbed Taron's chest as he came down from the peak of ecstasy, but when he finally opened his eyes, he realized Colin was rubbing his own cum in, as if he too wanted to mark Taron with his scent.

Seconds passed before Colin lay next to him, his one leg and arm slung across Taron's body while they both rested. In the silence broken only by ragged breathing, Colin played with Taron's chest hair, and once again it seemed there was something on his mind that he wasn't sure he should say. Taron could recognize the signs by now—the firm set to Colin's lips, his gaze becoming stern for no reason, and the unusually dense silence.

They cuddled up under the comforter until even their feet weren't cold anymore. When a total of five purring furballs decided to join them, Taron was sure they wouldn't be cold tonight.

"What is it?" he whispered, unsure he could stand the dense silence anymore.

Colin flinched, as if he'd been caught doing something

illicit, but in the end he rested his head on Taron's shoulder. "I was just thinking that this whole thing is so... comfortable. I haven't shaved my body in over a month, I'm not taking showers twice a day or preparing before sex in any way. I thought I would mind but I don't. And I don't think you do either."

Taron snorted and hugged Colin tightly. "You're perfect the way you are." So it came out sappy. Fine. He was allowed that much after orgasm.

Colin hummed, and while Taron couldn't see his face, he could sense his partner smile against his flesh.

"How big is this place?" Colin asked in the end.

Taron groaned. "Tomorrow."

CHAPTER FOURTEEN

The bunker was enormous. Whether it had been planned as a retreat for the local government in case of war or old McGraw's underground luxury villa, Colin didn't know, but his eyes got bigger with each room Taron led him through. The structure was made of retired shipping containers with walls reinforced from the outside and insulated to boot. There was some sort of ventilation system in place, and the labyrinth of corridors and rooms contained not only supplies, but also fully equipped bedrooms, a game room, as well as a large kitchen and canteen.

Despite Taron living there his own, the huge complex had clearly been meant to house multiple people, including children, as evidenced by boxes of old-timey toys and a playroom with a slide, swings, and even a small carousel, and cartoon characters painted on the walls.

Colin had been silent for most of the time, but when Taron showed him into a room that held two cars, one of which had wooden panels on the sides and a distinctly 1970s look, the dam burst. "I heard some cultures buried their dead with boats or carriages, but this is ridiculous. Is this where you're keeping my car too?"

Taron shook his head. <Drowned it.>

Colin should have suspected as much, but then his mind stalled. "With the body?"

Taron gave a curt nod.

Colin scowled. "Just great. They'll probably assume I murdered him if it's found one day."

The silence on Taron's part told Colin that this was exactly what Taron had hoped for when he'd gotten rid of the evidence. Fantastic. Ladies and Gentlemen, the guy Colin slept with.

Taron spread his arms with a silly grin, as if it was all beyond his control. <There's a system in place to take them above ground if needed.>

Colin rubbed his face in disbelief. "Why? Why would he hide his cars underground in the first place? Because this wasn't your idea, was it?" he asked, shocked by the sheer amount of work put into this ridiculous place.

<McGraw believed this container would work as a FARADAY cage.> Taron spelled out 'faraday' when Colin didn't understand it.

Colin knew who Faraday was, but the cage thing? He had no idea what it was about, and he told Taron so. Taron turned Colin so that they faced each other when he explained slowly how a solar flare or a nuclear bomb could induce an electro-magnetic pulse that would render all electronic devices, including cars, worthless, *unless* they were stored in a container that was resistant to such a pulse. It was a far-fetched worry, considering that, to Colin's knowledge, such a thing had never happened, but he still listened, because he was getting a glimpse of a world he had no idea about.

Taron chewed on his lip. <McGraw was preparing for war between the United States and Soviet Union, and he wanted his lifelong project to go into the hands of someone who would appreciate it. I was looking for a bunker far away from Yellowstone, so West Virginia seemed like a good choice.>

Colin's brain came to an abrupt stop. "Yellowstone? What? You're not local?" Come to think of it, even when he whispered, Taron didn't have a distinguishable accent.

Taron stared at him, as if assessing whether he should tell Colin where he was from. Why would it be a secret? Was he running from the law? Colin wouldn't be surprised.

<Wyoming.>

Colin watched Taron lean against the wall. Despite the warm-up after their return, Taron's health was in decline, as evidenced by the way he kept clearing his throat and the blurry look in his eyes. At least Colin had talked him into wearing two warm sweaters.

"Okay. Yellowstone *is* mostly in Wyoming. Did something happen there that you wanted to get away?" he asked softly.

He knew he'd hit a nerve before Taron even spoke, because of how his body language turned tense. <No. It was the sensible thing to do.> He spun around and waved for Colin to follow.

There was *more*?

The next few rooms were empty, and walking through them felt like being in a world beyond this one. "Why? I don't get it."

Taron turned around, and despite the tender night they'd spent together, the strangeness of the scenery had Colin's heart skip a beat in fear at Taron's sheer size.

<Why not? You think the government will take care of

you? You will drop dead within three days without water. If there is an economic collapse, you will be an easy target. And if there's a disease outbreak, you won't have anywhere to hide.>

Colin stepped back and raised his hands when Taron tore into his personal space. "But why would any of that happen? And what has the Yellowstone National Park have to do with disease?"

<It's stupid to be prepared for only one thing, but the Yellowstone volcano blowing up will annihilate half the country and cover loads more in ash.>

Oh no.

Colin rubbed his face. "So you're spending your life in solitude because you're afraid of something that might not even happen in your lifetime?"

Taron's expression hardened. <I'm not afraid. I'm prepared.>

Colin took a deep breath, watching Taron rub snot from his nose with annoyance. "Okay, I get that, but don't you think all this," he gestured around him to indicate the entirety of the bunker system, "is excessive? And if you really believe this catastrophe will happen and have so much supplies and space, why do you want to waste it on one person?"

<It was McGraw's idea to create an ark for the local families. I would have just settled on two containers.> Taron crossed his arms on his chest.

"But you're still keeping it to yourself, even though you think it could save people if the volcano blew?"

Taron's hair bristled when he signed, staring at Colin with wild eyes. Understanding him became possible only after he repeated it all much slower. <People are a liability.>

Colin frowned, stilling in a room that housed some

mechanical equipment and was likely meant to serve as a workshop of sorts. *"People* are a liability? You have how many cats?"

Taron's face darkened. In the pulsing light of the lamp above, his skin had a bluish hue, a sharp contrast to the reddish whites of his eyes. <They're family. They won't throw you under the bus, or scheme against you.>

"They also don't work for their keep and you can't really get much meat out of them when in a pinch. And you can hardly repopulate with them. I think that out of the two, people are less of a liability."

<You're don't understand. Who do you think will be the biggest threat when shit hits the fan? Who will come for your food and water? Other people. That's why McGraw didn't even tell his nephews what he was building here.>

Old McGraw sounded like a good people-reader.

Colin put his hand against Taron's forehead, sighing when he felt it burn, but Taron shook off his touch, aggravating Colin further. "You can't make blanket statements like that. People can contribute, make a community."

<Even then, trying to save those you love could be the nail to your coffin.>

Colin shook his head. "Oh, so everyone is a liability for you? Would you call me that too?"

Just seeing Taron ponder it for endless seconds was infuriating enough, but what followed was even worse. <Yes, but you're here, and it can't be helped.>

Colin's blood boiled, as if it wanted to evaporate any trace of Taron from Colin's body. "Did you really just call me a liability to my face?"

Taron spread his arms as if there was nothing wrong with any of it. <Sorry.> But with his stern expression, it looked very much like 'not sorry'.

Colin took a deep gulp of air and poked his index finger hard against Taron's breastbone. "What the actual fuck is wrong with you? Who would take care of you if you got ill?"

Instead of being cowed, Taron seemed to have built a new wall since the beginning of this conversation. <I heard cats had the power to pull sickness out of a person.>

Colin rolled his eyes, breathing through his nose as he paced around the room. "Oh, sure, they're gonna nurse you to health if you needed surgery or broke your back!"

He was shocked when Taron grabbed his arm to enforce eye contact. <I've created a network of like-minded gay individuals. We communicate over the radio and let each other know if there are bad times ahead. We have plans put in place in case anyone needed help. That's enough. I've managed on my own for years.>

Colin wanted to laugh, but the collar around his neck seemed to tighten. He couldn't believe it. Taron was literally telling him he had gay prepper friends over the radio, and that they were better than a partner in the flesh.

"Do you radio-fuck them too?" he asked, pushing at Taron's chest. The whole thing made him unreasonably angry, but once fury struck, he couldn't stop it.

<By Morse code?> Taron growled with a frown, but his cheeks got as red as the tomatoes in his garden. Maybe he'd just listened. Of course he fucking did.

"That is *so* not on! You have a real-life human here, who actually doesn't mind your weird-ass ideas, and who helps you out with everything, and you dare to call *me* a liability?" Colin shouted at the top of his lungs while his brain boiled in the pressure cooker of his skull. "I actually have medical knowledge. If anything I'm an asset on so many levels, but you can't even recognize this?"

He hated the smirk hidden in Taron's beard. <ASS,> he spelled out. <ASSet.>

Colin stood still, his throat getting so tight that for a moment he didn't dare speak. "Oh yeah, I *am* a nice piece of ass. And in this world after the apocalypse you want so much, your gay prepper friends will be dying to meet me."

The sudden tension in Taron's shoulders told Colin all he needed to know. <You're mine.>

Not so disposable then after all, but knowing just how much Taron secretly wanted him wasn't good enough. Colin had too much poison on his tongue by now to just let it go to waste.

"We shall see. Maybe you should fight them for me? Because I'd rather live with someone who doesn't think I'm a fucking shackle at their ankle!" Colin barked. "And who knows, maybe I'd like them better anyway. Maybe I could join a thruple for double the protection and resources."

The fury with which Taron grabbed him by the jaw shocked Colin, but his heart had already been beating overtime. Taron leaned close enough for them to kiss, and despite his anger, Colin's knees softened when the warmth of Taron's breath touched his lips.

"Stop fucking around."

"I'm being brutally honest. Just. Like. You," he said stubbornly and tried to jerk his face out of the grip, but it was no use. The rough fingers dug into his flesh until it was so painful Colin stilled, clutching at Taron's clothes.

"You want more cock or something? You'll get plenty from me," Taron growled, touching his forehead to Colin's, his whole stance combative, as if he were going to war.

Colin shook his head, trying to push him away, but Taron not only backed him against the wall, but also slid his other hand down Colin's pajama pants and cupped his crotch.

Colin's brain couldn't function anymore. Between the fury, disappointment, and the sudden rush of heat in his balls, he stared back at Taron, struggling for air. "I just want..."

What did he want exactly? Recognition? To feel safe where he was? For Taron to care?

And why? Was this all for easier escape when the time came? Because running away hasn't been on his mind much.

Taron's nostrils flared when he inhaled over Colin's cheek. "What?" His hold on Colin's cock became firmer, more insistent, and Colin knew it so well by now that it was hard to think about anything other than rocking his hips against that thick fist.

Colin swallowed, entranced by the forest-green gaze. Taron's beard tickled his cheek and neck, triggering a chain reaction that had him getting to his toes. The outburst rubbed Colin's ego in the most primitive of ways, but that couldn't wipe away any of what he'd said before.

"You said you'd rather not have me here in the first place. So what's your problem?" he whispered.

Taron grunted into Colin's ear. "You said it yourself. Cats are also a liability. I'm not kicking them out, am I?"

The mixture of emotional pain and physical pleasure was becoming unbearable, and he grabbed Taron's beard, twisting his fingers and tugging on it purposefully hard. "Don't fucking call me that!"

Taron groaned, but slid his other hand to Colin's chest. "Okay, okay. Asset." He kissed Colin's ear in the gentlest way, making the furious jerking off going on even more confusing. Still, Colin melted against him and frantically slid his own hand into Taron's jogging bottoms. The soft fabric stretched over his knuckles, accommodating their shape--such a contrast to the hard, rigid dick that dragged along his palm, greedily demanding satisfaction.

He pressed closer and hooked one of his legs over Taron's thigh, bringing their hips closer. "I hate you," he whimpered against Taron's lips before claiming them with a bite.

Their hands worked hard and fast, at one point joined in their rhythm, but Colin still got some satisfaction from the fact that he made Taron come first. Gasping for air, yet still hungry for kisses, Taron finished him off not long after. Colin wasn't even sure when the harsh touch from before became the hug that it was now, but he held on as if letting go would mean drowning.

His nose was buried in Taron's beard, and his hands moved up and down the firm back as they sat together, slumped by the cold wall. He wouldn't have to quickly shower and leave for classes. He had nowhere to go, nowhere to rush to. He couldn't remember ever being this peaceful in the arms of another man.

It felt good, and eventually, he pulled Taron's limp arm around him. Perhaps this was the break he so much needed, but being here, away from society did not feel like wasting time. Life was not passing through his fingers, because it was right here—in the daily work they were doing and in the companionship of a like-minded guy.

If circumstances had been any different, if it hadn't been for his parents pushing him to follow in their footsteps, maybe he would have ran into Taron at some point. Maybe they would have hooked up. Maybe the intensity of the encounter would have made Colin try to turn this whole thing into a date? Maybe Taron would have talked about the gospel of prepping for Yellowstone over lunch. Maybe they would have fucked the second time and arranged for Taron to teach Colin a skill that was really just an excuse to meet up again.

Maybe.

But if the supervolcano did erupt, this bunker would be the perfect ark for survival. It was one thing to live in the woods above, but being buried underground with a single person as the only companion forever? Taron wasn't annoying or noisy. He knew how to entertain himself, and his quiet demeanor complemented Colin's chatter.

What would it have been like to live here forever? Just the two of them.

If the tornado had actually been something more deadly, more extreme, what would Colin require to live a fulfilling life down here? Taron did have a point about people being a threat in uncertain times. The bunker, however, was well-hidden, and only a select group of people knew about its existence. In an apocalypse-style situation, Colin would rather stay far away from gun-crazy bible-bashers who decided it was their time to make the rules.

Taron lazily stroked his back, and the tender touch was an invisible chain, much stronger than the threat of the shock collar. Still, Colin felt safe in those arms.

It was cold underground sometimes. Maybe he could take up knitting as a way to pass the time in winter? It would be a useful skill in the future, one of the ways to show Taron that there were many benefits to having a companion.

Colin hadn't expected that Taron not needing him would be such a blow, but maybe he needed to rethink the size of his ego.

Next to him, Taron's chest expanded, and he then sneezed.

"Bless you," Colin said flatly but was surprised when Taron enfolded him in a tight hug that lasted for several seconds.

The embrace was strong enough to make Colin's ribs ache, but then he let go and kissed Colin's cheek as if nothing happened.

He was confusing. Like a cat.

<You want to see something special?>

Colin smiled and let his head roll over Taron's shoulder, staring at the flush on Taron's face. "Wow, there's more?"

Taron put his arm over Colin's shoulders and led him along the wall. What else could he have here? A shark tank? Ten freezers?

When Taron opened the door to the next container and turned on the light, words died on Colin's lips. Walls covered in small shelves would have been baffling if it wasn't for the handmade cat trees around them, the green carpet floor, cat toys, pillows and tiny beds scattered around the place.

He had no doubt this was Taron's addition to the compound. His fingers entwined with Taron's, and he grinned at him. "Really impressive. Do I also get a pet room dedicated to my needs?"

Taron leaned over to whisper instead of signing. "If you stay."

As if Colin had a choice in the matter.

Colin smiled at him, once again wondering if maybe there was some kind of middle ground. Technically, he could send his parents a letter informing them that he was leaving, or go to a police station to explain he'd been lost in the woods. Or maybe he could go back to his old life and keep in touch with Taron. Have a fresh start. He could alternate between staying at his parents' and with Taron while going to med school.

"I'll consider it, depending on your offer."

Taron pulled away and Colin already missed his hand. < Let's go and see if the tornado hit us, or if we were lucky and only have to clean up after the storm.>

Colin let Taron lead him, but his brain still lingered on the possibilities this place offered, on the cat room actually getting some use, and on that nice bed they'd slept in last night. Together for the first time.

"Or maybe... not?"

Taron raised his eyebrows and sneezed again as they walked the endless shipping containers that created a maze of rooms and compartments. He was getting ill and shouldn't be out in the wind and running around to fix things. Colin had already noticed Taron had the tendency to overwork himself. What he needed was bed rest and chicken soup.

"Since we're already here, maybe we could give this hiding underground thing a trial run? You know, just to see how we would cope."

Taron cocked his head, but the hook was in. <You'd want to?>

Colin swallowed, entranced by the hope in Taron's pale face. "I'm to stay, right? So I need to learn everything there is to know about this place. Just in case."

Taron nodded quickly and smiled. <I'll show you everything.>

Colin smiled back. "But bed first. Doctor's orders."

CHAPTER FIFTEEN

They spent almost two weeks in the bunker, with Taron leaving only to take care of the basic needs of the animals and to water the garden. It was for the better because for a few days Taron's cold had gotten pretty rough, and he needed the care and rest, no matter how much he claimed to be fine.

All in all, learning about Taron's entire setup, the different water sources, the air filters and so on, had been an interesting experience. Everything felt so hands-on.

Once they re-emerged from the bunker, Colin had considered escaping again, but that had only lasted until the June sunshine hit his skin. It wouldn't hurt to stay a while longer, so the next two weeks passed repairing the damage caused by the storm and looking after Missi and her kittens. Taron had even brought Colin more books from the library, all chosen to align with his taste.

He seemed to put a lot of thought into gifts. Earlier that month, he'd brought Colin his favorite chocolate bar, even though sweets weren't usually on the menu, and Taron didn't like spending money on things he didn't need.

Another time, he let Colin sleep past noon, just to surprise him with a breakfast in bed. Taron was a gruff guy, but he could also be very giving, no matter how silly his world view was.

Colin came back with fresh water from the well just in time for breakfast. The house smelled of butter, eggs, and rabbit bacon fried crispy—exactly the way Colin liked.

He thanked Taron and sat across from him, piling the eggs on top of toast. "Are you going out?" he asked, noticing that Taron wasn't wearing the old shoes he used around the homestead.

Taron nodded with his mouth already full. He was wearing a T-shirt, which showcased the broad arms that were such a treat to Colin. Perhaps later in the day, he would even take that off.

Colin rested his chin on his palm. Every bit of information needed to be ripped out of Taron by force. "Where?"

Taron made the gesture of casting with one hand. Fishing then. Colin's grandfather had tried to convince him watching a piece of plastic float on the water surface until a fish swallowed the bait was an excellent pastime, but Colin had hated it with a passion, so he never asked to join Taron. <South from the place where we found Missi. Close to where we saw that badger.>

"We could grill it outdoors. Could be a fun evening," Colin said, wolfing down his food. Taron wasn't the kind of guy who'd scold him for speaking with his mouth full.

Taron's eyes lit up. <In the firepit. Chicken, if I don't catch any.>

Colin grinned at him, but then memories flooded his mind, and his smile faltered. Taron picked up on that immediately and poked Colin's foot with a questioning look. Colin swallowed and leaned back in his chair, pulling closer the cup of herbal tea they drank instead of coffee.

"I was thinking about my grandparents, because Granddad liked fishing so much, and it just... hit me. I stayed with them for a few years when my parents were away. Now they're dead and I miss them."

Taron's shoulders fell. <Want to come?>

Colin shook his head. "No. I need to do some work in the garden. It's just... that maybe we could do something for my birthday. I never really had any parties thrown for me since my grandmom passed away. Well, I guess I could count that birthday threesome two years back as a party," he said, trying to pull himself together. The melancholic mood had come out of nowhere.

Taron frowned. <Birthday threesome? Seriously? We're not doing that.>

His serious face did it. Colin chuckled and gently rubbed his toes against Taron's calf. "No, but maybe we could do something else. There was this new *Avengers* movie I really wanted to see."

<What's that?>

Colin was confused for a moment, but then remembered that Taron had lived in the woods for the past fifteen years and was not up to date with modern pop culture. "Superheroes."

Taron smiled. <Like Batman?>

"No, not like Batman. They're the other ones," Colin said helplessly but ended up shaking his head. "Doesn't matter. But I've been following this series for years now, and this movie will be like the final chapter."

Taron stroked his hand. <Maybe we can get it on DVD in a few months. When is your birthday?>

Colin glanced at the warm, large hand covering his.

There was such comfort to the touch that for a brief moment he just stayed still. "In two months, August 13th."

<I'm sorry about the movie. But we'll do something special, okay?>

Colin squeezed Taron's hand, suddenly desperate to get out of there and have fresh popcorn while seated in an uncomfortable chair. Just because he wanted to. He usually preferred to watch movies at home, in peace, but the fact that he was forbidden from leaving made cinema a tempting perspective. "I could grow a beard in two months. Nobody would recognize me."

Taron stared at him thoughtfully, and only then it hit Colin that he was being scrutinized. That Taron was assessing if Colin would turn to the nearest police station, or make a scene in public.

<I like you shaved.>

Colin slid his hand out of Taron's grip. "Oh, come on! You really think I'd run? Still?"

Taron looked away and wiped his mouth with a towel. Since he'd cooked, the dishes would be Colin's to deal with. <I have to go. Fish don't wait for no one.>

They did, actually. There was loads of them and one annoyed Colin.

"Give me a break. It's just a movie. We'd be in a dark theatre, and we could go straight home after," Colin said, increasingly agitated. He could have fled a hundred times by now. Not that he could say that to Taron's face, but for all intents and purposes they were... close by now, and he didn't want to disappoint him. "When will you trust me?"

<I'll think about it.>

Did this mean he'd think about the movie, or think about trust? Colin didn't get to ask, because Taron rushed out the front door.

So they'd been fucking like newlyweds for weeks now, but Taron still expected a knife in his back?

Colin slowly followed him out, his gaze fixed on the broad shoulders. There was no point in arguing now, even though the collar, which he'd forgotten about, once again felt heavy and repressive. "Be careful," he said once Taron pulled his fishing supplies out of the shed.

Taron smiled at him and waved as if they'd never had the uncomfortable conversation. Of course. Taron was the master of evading topics. There was nothing else for Colin to do but do his thing in the garden and await Taron's return.

Or was there?

The fishing trip would take a couple of hours—more than enough time for Colin to reach the public road, even on foot. The weather was glorious, and he could even take water and snacks.

He wouldn't even need to tell the authorities what happened. He could claim amnesia, lie his ass off about surviving in the wild, or simply say he needed a break from his daily existence.

But anxiety stuck its claws into him, causing stomach cramps the moment he imagined Taron coming home with fish for their dinner, proud to show them to Colin, only to find the house empty.

He couldn't do that to him after demanding trust.

Colin bit his lips hard as he watched Taron disappear in the woods, but the tension didn't leave his body until he was done with the dishes. Once outside, the decision he'd made felt right. Taron was away at least twice a week, so it wasn't like he was missing his one chance today.

With peace settling in his gut, he gradually relaxed, going about his chores like most mornings. Once the animals were all fed, he went to the garden, where the leaves were still dewy, and which smelled of lush plants and rich soil. The sun lazily moved above Colin's head, so he put on Taron's straw hat and continued with yesterday's task—weeding. Few things felt more satisfying than tidying up the plots. It was hands-on work, and he could see the effects right away.

Too bad it left his brain unoccupied.

Would Colin never again go to the movies? Or would it take much more time to talk Taron into an outing. He could just go, of course, and celebrate his birthday however he wanted, without having to beg for favors. But then again, time passed so fast and he felt peaceful with Taron and his animals. Maybe he could wait until after his birthday, since it wasn't as if he could still graduate this year without handing in all the required papers. Perhaps late August or early September would be the right time to go. By that time, he would have spent a relaxing summer, fucking a guy whose company he enjoyed, and stuffing his face with organic food. What was not to like?

He didn't need the hassle of his normal life just yet, and in another month, maybe Taron could be convinced that it wasn't an either-or type of situation, and that Colin going back to his normal life didn't mean that they would never see one another again. In fact, being here over the weekend would have been so much more relaxing than Colin's home stays, which he sometimes evaded by lying to his parents that he needed to work on group projects with his classmates.

The cats provided a welcome distraction. Colin used a weed to play with Rio, who went crazy when he couldn't catch the tip of the damn thing. In the end though, it was back to work for Colin, and he cut some vegetables for lunch before walking behind the shed where Taron had planted some berries. Colin was excited for the wild strawberries, and he'd been watching them slowly grow and ripen for a while now, but when he scooted down next to the little plants, the bright red fruit made him smile.

Their size was perfection, and when he picked one to try it, it exploded in his mouth with layers of sweetness and taste. He was so proud of their mutual achievement he couldn't wait to see Taron try one too. Since he wasn't leaving just yet, he might as well join Taron by the river and have a picnic. And then fuck in nature. Just the thought of it had Colin grinning.

He ran back to the house to get a box for the fruit. It then went into a basket that also held some other snacks and the juice they'd pressed themselves a week back. Within minutes, he was off, following the narrow path that led to the river. The sunlight rubbed its warm digits against his skin as he walked, humming softly, but halfway there it occurred to him that he would reach Taron sooner if he took a shortcut.

Taron had told him not to go past certain areas, but by now Colin knew the collar wouldn't shock him, so he strayed off the path and strode across the expanse of lush grass covering the ground between thick bushes. What Taron didn't know wouldn't hurt him.

He'd never gone this way, and the sheer beauty of the untouched woodland made him contemplate just how much he'd missed this for most of his life. His attention was scattered from one tree to another, but it was the huge blooming rhododendron with its pink petals that took his breath away. He just had to get some for their home, even if Taron was to laugh at his attempts at making the cabin homelier.

Colin left the basket in the grass and approached the
bush, blinded by the sun that shone from behind the rhododendron. Every time he took a step, the moss gave under his
weight, but for once the ground was hard.

Something clicked—not cracked—in the serene glade,
and then he was knocked over, and fell without the ability
to breathe. The leaves and plants trembled above him in the
bright sun, their edges red, but as first shock wore off, Colin
became aware of the throbbing pain in his leg. Something
was wrong. So wrong.

He gave a choked cry and sat up, only to scream out at
the sight of iron clamping on his lower leg. His lungs ached
as if they couldn't inflate, but the longer he looked down at
the teeth digging into his flesh, at the metal jaws ruthlessly
pushing at his bare leg from both sides, the more the numbness in this area changed into unforgiving, pulsing pain.
Thinking was no longer possible, and his erratic thoughts
made him struggle, even though it was obvious he wouldn't
just slide out of the snares.

This time, he couldn't stop the scream that left his
mouth, and within a few heartbeats, he was scratching the
ground and clutching at grass, because there was no other
way to cope with the searing sensation.

"Taron! Taron," he cried, shaking in fear when something
shifted inside his leg. This couldn't be happening. It couldn't...

Sweat beaded on his back, cooling his skin, and he went
frantic when he realized the basket was far away. He didn't
check for ants, had he? What if ants overran his picnic
basket and ate everything?

Tears stung his eyes, and he rolled down again, shaking
all over. So far off the path, he might bleed out, or he could
be found by a wild animal here, trapped and unable to

defend himself. He knew he should be able to do *something*, but staying up was impossible, and looking down at that metal squashing his limb made his guts twist.

His brain shut down, but when his fingers suddenly traced a piece of metal hanging off his neck, hope flashed inside him, bringing logic back on.

The whistle. He had a whistle.

Colin's lips found the metal mouth as if it was a bottle of water in the desert, and he blew at the top of his lungs. Time and time again, despite the sobs choking him, Colin blew the whistle.

He didn't hear the footsteps, and when Taron appeared above him, his touch seemingly came out of nowhere. He squeezed Colin's shoulders and kneeled in the grass with a tense expression. He wanted to say something, but he was so frantic it came out as a mix of grunts, so he took a deep breath and signed.

<What are you doing here?>

With absolute focus, he examined the snares taking a bite out of Colin's leg.

Colin looked at him and blew the whistle weakly, shaking from the cold. When had the temperature dropped? "Picnic," he said and waved his hand toward where he thought the basket was.

Taron inhaled through his nose. <I told you not to come here.> He fiddled with something by the snares, and Colin was so desperate for help he wouldn't even argue with Taron.

"I wanted to get to you faster."

When Taron yanked the snares open, hot white pain flooded Colin's whole body and made him scream. He twisted in the grass, kicking about with his untouched foot, but his hands already found Taron's clothes and held on, just in case he wanted to leave. "Don't go."

Taron shook his head and made the short sign for 'never'. He slid his arm under Colin's knees, the other behind his back, and when he picked him up, Colin instinctively embraced Taron's neck.

His illogical brain told him that with the snares gone, the pain should be subsiding, but instead it only became worse, ripping the fibres in his muscles one at a time with every step Taron took. He didn't want to look down, so he focused on Taron instead, breathing his scent and watching for any indication of what he was thinking. "I have all the wild strawberries in there. We can't just leave them."

Taron opened his lips as if to say something, but instead, when they were passing the basket, he leaned lower for Colin to grab the handle. Colin pulled the basket to his chest, but as he was leaning down, his gaze caught the swollen flesh torn by the teeth of the snare, with drying rivulets of blood crisscrossing the purplish skin. He took a deep breath, halting the sudden nausea and clutching the basket to his chest.

"Fuck. Oh fuck. It's broken. I'm sure it is! How far is the nearest emergency room?"

Taron glanced to the leg, then to Colin's face. He said something, but with the blood pounding in Colin's head, he couldn't hear a word, so Taron repeated.

"No hospital."

For a moment, Taron ran in silence, securely holding Colin's body despite gravity weighing them down. But Colin's brain eventually caught up, and he shook his head, trying to forget about the injury. "What? Of course we're going! I need an X-ray. Maybe surgery..."

"We can't go. We will set it here." Even Taron's strong

grip wouldn't give Colin comfort now. He'd entered the Twilight zone, and he would die here. Bleed out, get an infection, walk with a painful limp forever, get sepsis, or suffer endless horrific consequences.

"What do you mean we can't go? There's nothing stopping you from getting me real help. If someone knows who I am, just tell them you found me in the woods," Colin uttered, clutching at Taron's neck while his own pulsed under the shock collar.

"You know why we can't go."

This couldn't be happening to him. His first ever broken bone. Endless information about how to treat it vibrated inside his skull, yet all he could think of was the horrifying state of his leg.

"No, I don't. I need help. I really need a doctor. This isn't a joke. Taron, please," Colin whispered, looking straight into his eyes despite the aching pain telling him to just curl up and cry. Even his grip on the basket was becoming too weak.

"It will be fine. I'm not going to prison." The unyielding look in Taron's eyes broke Colin's heart in two. This was it. Taron didn't trust him, and wouldn't be changing his mind about it, even if it meant Colin suffering the consequences.

"Please, Taron. I beg you..." He couldn't help another sob, but Taron wouldn't budge.

Every step Taron took created an impact that shook Colin's leg, and the pain became too much. Colin faded out. The last thing he saw was his basket falling to the ground.

CHAPTER SIXTEEN

Taron got Colin drunk on the moonshine, but even the copious amount of alcohol couldn't numb him to the pain of having the fractured limb handled. Colin tried to assist him and by trying to reposition the broken bone himself at first, but ended up hesitantly probing at the swollen flesh, unable to make himself push. Each twist of Colin's face, each sob was a scar on Taron's heart, but he needed to stay firm. Regardless of what Colin believed, this could be dealt with at home, without endangering everything Taron had worked for. People had done so for millennia, without antibiotics to make sure the wound didn't get infected.

Colin hadn't broken his leg on purpose, but if he ended up in hospital, he'd be gone from Taron's life forever, even if he decided not to press charges, which was highly unlikely. Preparing for a disastrous future meant Taron had also studied first aid and medical basics. He'd been ready to one day have to deal with a fracture himself. He just hadn't expected needing to help someone else.

His hands were covered in blood, and he had to kick all

the cats out of the house when they wouldn't stay away from the makeshift operating table, but there was barely any dislocation, so he figured the injury would heal with time. Colin hated him right now, but despite what his drunken slurring suggested, he would eventually come around.

The swollen flesh was hard to look at, but once Taron set his mind to it, he just wanted to get through the process as fast as possible. In a way, Colin fading out of consciousness again was a blessing.

The whole ordeal took ages, and by the time Taron transferred Colin to his bedroom with the leg secured with wooden planks and rope, he didn't feel better at all. Colin gasped for air, stirring in his shallow slumber, and Taron returned with cold water to wipe sweat from his pale face. He'd already taken the antibiotics he'd requested, so even if he was feeling awful at the moment, in a few days, his condition should improve. After all, the bone hadn't broken through the skin or anything horrid like that. And without the traditional cast, Taron could take care of the puncture wounds left by his trap with ease.

Once everything was over, tiredness settled on his shoulders, and he resorted to making himself a rare coffee. He sat on the bed and gently dabbed the bleeding wounds with a cold, damp cloth. His heart couldn't bear seeing Colin in so much pain, and if he only could, he would make Colin sleep until he was healed.

Colin suddenly stirred again, looking around with reddened eyes, but as he tried to sit up, his leg must have hurt, because he dropped right back into the pillows, clutching at his thigh with a hiss that twisted his features.

"This was not a fucking dream..."

Taron stroked the healthy foot. <It's okay. It's done.>

Colin's eyes opened rapidly, and he kicked Taron's

hand away with the healthy leg. "No," he said, breathing harder by the second. "Why are you here?"

<Where else would I be?> Was Colin delusional after too much moonshine?

Colin shook his head, shifting away from him. "Away. Go on. You wanted to fish. Then go."

Taron patted Colin's shoulder to make sure Colin looked at him. <I'm not going anywhere. I'll be here whenever you need me.>

Colin pushed his hand away as if it were dirty, his face freezing into an angry grimace. "I don't need anything from you. This is all so convenient. I should have tried to run once you left, not gone for a fucking picnic."

Taron's heart sunk, all his worst fears confirmed. Colin still wanted to leave, no matter how much he seemed to enjoy living with Taron.

<I hate seeing you hurt. I will take care of you.>

Colin took a wheezing breath, his eyes wide. "No. You don't really care. You're just angry that I'm not fit to help around anymore. You don't care how I feel as long as I don't get you in trouble," he said in a high-pitched voice, clawing the covers.

Every word was meant to cause maximum damage, and wreaked havoc inside Taron. Was this really how Colin felt about him?

<You know it's not true.> He leaned down to hug Colin, but got a slap to the face so harsh he backed away at once.

Colin rolled farther away on the bed, his face flushing, eyes unfocused as he landed on his stomach. "I can't believe I actually trusted you. You are a sick man. You're *sick*! My leg could be damaged forever, but you'd rather keep me here without help."

Taron slapped his own chest hard. <I helped.>

Colin shook his head, pulling the blanket over him, and the fabric trembling over him made the tremors passing through his body even clearer. Everything inside Taron told him to offer Colin comfort, but he knew it was unwanted.

"You did shit. For all we know, you might have made my leg worse, and there's no way to know. You're selfish. Whatever you say, you don't care what happens to me."

Taron *did* care. He cared for Colin never leaving, and that did make him selfish. He'd also murdered a total of three men in his life, and had abducted Colin, so he didn't have a claim to goodness. He didn't have to reflect on it much most days, but today, he'd been confronted with a reflection he didn't particularly enjoy seeing.

<You will be fine. I will make sure. I will talk to Gus on the radio. He has a doctor friend.>

Colin grabbed the pillow and tossed it into Taron's face. "There's doctors in the nearest fucking town! You're delusional!"

Taron ducked with a groan. <If the world wasn't there to offer help, we would have needed to deal with it ourselves too. Being self-sufficient is best.>

Colin showed his teeth and sat up, struggling in his drunken state. He looked like a cornered animal that didn't know why it was bleeding. "But we're not! Even if the end of civilization might fucking eventually happen, it hasn't happened yet. We *can* ask for help, and if you're not gonna help me, I will do it myself!" he said, dragging the injured leg behind him.

Taron pushed Colin's shoulders, holding him down before he could stand. <Where are you going?>

Colin punched at his chest so hard it made Taron's breath stall for a moment. "To town. Where else would I go with a fractured leg?"

Taron groaned and dragged his hand down his face. <You're not going anywhere. You will rest. Heal.>

Colin pinched him hard and kicked at him blindly with his healthy leg. "Let go. Don't fucking touch me."

<Then lay down. Do I need to cage you?> Taron let out a groan to drive his point home. For once, he wished he could just scream out his frustration, like most people.

Colin stilled, and anger was gone from his face, replaced by such despair it broke Taron's heart in half. "You'd do that to me again? Really?"

<Only if you're a threat to yourself.> Taron clutched at his hair in frustration and stepped away. He couldn't believe this mess. If there was something he'd never prepared for, it was ending up with a partner. He was supposed to be self-sufficient, and the only reason he'd learned about dealing with fractures was because he'd assumed he might have to help himself at some point in the future. And now here he was, falling apart for a guy who hated his guts yet unable to let him go.

Colin snorted, shaking his head. "It's you who is a threat to me. And because of *you* I will be miserable forever."

Taron leaned against the wall with his arms crossed. There was no way out of this situation, because even though Colin was now a ticking time bomb, Taron would never be able to bring himself to dispose of him. He'd fallen into the trap he'd so desperately tried to avoid—caring for another person.

<You will learn to live with it,> he signed in the end.

Colin screamed and punched the nearest pillow. "Fuck! You! What do you know about being trapped and helpless? I could be home in an hour and a half, but you keep me here like a fucking pet bird, even though I need help. You don't understand shit!"

Taron wanted to sign to Colin that he wasn't ignorant to the things he was feeling now, but as soon as he started he worried about his meaning getting lost, or Colin being too drunk to understand his frantic gestures. When he opened his mouth, putting his grief into spoken words proved too hard, so he grabbed a notebook and started scribbling furiously.

Tears prickled his eyes, even though the events he wanted to describe had passed so long ago. This should have been behind him. He'd chosen a path that allowed him to protect himself from history ever repeating itself, only to walk into invisible snares. His fingers got trembly by the end, but he handed the open notebook to Colin, hoping that finding out about Taron's past would help him understand.

Colin glared at him, but started reading with an annoyed sneer, as if having to deal with Taron's disability infuriated him.

I just believe in being prepared for the worst, and your leg is a minor setback. We've dealt with it, and even if it hurts now, you will get better. You should be prepared for things in life. My family wasn't. I was eighteen when our hometown was flooded. We were told to evacuate, but my parents thought they knew better, and that everything would just blow over. When the worst flooding came, it took my family by surprise. My dad sent off my mom and my two younger sisters on a boat to reach safety, and we stayed because the dinghy was too small for us all. We were to climb to the roof if things got bad.

Before that even happened, looters came to our house. Dad tried to fight them off. He shot one, but got thrown out of the window, and into the flood rapids. I killed the other one, and then stayed in the house for a week. I was waiting for mom to come back for me. For dad to maybe find his way back, injured. I needed to be there for them. Our house had barely any supplies, and I ended up living on my sisters' Halloween candy stash and water filtered as best that I could.

No one of my family survived. I refuse to be caught in a situation like that again. I thought I could do it all on my own. Start a new life, and be only responsible for myself, but now you're here, and I want you here, and I don't want to lose you, so we both need to learn to handle shit on our own.

Colin's chest moved up and down, and as he read on, the frown on his forehead deepened, making Taron feel like his heart was getting dissected while still beating. Seconds passed in growing tension.

In the end, Colin finally met Taron's gaze, but his own was sharp as ever. "You actually think this explains what you're doing to me?"

The harshness behind his words was worse than the slap had been. Taron hadn't told anyone this story since its aftermath, but he so desperately craved for Colin to under-stand that he'd bared it all. <Yes. The government won't help, so you have to learn to deal with things on your own.>

Colin swallowed hard, and tore the page in two. He then put the two halves together and tore them again, never looking away from Taron as he minced his soul with this simple gesture. "There is no *us*. I told you what I want, and you still bent me to your will by force. You don't trust me. You don't even respect me. I don't want to be around you. I don't want to see you. I don't want to hear your excuses. I hate you."

Taron watch the pieces of paper float to the floor. His heart went numb. This was exactly why he'd avoided relationships with people. <You don't want to be with me?> It felt needy to ask, but he still did.

Colin swallowed but kept up the eye contact, despite his brows lowering. "Are you really asking me if I want to be with a man who abducted me, kept me in a cage and doesn't listen when I tell him I need a doctor?'

Taron hung his head. It seemed the honeymoon period was over. He should have never let Colin steal his heart.

He said nothing and picked up the shredded paper. He would manage this somehow.

He always did.

He'd been fine on his own.

CHAPTER SEVENTEEN

I f there was a zombie apocalypse, the bunker would have been the perfect hideout. Well-hidden, supplied not only with dry food but also means to grow more produce. First and foremost—safe. They could stay underground for at least three years, and if it became necessary to leave it all behind, Taron would have surely been the perfect companion to have on your side.

Brave, strong, and resourceful, he would have made sure nothing bad happened to Colin. He knew how to forage, how to filter water, how to make a fire... And if, by any chance, Taron got bitten by a zombie, Colin would have been there to amputate the limb and save him.

It wouldn't have been so bad to face the cruel world together.

And in that kind of hypothetical scenario, Colin would have understood, appreciated even, Taron's ability to treat a fractured leg. But they weren't under siege by brain-hungry monsters, and no matter how much he liked the bunker and *had* enjoyed Taron as his man, Colin should have been taken to the hospital.

And two weeks on, he was still worried about how his limb would heal, still imprisoned and collared. This might as well have been a reinterpretation of Stephen King's *Misery* if it wasn't for the fact that Taron didn't demand anything from Colin, and for the most part just let him be. Colin refused to speak to Taron or otherwise acknowledge his existence, beaten down and hurt after the disastrous afternoon when one of Taron's snares had broken his leg, but Taron still tried to get some brownie points by cooking Colin's favorite meals and bringing him interesting books. Following his latest trip to town, he even brought Colin some superhero-themed DVDs

All of this would have been adorable if their relationship were voluntary and based on mutual respect, not force.

One of the luxuries afforded Colin was taking hot baths. Down in the bunker, with one of his legs hanging out of the tub, Colin enjoyed the tranquility of being alone. Of course, the injury meant that he needed Taron's help to enter the bath, and his touch had only agitated Colin further. Why was it that after two weeks of celibacy, even Taron's scent made Colin think back to all the sex they'd had in the past? A man like Taron didn't deserve to star in Colin's fantasies.

But here Colin was, thinking of long days and nights under Taron's heavy, strong body, of his rough hands that could be so gentle, of the intensity in his green eyes that spoke of a hungry desire Colin had never experienced in a world where sex was plentiful.

He submerged his head until all he could see was the trembling surface above. The bath was getting cold, but the sense of peace it gave him was something he didn't want to give up just yet. Days in Taron's presence were slowly becoming unbearable, and the silence that he himself enforced choked Colin whenever they were in the same room. But what was he to do? He did not want to fall back into a guy who didn't really care for him and who refused him the necessary medical care for selfish reasons.

And it would have been so, so easy to just roll into Taron's arms again. After two weeks of zero sex, even the sight of Taron's forearms was enough to make Colin salivate, and since it had been so hot recently, Taron insisted on walking around shirtless, with his firm, hairy chest on show. It made Colin wonder if the fucker did it on purpose, well aware of his prisoner's weakness for him.

But Colin would not be tempted, even if he was to tear the skin off his cock from too much masturbation.

Just as Colin was about to indulge in just that, Taron walked into the room. Knocking wasn't something Taron was a fan of, so Colin always ended up startled.

In an ideal world, Colin would have remained still and pretended that he hadn't noticed another person's presence, but he didn't have gills to breathe underwater, so he pulled his head out, not bothering to shake off the cooling droplets.

Taron didn't even meet his gaze, but he was topless, and his skin had that reddish flush of a fresh tan. He'd brought towels, fresh dressings for Colin's leg, and laundered clothes.

<Done?> he signed without looking up. That was the extent of their recent communication, and while Colin hated the awkwardness of it, at least he got some satisfaction out of the fact that Taron seemed to hate the situation just as much.

He was determined to never talk to Taron again, so instead of providing an answer, he pushed his body up, trying to leave the tub without help. It was a lost cause since the injured leg was a dead weight, but at least he'd tried.

Needing Taron's care was even worse than the pain and

discomfort caused by the leg brace combined, but he still appreciated that Taron appeared the moment his help was necessary. He easily assisted Colin out of the tub, the big body sturdy enough to trust. Skin slid against skin, and Colin had to wrangle all the sexual thoughts that galloped through his mind, and herd them toward a cliff. His naked-ness wasn't helping, but it wasn't as if it could be avoided in these circumstances.

He grabbed Taron's shoulder to steady himself but wouldn't look at him, even though the scent of sunshine and woodchips beckoned him to Taron like light in a dark forest. Taron carried him with ease, as if there were no bounds to the strength in those thick arms.

In the silence that remained a heavy presence around them, even the tiniest sounds were amplified, from the splash of water in the tub, to the squeak of springs in the mattress. Taron left Colin a towel so he could dry himself, but kneeled to change the dressing on Colin's leg.

Colin swallowed and started with his hair while damp-ness cooled his warm skin. He sensed Taron cleaning the healing cuts, adjusting the planks that kept the lower leg stable, and tried hard to look everywhere but at the head between his bare knees. It had been too fucking long without sex.

Exams. Think about exams. Or better yet—about the face Dad made when you told him you weren't sure if you should become a surgeon after all.

But Taron was there, kneeling between Colin's legs. Touching him. It would have been so easy to just fuck. He had no doubt Taron would go for it. Taron fucked like the monster he was, and Colin hated and loved him for it at the same time.

When he stole a glance from under the towel wrapped

around his head, he caught Taron staring at his cock, and stilled, his mind as blank as the white fabric he'd used for drying.

Seconds stretched, and his sudden stupor finally caught Taron's attention. The moment his eyes darted up from Colin's crotch, the connection was made—so electric it trailed fire all the way up Colin's legs. He'd expected Taron to flinch, pretend he hadn't been caught red-handed, but that wasn't what happened.

Colin couldn't look away from the thick beard, masculine features, and most of all—the hypnotic eyes communicating the same hunger that ate Colin up every day.

Endless seconds passed, and, without ever breaking eye contact, Taron inched closer, forcing Colin to spread his legs wider. His hands glided up. First to Colin's knees, then to the inner thighs, and their touch shut down Colin's ability to move and speak. He just sat there, entranced by the sudden change in their dynamic while the flames spread through his body, like a disease he had no immunity from.

His mouth opened only to take a long gulp of air, because his cock was already throbbing, so close to Taron's hand, its warmth was palpable on the defenseless flesh.

The clock in Colin's head ticked, counting the split seconds remaining to the moment when he'd feel Taron's fingers, but Taron did something he hadn't before. He bowed his head and licked up Colin's cock. In that moment, Colin's defences crumbled. He gave a helpless moan, clenched his fists, and curled his toes.

Taron's beard was silky against Colin's sensitive balls, and he spread his thighs without thinking, to get his head around the unexpected sensation. He rested his elbows on the mattress and glanced Taron's way, legs already trembling.

He could do this. He didn't need to *like* a guy to fuck him and enjoy it. During his online hook up times, he'd often wished his partners would keep their mouths shut so he wouldn't have to deal with whatever shit they had to say. This would be the same. Just a fuck. He wasn't a monk planning to spend the rest of his life celibate just because Taron had decided to keep him here.

Taron sucked in the cockhead, making Colin's thighs tremble from the pleasure. His ass flexed, rising from the mattress ever-so-slightly as the instinct to go deeper settled at the back of his mind. It had been a while. Taron had jerked him off too many times to count, but he'd never been even remotely interested in giving Colin head—something that couldn't be explained for fear of losing his dick. And now? Colin's resolve that he didn't need Taron for anything melted away, leaving behind raw lust, which he channeled into the hand he tightened on Taron's hair.

He wasn't giving in. He was taking whatever he needed, and that was his little victory. Taron rubbed those strong hands up and down Colin's thighs, and sucked his dick as if this was the last blowjob he'd ever get to give. For once, Colin felt in control. Even if Taron had hurt him so badly the wound would never heal, he still held the reins at this moment.

Or was he just delusional because he craved sex too much?

His cockhead popped out of Taron's mouth with a loud damp noise, and the cool air on the sensitive flesh sent Colin's brain into overdrive. The moment Taron sucked him back in, caressing his balls with one of his big, skillful hands, he knew this wasn't enough. Taron's tongue was hot and soft as it caressed the shaft, but the sweetness of this blowjob only fueled Colin's anger.

He hated it, and he hated Taron for showing his true face two weeks ago.

Choking on a growl, Colin grabbed Taron's shoulders and pulled him up, his legs already spread as wide as the bed allowed. He hissed at the pain flashing through the healing one, but the makeshift brace was secure enough. All he needed was to get this fuck out of his system. For Taron to plow him senseless. No kisses or caresses, just a dick doing its job.

Taron didn't need to be a nice person to give that much.

But Taron's hungry eyes pinned Colin to the bed as the two of them landed face to face. His heart stopped beating.

No. He didn't want to look at Taron. He just wanted the fuck. Rough, hard, and fast. As wicked as Taron.

That bastard was holding his heart in his oversized fist and squeezing it so hard Colin had to get away from him. He rolled over with so much haste his leg slapped against Taron's thigh, but the sudden discomfort wouldn't be enough to stop him, because the pain in his heart was way worse than any physical injury could have been.

"Lube," he barked, burying his face in the sheets that had already absorbed some of the dampness from his body. Taron wasn't on him yet, but Colin could sense the heat radiating from him as if it were physical touch. For once, he was glad Taron was barely able to speak, because the bastard wouldn't be asking any unnecessary questions.

He waited seconds until the thick fingers he knew so well slipped between his buttocks, and he resented just how much he welcomed their touch. Two elements fought inside of him. Fire—making water evaporate, and water—extinguishing fire. He loved and hated all at once, and it was all Taron's fault. He'd been just fine with lukewarm fuck dates and feeling absolutely nothing for his lovers, other than lust for their bodies.

With time, that would be all he felt for Taron too, but first he needed to forget all the good times and focus on what a crappy human being he was. Taron was a murderer, an abductor who kept Colin in a collar and used him for sex. None of their times together had been consensual in the true meaning of the word, so Colin refused to have any qualms when it came to using Taron for his own satisfaction either.

He wanted to be fucked hard enough to forget all the memories that were confusing him about the kind of relationship they had.

Colin gasped when Taron's finger teased his hole, but with the improvised leg brace, their current position was distracting him from the sensations he craved. Biting his lips in anger, he backed away, placing both his feet on the floor, and speared himself on the digit.

He was glad the new position forced Taron's weight off. He stood behind Colin, and his ragged breathing was the only thing Colin wanted to hear. The quick finger fuck sent shivers all the way down Colin's legs, and he had no doubt Taron's cock would soon be buried inside him, because the greedy bastard pulled out his fingers.

When Taron ran his hand up Colin's spine, he shrugged it off. He wasn't a cat to be petted. He was a person, who had decided he wanted cock, and Taron was to provide him the satisfaction. What did Taron not understand about that? Wasn't access to sex a good enough bargain for him?

So Colin chose to be more explicit about his needs and pushed back his hips, obscenely moving them from side to side while clutching on the sheets with his hands. He wanted the dick. Just the dick. If Taron was forced to stand behind him, there would be less touching.

Colin held his breath when Taron aligned his cock with Colin's hole and thrust the head in with ease. Sparks exploded under Colin's eyelids, and he clenched his ass on the thick rod.

Taron grabbed Colin's sides and rocked his hips to force more of his dick in. This was the Taron Colin expected. The Taron he'd grown to love and hate. Taron had to know how wrong this was, but being an opportunist, he took advantage of the situation as soon as he got a green light to fuck without the victim accusing him of rape.

Fair enough. They could both use one another at the same time. Maybe once they got rid of some steam, the next week or two would prove a bit more bearable. His other thoughts melted away, because the way Taron grabbed his hips—roughly and to the point—made Colin's body sizzle even before the heavy balls slapped against his bare ass.

The groan that left his lips when Taron slammed home didn't even sound like him. It was the cry of an animal hunted down by a wolf, already bleeding and about to die soon. The fast penetration made Colin's body tense, causing inevitable discomfort, but the pain was gone a few deep breaths later. And once Colin was ready, he braced himself for what was to come and tilted his hips.

He spread his legs, inviting more of this delicious agony, and he didn't have to suffer through hugs, licks or kisses, because the only place their bodies met was where Taron slapped his hips against Colin's ass again and again.

Taron didn't always position his cock exactly right to stimulate Colin's prostate, but of course, of all the times they'd fucked, this had to be one of those where Taron hit the nail on the head. Over and over again, making Colin squirm, moan and gasp for air.

The fucking was so good his head became light, and he could forget the mess of his situation. All that counted was how heavy his balls were, how his stiff cock leaked pre-cum, and how his prostate sent jolts of pleasure through his body. This was selfishly his, and he didn't care if Taron was also getting a kick out of it, because this wasn't for him.

When the thrusts got faster, Colin dropped to his elbows, which left his broken leg at an awkward angle, but he no longer cared. All he wanted was for this amazing cock to purge his brain, until he could no longer think or feel. And when the hot tingles that had earlier climbed all over focused on his dick, he finally got what he wanted. He hurriedly pumped his cock, tugging on the incredible sensation inside it. Each of Taron's precise thrusts was like an explosion of fireworks pushing through the inside of Colin's shaft.

He closed his eyes when he came, desperate to forget the world around him. That his leg was broken, that he had a shock collar around his neck, and most of all—that he did want a hug.

His ass clamped down on the thick, meaty cock, sparking yet more pleasure and then back down to his dick, in an endless cycle. He'd considered backing out, telling Taron not to come inside of him as some ultimate diss to make sure Taron understood he wasn't welcome, but to hell with that, because he loved going bare. He'd let Taron come inside him not for Taron's sake, but because *he* enjoyed feeling sticky cum drip down his balls.

He was gasping for air, sliding forward on the bed, but the grunts behind him were sure signs Taron was coming.

Heat throbbed in Colin's cheeks, in his ass, in his stomach. The world whirled around him from the animalistic pleasure of it all. Maybe Taron was the predator here, but Colin got his satisfaction.

He cried out, because having Taron come inside him always gave him that fleeting sensation of almost orgasming again himself, but that was the end of it. It was over. He should've already been pulling away, but Taron didn't let him, leaning down and pressing his hairy chest to Colin's back as he rocked his hips against Colin's ass.

It felt too good, but Colin didn't want to enjoy it, so he twisted his hips until the softening cocked popped out of him. His legs were goo and he still hadn't opened his eyes, but Taron sent him back on the bed, and laid on top of him. The strong arms wrapped around Colin's body, like pythons ready to choke him, but it was Taron's words that were the venom.

Quiet, barely there, yet heavier than the door to the fucking bunker.

"I love you," Taron whispered so close to Colin's ear he brushed his lips over the skin.

Colin's heart imploded so rapidly the physical pain of it made him want to stand up, to regulate his breathing and make sure he wasn't dying yet. Without thinking, he pushed Taron away, frantic and already growing fresh spikes. "Shut up."

Taron slipped to Colin's side and watched him with the eyes of a Golden Retriever who'd gotten his bowl of food taken away before he could finish. He had no right to sadness. Hadn't he gotten his fuck? Did he have to ruin even the few pleasures Colin had left in life?

Colin stumbled away from the bed, dragging the

injured leg awkwardly until his back hit the wall. He shouldn't have been running away. He wasn't scared, or sad, or happy. He was angry. No, he was furious!

"Don't look at me like that! You think I'm stupid? You're not gonna manipulate me!"

Taron's expression hardened, and he sat up on the bed, watching Colin's every move. <I said I love you.>

Each one of those last three gestures was hard to watch. Colin didn't want to see them. He wanted to claw his own eyes out and never see them again.

"And I said shut the fuck up! I wanted a cock up my ass, not lies."

Taron shot to his feet and, before Colin could even comprehend what was going on, slapped him hard. The sting made Colin grab his cheek, but his pride hurt more. How dare Taron act as if he were the hurt one.

Colin's teeth clattered, and he pushed back against the wall when Taron raised his arms into the air and made noises that were hardly words.

"Don't do that. You don't love me. If you loved me, you would have listened to me when I said I needed a doctor. But you always just do whatever you want. You keep me locked up. In a collar," he said, despite choking when he yanked at the metal ring around his neck. "I don't fucking know, maybe you *think* you love me, but really I'm just the most convenient fuck you've ever had. I just happened to fall into your lap!"

When he finished, the ache in his throat told him that he'd just screamed at the top of his lungs. His ears rang, but he wouldn't back down. He wouldn't be Taron's fuck-pet.

Taron was heaving as if he were the victim here. In this bunker where no one would hear just how loudly Colin was screaming, would Taron become more violent at some point? Colin braced himself for impact, watching his captor's every move. Had he made a mistake? All his life he'd held back on telling people what he thought of them, but even his politeness had a breaking point.

Taron tucked his cock back into his pants and approached Colin with a scowl. When Colin stilled, expecting to be hit, Taron reached for the door and opened it. He pointed to the corridor with a decisive gesture, and grabbed Colin by the arm.

God. No. Was he being taken back to the cage?

Colin hesitated, but when Taron's grip tightened, he left the room, limping along without a word. He didn't want to give the bastard any ideas. Whatever chance for true companionship they'd had in the past was now gone. And rightfully so, because that chance had been built on a foundation of violence and lies.

Colin's throat was choking him, his entire leg hurt from the effort of walking fast, and worst of all—there was cum between his buttocks, which right now felt like a sign of humiliation rather than pleasure.

In the silence, with Taron's grip branding his arm with bruises, the walk itself was torture. They didn't stop by the cage though, which made Colin's heart lighter. Having to be helped up the steep stairs was as undignified as it was uncomfortable, but once above the surface, they headed straight for the porch. New horrors sprung to Colin's mind. Would he be kept in one of the sheds? Those got hot and humid during the day, not to mention how isolating and scary it would be to stay in one at night.

But Taron sat Colin in the cushioned wicker armchair where Colin had been spending many of his days lately.

<Stay,> he signed, as if Colin were a dog, and went back into the house.

Colin flinched when the door shut, but once he was alone, the atmosphere became peaceful, leaving just his nakedness and the quickened heartbeat as signs of what had just occurred.

The sun reached halfway up his thighs, and when he took his first full breath since the sex had finished, the scents of the forest made him lean back, somewhat calmer despite the shadow of Taron's axe still hanging all too close. Rio opened one eye and peeked at Colin from the corner of the porch where he enjoyed the warmth of sunshine, sprawled over Colin's crutches.

Without Taron present, out of the dark bunker, the world seemed at peace. Rattling inside the house was the only sign that something bad was still going on, and he was sure he wouldn't like what was to come.

Taron came out with a small backpack and some clothes in his other hand. He threw the bundle of fabric into Colin's lap and pointed at the bag.

<Food and water.> He leaned over to Colin and pulled on the collar so abruptly Colin expected a shock, but instead, he heard a click, and the metal band was off his neck. Taron threw it into the grass without even looking where it had fallen. His eyes were reddened when he signed. <I want you gone. I don't care if you tell the cops. I had a good life here on my own, and you broke me. You wrecked everything. Go. You're free. Go to a fucking doctor. I don't care.>

Colin stared at him, unsure if he understood Taron right, but he didn't dare ask. His neck was uncomfortably light without the weight of the collar, and in the shadow of Taron's accusatory stare, he felt so small and insignificant he might have as well been a speck of dirt. He said nothing, watching in disbelief as Taron slammed the door behind him and left him alone.

The collar was off.

Colin was free.

CHAPTER EIGHTEEN

Colin was glad his leg hurt, because the constant ache caused by the wooden brace rubbing against skin was providing him something to focus on other than the never-ending corridor of green and brown. Branches reached far above the path, trying to grab him, but his brain remained focused on the damp mud filling the deep grooves of tyre tracks left by Taron's car. His crutches and feet kept slipping on the uneven ground, so each movement needed to be perfectly executed if he didn't want to fall and cause further damage to his leg.

Sweat had built up all over his skin, making him crave water, but he was determined to trudge on, because it had been late in the afternoon when he'd left the homestead, and he had no idea how much longer it would take for him to reach the asphalt road. If he couldn't make it during daytime, would it be safer to walk or lie down somewhere in the grass? He had no flashlight and no phone. He had barely anything beyond the sparse provisions and clothes that were way too large for him.

He was starting to fear that the brace had rubbed his

flesh raw under the sweatpants, but it wasn't like he had anything to dress the new wound with anyway, so he chose not to look.

With his attention focused on the slippery road, he had no choice but to see the tyre marks left like crumbs for him to follow.

Colin stilled when one of the crutches skidded on a small rock, forcing him to stiffen his body in order to remain standing, and a low sob left his throat when he thought back to the warmth of the porch and to Rio playing with the straps of the backpack following Taron's departure. Colin had stayed in the chair, naked and shocked, for minutes, because his brain kept telling him that Taron wouldn't have let him go. That it was bound to be a cruel joke to taunt him.

But Taron had never come back, so Colin did the only logical thing to do—he dressed in whatever was provided and headed for home. Anyone would have grasped that opportunity for freedom, yet after three months of isolation from the outside world, he was freaking out.

Even the fucking collar around his neck had given him a sense of stability, of belonging. Released from it, he was floating in an endless sea of choices. What would he say to authorities or to his parents? He'd told Taron he hated him, but he wasn't sure if he wanted to report Taron to the police. His brain was mush.

The crutch slipped again, and he cried out in frustration, slamming it hard against the nearest bush as soon as he regained his balance.

"Fuck. Fuck you," he screamed at the top of his lungs, looking around the forest bathed in warm sunlight. There was no one to hit back at him, and the sense of emptiness this caused made his heart squeeze as if an invisible hand were trying to rid it of blood.

Fucking Taron. How dare he play with Colin's mind like this? He wasn't supposed to be nice. He was supposed to be a monster who mistreated his victim until Colin managed to flee. But no, the fucker had somehow twisted Colin around his finger, made him feel like there were advantages to the situation. It had all been lies. If someone's pet needed medical attention, the proper course of action was to take it to the goddamn vet. Surely, Colin deserved the same treatment! And likewise, a wounded dog that barked because it was helpless and scared shouldn't be just sent away the moment it stopped being playful.

What the fuck. What the actual fuck?

Colin's eyes stung, and he squeezed them shut, hugging the crutches as his entire body throbbed, itching for release of the tension that had been building up inside him for the past two weeks.

If anything, Taron should have been grateful he'd finally gotten laid. Just like Colin *should* be exhilarated by his upcoming freedom, yet all he wanted to do was cry. He'd never been such an emotional mess. Even in the first days after his abduction, he'd cried for hours, but his situation then had been clear enough. Now? He was angry at Taron for... what? Letting him go? Wasn't that what Colin had wanted from the beginning?

The problem was that the freedom ahead came with pain, and noise, and people asking him questions. With exams, a future to think about, and guys who he only cared to meet if their dick measured more than six inches. Whatever happened, Taron wouldn't be a part of that future, and neither would the bunker, the physical work that gave Colin peace and meaning, nor the comfortable silence.

He sobbed when his leg twitched but went on, focusing on the road ahead. He'd woken up from a very long dream, and it was time to face reality. He just wished the future could still hold Taron's arms around him. Which was pathetic, but he was done making excuses for his emotions.

He hated Taron. But even more, he hated that hurt look in his green eyes when he'd tried to confess his love a second time. Colin should have been happy he'd managed to wound the monster, but he couldn't bring himself to feel any satisfaction from Taron's pain and just sobbed again.

No matter how illogical it was, he felt like he was leaving behind a part of himself that could never be recovered. A part that made jokes that weren't mean, that liked getting up in the morning without hitting the snooze button ten times in a row. The person who felt truly comfortable with himself despite the collar, the lack of internet, and the absence of his family. The person who didn't consider cuddles a waste of time and liked watching stars at night while a cat sat in his lap and a heavy arm weighed down his shoulders. The person who felt like he was *enough*.

Colin stilled when his eyes blurred over. The crutches were cold, hard, too thin, but they were the only friend he had, so he clutched them to his chest, wondering if all the tears spilling down his face would end up in dehydration.

He stilled at the hum of an engine behind his back. There was just one person who could be driving from that direction. Had Taron changed his mind? Colin's brain was saying 'hide!', but his whole being craved to be found and taken back to the man for whom he was the center of the universe. The man who'd told him he was perfect the way he was, and who didn't hold back mocking Colin's lack of survival skills just to endear himself.

Shame curled at the pit of Colin's stomach, and despite

the pull dragging his mind toward the noise, he turned around and resumed his trek, shoulders aching the moment he rested his weight on the crutches again.

But the vehicle was faster than Colin, and soon enough he could sense the weight of Taron's gaze on his nape, like a rope tightening around his neck to haul him back. The sound of the motor was like the purr of a pleased cat, but Colin refused to acknowledge it in any way.

Taron drove past him, but then stopped the pickup truck across the road and got out. If he expected having to fight Colin, he would be pleasantly surprised. Colin was too exhausted to resist.

Taron seemed refreshed when he approached Colin in the dying sunlight. The button-up plaid shirt only made him more of a hunk, and his groomed beard said *I care what people think*, not *I murdered a man on this road three months ago.*

He stopped in front of Colin with a strangely neutral expression. <You shouldn't be walking. Get in the truck. I'll take you home.>

Colin swallowed hard, clenching his hands on the handles of the crutches, desperate to keep his face in the shadow. He knew he looked like a mess with flushed, puffy cheeks and red eyes, and he didn't want Taron to see him in such a state.

He was so pathetic, but the offer to be taken back made his chest pulse with warmth, and he couldn't help it. Maybe he had Stockholm Syndrome by now. Maybe he was weak or stupid. But the offer made so gently broke his will.

If Taron took him to his bed, would Colin's other barriers break as well? Would he be the obedient pet again and never ask for anything forbidden, just so that Taron didn't have to refuse him?

Not trusting himself to talk, he just shrugged.

Taron wrapped his arm under Colin's to help him move, and the gesture alone made Colin release another sob. Taron was so warm, so big and steady he could have stopped the whole world from crumbling on Colin's head. He didn't mock Colin's tears, or act angry anymore.

He led Colin to the pickup truck, and helped him into the passenger seat. Colin couldn't contain his relief. Since he'd fractured his leg, Taron's support was something he'd grown as accustomed to as having two hands. He would pick it over all the hot bodies in the world.

Colin bit his lips to hold in another sob when Taron shut the door and walked around the vehicle. The backpack was his safety net, and he held onto it as if without it he were at risk of drowning.

Taron took his spot behind the wheel and started driving down the narrow road without as much as a glance at Colin. At first, Colin was sure they would drive to a spot where the path offered enough room to make a turn toward the homestead, but after they passed two wider parts of the road, he was beginning to get antsy.

He wiped the sweat and tears with his forearm and peeked at Taron, trapped in his indecision. He spotted his driver's licence in the cup holder between the seats. He picked it up in shock and stared at a face he barely recognized, even though the photo had only been taken two years ago.

His pulse quickened so fast he was feeling it under his jaw. "Where are we going?"

<Home,> Taron signed.

Something passed ahead, and Colin froze, realizing they were approaching the asphalt road he'd been trying to reach all along. He looked through the window at the back of the truck and helplessly raised his hand, pointing toward the homestead. "But..."

Taron stopped the car to communicate. <Your home. I shouldn't have let you go on your own. I'll take you home. Then, you'll do what you feel is right.>

Colin knew he should've been overjoyed. But he felt no happiness at the prospect of seeing his family, staying in his room, or even getting to see that new *Avengers* movie. Taron's words were a punch to the chest, of the kind that could stop a person's heart, and in this moment Colin didn't feel far from it. As his mind blanked, going dark at the edges, Colin leaned into the seat, not trusting himself to answer. A numbness spread through him, and the confines of his own body were far worse than the cage had ever been.

Taron waited half a minute, or forever, but then started the engine and drove onto the asphalt. The crunching under the wheels was too loud, the air in the car—too stifling. Nothing felt right. Colin's leg hurt again, and he regretted yelling at Taron earlier even though at the time he'd meant everything he'd said.

They remained silent as Taron joined the afternoon traffic and passed the first signs of civilization. Houses, mail boxes... Colin wondered whether Taron had one. Did he even have a bank account? Surely, he had to if he owned a car and property, but Colin couldn't bring himself to speak and sank deeper into the seat as they drove into the very town he'd intended to pass through on his alternate route home. It seemed so long ago that he could hardly believe his past life had been real, even though it was his relationship with Taron that had been the mirage.

Road lights and power cables were such an abominable sight, crisscrossing the sky like an ugly spider web intended to catch people and suck energy out of them bit by bit. The

cars passed at far greater speeds than he considered reasonable, and for once he wondered what would have happened
if Taron got into a serious traffic accident while running
errands. What would have become of the cats? And what of
Colin, trapped in the woods that had by that point become
his wall-less jail?

And if Taron did go to prison for the abduction and
murder, would Colin be allowed to take care of his animals,
or would the state take them away? He glanced at Taron
when they stopped at a gas station by the road. Blue neon
light illuminated Taron's beard, even slipping through his
longish hair to create strange patterns. Everything about the
plastic flashing sign with the gas prices felt too crisp, too
real. The world in which Colin had lived in for so long was
now alien, and he could only hope that the feeling would
pass at some point.

Colin glanced toward the store and colorful candy he
knew would feel too sweet on his tongue after eating a
wholesome diet of organic vegetables and meat sourced
from their own little farm. His hand darted to Taron's
forearm and squeezed it. "I won't tell anyone."

Taron gave him a long, indecipherable look before
leaving the pickup. If he was such a monster, why did Colin
care what Taron thought? The guy was evil. He'd
murdered. He'd locked Colin in a cage. He didn't need or
want to hear Colin's thoughts.

Colin bit his lips so hard they went numb, and wouldn't
let Taron out of his sight as his captor filled the tank and
then made his way into the shop. And as if Colin were
Taron's guardian angel, a commotion started the moment he
briefly averted his gaze. Yelling he couldn't work out
reached his ears, but Taron was already leaving the small
building with Tom McGraw on his tail.

Colin sank lower in the seat, in case McGraw, who held a grudge the size of the Grand Canyon, recognized him and turned Taron over to the authorities. The two men moved between parked vehicles, Taron leading the way with an expressionless face and McGraw hissing at him like a vicious animal. A woman fueling her car followed them both with a shake of her head, but other than that there was no one else to witness the exchange.

Colin evened out his breathing, hand resting on the handle, in case he needed to intervene and support Taron, but the driver's door opened and Taron stepped inside. He sat behind the wheel and drove off with his wheels squeaking against asphalt. McGraw threw a half-empty can of soda at the pickup, but other than some of the drink landing on the back windshield, that was that.

They headed for the highway Colin had avoided all those months ago.

~~~~~

The cul-de-sac where his parents lived felt like a place from another planet. The greenery here was only of the kind that had been carefully chosen, and the picture-perfect facades of homes, each with a double garage and red mailbox at the front, felt strangely uninviting. Taron didn't want to park right on front of the house, so he stopped nearby, behind a large bush that obscured the car on Colin's side. It was already dark, and in the nearest window, Mrs. Mitarashi was serving dinner to her family. It wasn't a common occurrence in Colin's home, because both his parents worked at the hospital, and synchronizing meals was nearly impossible.

Not that he minded. More often than not, he'd

preferred to eat on his own, in his room, where no one would bother him or criticise the fact that he was watching a TV show while chewing through dinner.

He'd never missed TV when eating with Taron.

Taron turned to him with a low exhale. <If you do decide to go to the police, you have to promise me the cats will be taken care of.>

Colin's throat closed, and he stared back into Taron's eyes, which in the low light looked like two wells leading straight to the centre of the world. "What are you talking about? I won't go to the cops!"

<You might change your mind in a week or two.>

Colin wanted to protest, but the familiar shape of a woman walking past the car across the empty road made him stall. His mother was in her favorite jeans and a white T-shirt, the wavy hair with a texture just like his, pinned at the back of her head. His heart skipped a beat when he noticed a fluffy dog following her on a lead.

The sight of the creature had him lean back while the cogs in his brain jarred, struggling to adjust to all the new parts that had just been added to the mechanism. It was as if years had passed, not months since he'd been gone, and he felt more upset that she'd gotten a goddamn dog than that she hadn't noticed him yet. But then again, he was the one still sitting in the truck instead of running toward her. What was wrong with him?

"I didn't know they got a dog," he whispered. "What is that? A Pomeranian?"

Taron's head turned her way, but Mom was already walking back home. He shrugged, leaving Colin to twist his fingers with uncertainty.

It was a quiet neighborhood, and at this time of the evening—deathly quiet, but for some reason the silence in the car felt more comfortable than the peaceful air that awaited Colin outside.

"You think she got the dog to pick herself up after I was gone?" Colin tried again.

Taron sighed. <Maybe. You're worth much more than a dog, Colin.>

Colin swallowed hard and clutched at the fabric of the oversized pants. "I don't know. Sometimes I feel they didn't really want to have me, and that's why they let my grandparents raise me until I was old enough to meet their expectations."

He rarely expressed those ideas in any way, but in the quiet of Taron's car, with the one man who seemed to think that he didn't have to become anything other than what he was in order to fulfill his purpose, he let out his darkest thoughts.

Taron didn't say anything, but he listened. He didn't look away, or interject. He always took in what Colin was telling him. So Colin let it all flood out of him, because this was his last chance to do so.

"I didn't even choose to be a doctor, but my dad wouldn't accept it if I wanted a different career path. I was always good at studying, and since I didn't have anything in mind, I chose my electives accordingly. I always played it too safe. Even now, when I think about going in there, I'm panicking that my dad will just say I disappeared to evade responsibility for a couple of months. I never really felt like they loved me. When I was a kid, I convinced myself they had to, as my parents, but I never really felt it," he choked out the last words, but whatever he believed about his parents, it was obvious Taron wanted him to leave, so he frantically opened his seatbelt, choking on the sob pushing at his throat. When had he become such a softie? He was ridiculous and had no control over his emotions--something that would surely be a stain on his future life. And now, he was unloading all this on a man who shouldn't have to care about Colin's meaningless family drama when his own was long gone.

"I just think they had a kid because that's the thing to do. And they support me, because that's another thing you do. Just like I'm studying, because that's the thing to do if there's money to pay for it."

His life was such a swamp, dragging him down the moment he stepped into it again.

But it was time to cut the cord and leave his abductor, because that was another *thing to do*. No one in their right mind would have stalled.

Taron reached out to Colin and grabbed his hand, but when Colin froze, torn between running off and letting himself be recaptured, it occurred to him that Taron passed him something. He opened his palm and saw a rabbit paw on a leather string.

Taron signed to him when Colin looked up. <For luck. It was supposed to be for your birthday.>

Colin's lips twitched, and he stared at the gift, at loss. "But... we didn't speak to each other," he said helplessly, clutching the item in his hand. It was imperfect, with crude stitching. Taron must have made it himself.

<I hoped we would be by the time your birthday came.> Taron took a deep breath and ran his fingers through his hair, his sun-damaged skin touched by a ray of light coming from outside.

Colin rubbed the paw with his thumb. Wasn't that the thing to do for luck?

This was the moment to leave, and he should be removing his toxic presence from Taron's car in order to reclaim the life he deserved, but his body was numb around a heart throbbing with loss.

"I'm sorry about your family. I know what you were trying to tell me. I didn't mean to be so harsh. It was just... the situation," he said, pathetically prolonging the inevitable for a few more seconds. He'd been so cruel to Taron, lashed out, yet Taron still brought him here, to a place Colin no longer considered home.

When Colin put his hand on the door handle, Taron pulled on his arm again.

<I know you hate me, but... if something awful happened in the world, if you needed shelter, you can come to my bunker, okay? No strings attached.>

He might have as well put Colin's heart into a meat grinder, because for once all Colin wanted was for the world to end around them and leave them with no ties to anything outside the bunker. If Yellowstone really did blow up, he'd have the perfect excuse to never leave Taron's side.

He leaned in, eyes fixed on Taron's, and the need to be close to him again became so overwhelming that the cul-de-sac and reality melted away, leaving them in a dark pickup truck.

Breathing in the scent of soap and wood, he put his hand on Taron's knee and moved it up his thigh, overcome by the need to taste him, even just this once. Would Taron trust him to do that away from the homestead, the cage, and the collar?

Taron's breath hitched, but he didn't move away. Instead, he placed his fingers over Colin's. For a moment, they both stayed still, waiting for the other to move, but when it became clear Taron would not take initiative this time, Colin moved his hand to the front of Taron's pants, rubbing the familiar shape of Taron's dick.

He loved how thick it was, and what Taron could do with it, but at this point Colin only cared that it was Taron's and that he needed to have it in his mouth.

He pulled down the zipper without looking away. Taron swallowed loudly and stroked Colin's shoulder. He was such a piece of man, yet Colin's need for connection was way beyond lust. He craved to never leave this car and never have to make a choice. A state of permanent limbo where he sucked on Taron's cock forever sounded like a plan.

His own dick was reacting to the sudden change of atmosphere when he slid Taron's jeans lower and took his cock out. Still soft, it was warm, and smooth, and so lovely Colin wished to wake up to it every single morning. Their final act would happen without words, because Colin couldn't possibly make a coherent sound, so he cupped Taron's balls and rolled them in his fingers while he leaned forward, their eyes locked.

Neither of them spoke, and yet Colin understood the depth of Taron's emotions, without words. Even if he still worried Colin could've been out for revenge, he didn't care, which made the memory of the sex they'd had earlier even more sour. Where Colin had tried to detach himself from feeling anything, Taron had been there with him, with his heart on his sleeve—skinned and bleeding.

Colin wanted to say sorry, but it was too late now, so he communicated his feelings the only way he'd learned. He still feared Taron would reject him, but when he pumped Taron's dick and buried his nose in the soap-scented sac, Taron's thighs tensed under him, his hips rising to meet Colin, who tasted the smooth skin with a small lap first.

A shudder went through him, and he closed his eyes. Giving blowjobs had been routine in the days before Taron, a quick and easy fix of sex. Never before had it actually meant something.

With Taron, this was so much more than gorging himself on dick.

Licking the underside of Taron's thick cock was hot, sucking in the head—even more so, but the emotion that overflowed within Colin was about much more. He didn't just care about his own pleasure. He desperately craved to communicate how much he cared for Taron, how he wanted to be good to him, and give him even the things he hadn't asked for. He wished he had more hands and tongues to touch all of Taron at once, but he did whatever he could to caress, squeeze, tug, lick, and suck all the sensitive spots he could reach. When he suckled on Taron's balls, keeping the pressure low so it would all last longer, his hands played with the dick and drew circles on the inner side of Taron's thighs.

And when his lips kissed the tip of Taron's cock, drinking up the saltiness of his pre-cum, his entire being longed for this to never stop. He worked his tongue around the head and sucked all of Taron's length into his throat, opening up despite the discomfort that came with its girth. This was his last chance to let Taron know that their odd relationship meant something to Colin, and that he would never be forgotten.

Taron tangled his fingers in Colin's hair but didn't press or pull, just caressed Colin's scalp. His moans were subdued, but as Colin bobbed his head, feeling beyond safe between Taron's legs, the twitching of his cock told Colin that the orgasm was coming, and no matter how much Colin wanted to prolong this moment, Taron was already reaching the edge. His firm thighs kept tensing under Colin faster and faster as the rhythm of their connection increased. Colin squeezed the base of the cock in his hand and focused his attention on the head. He needed to taste all of that hot cum. Just this once, it would be kept warm in his mouth and then drizzle down his throat so he could keep Taron with him that bit longer.

Taron made a strangled grunt when he came. Colin greedily swallowed, sucking on the cockhead until there was no more left. Taron was still gasping for air, but their time together had to come to an end, and Colin needed to remove himself from the car.

From Taron's life.

He'd never been so unhappy.

With Taron's warm taste still lingering on Colin's lips, he sat up, struggling for breath as his lungs refused to accept any more air. Colin took his hands off Taron and rubbed his shoulders, looking out at the fake normalcy of life that awaited him.

Taron squeezed Colin's hand. For a few seconds, he just watched him, but then leaned in for a kiss, grabbing the sides of Colin's head. He was a fast learner, because since their first kiss, Taron's first ever kiss, his lips had become Colin's addiction. A day hadn't gone by without a make-out session somewhere. Taron put all of his passion into their locked lips, but it only prolonged the agony of having to leave the truck.

Colin broke it off, gasping loudly the moment he was back in his seat. The darkness provided just enough light for them to see each other, and he was ashamed that Taron was seeing him with the twisted features, once again so near tears Colin couldn't trust himself to speak.

So he signed. <I love you.>

<I thought you hated me,> Taron answered without a

smile. He wouldn't blink, as if he didn't want to lose even half a second of Colin's presence.

At loss, Colin exhaled, struggling to explain it himself, but eventually he settled on, <I'm stupid. I was angry. I'm sorry I hurt you.>

<I understand your life is out here, but if you wanted to visit sometime-->

Colin leaned forward and took hold of Taron's hands, desperate to be understood. "No. I only feel like myself when I'm with you. And if you still want that... please, take me home," he ended in a whisper.

Taron smiled and pulled Colin's hands to his lips for a kiss. He had to let go to sign, but it took ages until he responded. <You're not a liability. I love you. With you, living isn't just about the future collapse anymore. It's worth living now.>

Colin nodded and put his arms around Taron's neck, leaning above the handbrake digging into his side. A sense of peace settled over him the moment Taron held him close, and he rubbed their cheeks together, wishing to mark Taron with his own scent, even though there wasn't anyone trying to take his man away.

Maybe that fucking audiobook had been right. Maybe change was always good, even if difficult.

CHAPTER NINETEEN

Colin's hand was warm on Taron's. It was no longer smooth and soft, like when they'd first met. After weeks of physical work, there were rougher patches on the palm, and even a recent cut that Taron could sense against his skin.

For once, the air was clear of lies, and secrets and with no more words needed to express how they felt about one another, the two of them settled into a comfortable silence. Taron could hardly believe Colin had the choice to go home, and had decided to stay with him instead. Despite all the pain and fear Taron had caused him, despite the fight they'd had earlier, Colin still wanted to stay.

Throughout the drive home, Colin shifted closer, until his head ended up resting on Taron's shoulder, one arm curled around Taron's.

Their life would look different without the collar around Colin's neck. They had to plan for a future together, one that was built for them both. Perhaps they would have to eventually reveal Colin's whereabouts to the authorities, even if just for their peace of mind, but it wasn't something they needed to concern themselves with just yet.

Some parts of Taron were still aching and tender after the hateful words Colin had thrown at him, but none of that mattered if the outcome made him glow with happiness. There was peace in his heart, and knowing that the man he loved felt the same about him would heal any wounds he'd caused. Neither of them was entirely blameless anyway.

Once they drove off the asphalt road and down the familiar path into the woods, he moved his arm to rest around Colin, smiling when he remembered him asking to be taken *home*. They would soon arrive, and Taron would take all night to show Colin just how welcome he was.

Having another person around would mean changes for the homestead, but Taron was more excited than worried about that for the first time. Colin spoke, as if he'd read his mind.

"I wonder if they held a vigil for me at the university. There was this one professor who liked me, so maybe she cared to organize something. I bet the people present would have been a collection of my past hook ups and some people who feel everyone deserves to be remembered."

Taron groaned. The last thing he needed was to hear about Colin's hook ups. He stroked Colin's jaw with his thumb, wondering what else Colin had on his mind. Would he still want to go to the cinema for his birthday? And if he did, would he wear a disguise or just not care about being found?

Colin crooked his neck, arching into the touch like a cat and moved one hand to the middle of Taron's chest. It felt so comfortable to be touched like this, as if they'd never parted or started this relationship on less-than-ideal terms. "We'll need to think about logistics though. I guess there are people who do care what happened to me. Maybe I should just eventually reveal myself and tell the police I wanted to escape from it all. I'm an adult, so I can technically leave everyone in the dark about my whereabouts, even if that makes me an asshole."

Taron snorted. Colin was a bit of an asshole—that much was true. He nodded, eager to keep Colin to himself, for none of his old friends and family to know where he was. Judging by Colin's confession by his parents' house, he wouldn't have too hard of a time convincing him.

Colin shifted in his arms and rubbed the tip of his nose against Taron's cheek, just above the line of his beard. The touch was soothing yet titillating, and Taron struggled to focus on the narrow road. "But I feel best when I'm just with you. Without all that external noise. All in all, I wouldn't mind seeing other people once in a while, but being here opened me up to the idea that this kind of quiet life is even a possibility."

Taron frowned. <Seeing other people?>

Colin blinked, but then his mouth twisted into one of those mean smiles that Taron found so endearing. "You're jealous! That's so adorable!"

Taron nudged him with his elbow, dying to be home already, so that he could fuck all that attitude out of Colin. <No.>

Colin chuckled and started combing his fingers through the long beard. "You want to keep me hidden, so that no one can even imagine putting his hands on me?"

Taron nodded begrudgingly. That would be the ideal situation. Just him and Colin, and their cats.

Colin's arms tightened around Taron, and he gave him a loud kiss on the cheek. There were words still hanging in the air, but it took Colin a couple of seconds to voice them.

"I can't believe I found someone who wants me this much. Sounds like a plan."

Taron also gave Colin a kiss, soothed by the fact that they could finally communicate without the threat of lies, without having to wonder if Colin was playing a game, and without Colin fearing for his life in case he angered Taron. Things have changed between them, and were on the road to a new start.

It felt right, no matter how much Taron had tried to prevent this kind of attachment in the past. He would make their relationship work, and protect Colin at all cost.

They were already approaching the clearing where they lived, but as he focused on the narrowing at the end of the road, Colin stiffened beside him, untangling himself from Taron. "It's someone's pickup."

Fuck. Fucking fuck. Tom McGraw.

Taron sped up and parked his own truck to block the intruder's way. If there was a hair missing off any of his cats, McGraw was going the way of his brother.

<Stay,> he signed to Colin, and jumped out of the vehicle as soon as it blocked the only way out. He left the headlights on, so they illuminated the yard, but their pale glow wasn't enough, and as Taron approached the porch, he regretted that he'd been in so much hurry to catch up to Colin that he'd forgotten to take one of his guns with him. Staying armed and ready was the ABC of living off grid, and he'd failed the test.

The illumination revealed the open door and the first line of trees surrounding the house, but everything else remained in the shadows—a single black mass with no shapes to discern. He was about to grab one of the planks piled by the steps when the car door behind him opened.

Fuck. Could Colin ever listen to orders?

He turned to show him back to the truck, but his blood went cold the moment he saw a shape moving behind McGraw's pickup. The fucker must have heard them approach and made it outside. Taron grabbed the plank without care for noise anymore, and ran back, hoping his rushed movements would be enough of a warning.

Colin stumbled back, unstable with the crutches in both hands. His eyes went wide, his face elongated when he opened his mouth, but he didn't get to turn and assess the real danger.

McGraw's hand was huge and covered Colin's entire throat, squeezing him so viciously Colin yelped and dropped one of the crutches to remove the fingers from his neck.

A heartbeat later, Taron stood still too, clutching at the plank so hard the rough wood scratched his skin. In the ghostly light, the gun pressed against Colin's vulnerable cheekbone shimmered as if it were a prop, not the real thing. But Taron knew exactly what kind of weapon it was and what would be left of Colin's face if McGraw pulled the trigger.

He dropped the plank and put his hands up, still taking tentative steps toward them. His heart was a black hole of fear, and he regretted Colin hadn't left him after all.

He let out a helpless grunt. If only he could yell at McGraw, tell him to let go of Colin, promise some kind of agreement about the land.

"Listen to me carefully, Hauff!" McGraw yelled, the gun all too close to Colin's lovely skin. "Stay where you are or this fucker gets it. And then, you will—"

Something abrupt flashed in Colin's eyes. The remaining crutch rapidly descended and dug into McGraw's shin. Taron's mind blanked when the gun went off, deafening him for a few moments when Colin dropped to the ground, his body moving into a convoluted twist. There was blood on his T-shirt, a red spray that looked eerily bright in the white glow of the headlights.

McGraw stalled, his eyes wide, as if he hadn't meant to shoot. Taron wouldn't wait another second. With a growl he hadn't even known his throat could make, he charged McGraw's way. Grit crunched under his shoes, and he was a one-man stampede when he smashed into the bastard with his whole weight. The gun dropped somewhere, but all Taron cared about were Colin's cries.

As soon as they both dropped to the ground, he clenched his fingers around McGraw's neck, thirsty for blood. The world trembled around him, sharp in its contrast between light and shadow. McGraw's knee went all too close to his crotch, but Taron blocked him, numb to the discomfort of the fist continuously punching at his flank. His brain was fuzzy from the onslaught of questions, and he couldn't focus on the fight without glancing Colin's way.

His lover lay still, a bloodstained hand clutching at his arm, but his teeth were clenched, and his stifled moans were a sure sign of li—

Pain radiated all over the left side of Taron's face and neck, but when he tried to pull away from it, he took McGraw's face with him. Teeth dug into the flesh at his jaw so hard that if it weren't for the beard, the bastard might have been drinking blood already. From the corner of his eye, he saw Colin crawl away.

Good. He couldn't be an equal part of this fight. Not injured. Not ever. Taron didn't want him hurt by the likes of McGraw.

He rolled over, and fortunately, McGraw was a coward. Instead of attacking again, he crawled the other way, gasping for air and choking. Taron pawed at him, dragging him back by the shirt, desperate to finish this, so he could take Colin to the hospital. How much was he bleeding? Had his bone been hit? It couldn't have been a major artery, because Colin would have been done for already, and Taron could still hear him move, even through the noisy gasping right next to him, or the crunching of leaves and dirt.

McGraw punched his side again, in the very moment when Taron's muscles relaxed, and the pain in his vulnerable ribs turned everything red. He struggled for breath, pushing on top of his opponent, but his gaze only met McGraw's for a split second before something collided with the side of Taron's head.

The world spun, and the unexpected stab of pain bubbled up until it filled his entire skull, pressing on the bone from the inside. The loud cry might have been Taron's, but he dropped into the dirt, paralyzed by the sense of dread that came with the loud thudding in his ears. A shadow rose from the ground right in front of Taron's face, menacing in the way it just loomed in silence. But before McGraw could have struck again, a gurgling noise and the creak of breaking wood snapped him out of his stupor.

Taron managed to roll to his side, still frenzied after the blow to the head, when McGraw dropped next to him like a log. Blood was foaming up in the twisted lips, but when McGraw tried to speak, his eyes wide and fixated on Taron, all that came out was a gurgle.

In Taron's hazed mind, all was still a blur, but he grabbed at McGraw's neck weakly, desperate to fight, to protect Colin. His hand went still when he realized where the blood was coming from. A pitchfork stabbed through McGraw's neck in two places, pegging him to the ground.

Above them, Colin heaved, supporting his weight on the wooden handle of the tool.

When Taron looked up and saw the deer-in-the-headlights expression on Colin's face, he kneeled over McGraw's body, and as the man tried to rise, Taron grabbed his head and twisted it with a final snap. He didn't want Colin thinking the murder was just his doing.

McGraw went limp, and the homestead was once again peaceful, with the only sounds coming from the forest and the gentle hum of the nearby pickup.

Colin took a deep breath and stepped back, taking his hands off the murder weapon as if it burned him. His legs gave under him, and he landed on his ass, watching the fresh corpse from between his spread legs.

"Shit," was all he said, going from flushed to so pale Taron worried he might faint.

Taron was still dizzy when he got up but shielded Colin from the gruesome sight. <Let's go inside.>

Colin drew in a sharp breath and looked up with a forlorn expression. He'd mentioned that he'd seen dead people, but it was a different thing to see someone who was already dead than witness their violent demise. Or be the cause of it for that matter. He raised his hand to Taron, wordlessly asking for help.

Taron kneeled by his side, and when Colin struggled to move, he picked him up, wary of the blood dripping down Colin's arm. As soon as the gunshot wound came into view, Taron wished he could have killed McGraw all over again.

Colin cuddled up to him, as if touch was exactly the thing he needed. "I killed him," he whispered, staring toward the lifeless body that Taron wanted as far away from him as possible.

He walked to the open door to the house with Colin in

his arms. He wished to soothe his lover, but words wouldn't come out even as he tried to whisper, so he settled for a kiss.

The smell of gasoline hit him before they even entered the house and Taron stopped on the porch with a scowl. Colin stiffened in his arms, and pointed at two canisters right beside the wicker chair.

"Where are the cats?" he asked, twisting in Taron's arms as he tried to stand on his own again.

Taron snarled. No matter how much he loved his pets, Colin's wound was a priority, but the stubborn boy wouldn't listen and limped inside, so Taron followed his lead. The cabin stank of gasoline and once the lamp was on, the dark stains on the floor were a clear indicator of where the fuel had been spilled. There was no cat to be seen, so all must have hidden somewhere upon McGraw's arrival, but when Colin limped toward a little nest built for Missi and her kittens out of an old basket, he found all of them were cooped up inside, under a gray blanket stained with gasoline.

Colin rubbed his face, his teeth pulling over his pretty lips. "No. I take everything back. I will not be agonizing over this bastard's unworthy life," he said, and only the presence of the kittens must have prevented him from slamming his hand on the closet right next to the basket, because he halted halfway through the movement.

The kittens shivered by their mother, releasing tiny noises of distress. Taron couldn't believe what McGraw had wanted to do. Colin's reaction was something new, though. Colin wasn't exactly a Sunday church boy, but hearing from him that he understood some people didn't deserve to live filled Taron with pride.

<I hope he rots in hell,> he signed when Colin glanced over his shoulder.

For a moment, Colin contemplated this, his throat working. "What will we do with the body? This can't be traced back here."

<Your arm first.> Taron swallowed. <Hospital.> It wasn't convenient, to say the least, but Colin needed help, and Taron never again wanted for Colin to think he didn't care. The issue of trusting Colin to not go to the cops about the murder and kidnapping was long buried as well. <I will tell them it was self-defence.>

Colin met his gaze, breathing more evenly now, though he kept blinking, as if there was sand under his eyelids. "No. It's too risky. You can't afford a decent lawyer."

Taron swallowed and looked away at that blow. <I'll work something out. Let's go.>

Colin's chest started working faster, and he grabbed Taron's forearm with the healthy hand. "No. They might start digging and find out about his brother. This is," he swallowed hard and stared at the blood-soaked sleeve, "It's a flesh wound."

Taron stalled. <You don't want to go to the hospital?>

Colin took a deep breath and tentatively pulled up the sleeve, revealing red-stained flesh and a ragged wound left by the bullet. "Can you see two holes or is the bullet still inside?" he inquired, taking a deep breath and presenting his arm to Taron. It was a relief to see both the entry and exit wound, and as Colin moved all his fingers with little issue, his body gradually relaxed.

"No. We'll deal with this on our own."

Taron pulled out a gasoline-stained chair out for Colin. He smiled and stroked Colin's sweaty hair. He'd found a most precious gem in the deepest mud, and he would never let go of it. He leaned down for a kiss.

<Together.>

EPILOGUE

In the three years since Peter McGraw's death, Colin had left the homestead a total of seven times. Three times to celebrate his birthday with something special, once to inform the police that he was in fact alive and not at all lost, once to visit the livestock market, once to go to a prepping conference, and once to go to the dentist. He was all for living off-grid now, but he wouldn't lose a tooth for the sake of principles when the apocalypse was still a distant concept.

Colin switched off the gas stove and pulled the tray of mason jars layered with cut apples and spices closer. He used a ladle to pour the boiled water with vinegar and sugar into the jars and then screwed the lids on before turning each container upside down. Once this was done, he faced his German Shepherd mix, Zeus, and the dog made a puppy-like squeak when it saw a piece of apple in Colin's hand.

But Colin found himself salivating too when he glanced through the window. Taron was wearing a woolen hat Colin had made for him last winter, but the hard job of chopping wood must have made him so hot he'd taken off his jacket and stayed in just the T-shirt. Watching him being proficient at stuff never got old, but chopping wood was Colin's particular favorite. Taron's chest expanded when he lifted the axe and his arms tensed when he brought it down.

He absentmindedly gave Zeus the piece of apple, but the pie Taron had baked before must have cooled down by now, and since Colin wasn't an asshole who'd just steal some and eat on his own, he cut two pieces, put on his sweater and left the house with a wide grin. Sugar wasn't often on their menu, so this was a treat to cherish.

Zeus followed him outside as soon as he swallowed his treat and joined his two sisters, who played in the grass close to their master. The three dogs—then still puppies—had been a surprise for Colin's birthday, only weeks after he'd decided to stay with Taron for good, and they had proven to be excellent companions. With twice the workforce Taron decided to purchase a couple of goats, and they since produced their own dairy, becoming even more self-sufficient. Three years on, the homestead was Colin's life, and he didn't mind it in the least, especially that with a new viral disease killing commercially-reared cattle by the thousands, he and Taron could feed themselves in the peace of their little world.

"I think you deserve a break," he said, approaching Taron with the pie.

Taron smiled and put down the axe, eager for the treat. He was still their main cook, and organized the jobs needed around the home. Despite Colin once claiming that he was a fast learner and could master prepping in a matter of months if given the right books, Taron always had some knowledge up his sleeve to surprise him with. On the other hand, Colin had made their health his job, and had

managed to outlearn Taron in terms of herbs, natural reme-
dies, minor surgery, and also made sure he had all the equipment necessary.

    <Thank you. It's gonna be a long winter, so I want to get
a head start with the wood.>

    They sat on a bench carved out of a thick tree trunk,
and Taron watched Colin take the first bite, eager for praise
like Zeus was for a treat. The pie was fantastic, with just the
right level of sweetness, and a surprising hint of rosemary.

    Colin smiled at Taron and gave him a peck on the lips
before pushing closer.

    He liked it that they only had each other. Whatever
scuffles happened on the way needed to be resolved in one
way or another, and because there were no other people
around, both of them were supremely motivated to make
things work. Or perhaps it was just that they were a perfect
fit. Either way, Colin never felt tempted to flirt with anyone
else or seek other company during the few times he was
away from there.

    As time passed, unfamiliar people became more of a
nuisance, with their petty problems and lack of focus
caused by the informational avalanche of the outside world.
In the woods, he and Taron could live in peace, focused on
things that mattered and unbothered by distant issues they
couldn't do anything about.

    They ate in silence, enjoying the view of yellowing
leaves dropping from the trees one by one. Colin had never
known such peace before making this place his home. Even
though he'd considered Taron's prepping crazy at first, out
here, in the forest, he'd grown to feel safe knowing there
was a massive bunker under their feet where they could
hide if the world around them crumbled. Preparing for that
possibility was now a way of life, so Colin had learned to

make provisions the same way he'd learned to use a shotgun.

They sat together for a few minutes after they'd finished the afternoon snack, but there were only so many hours left until dusk, so Colin gave Taron a kiss and stood, returning to the kitchen. The chickens likely wouldn't lay any eggs in winter, and while they could always buy some in the winter months, Colin no longer wanted to leave his future to chance. So maybe the apocalypse wasn't coming yet, but with all those cows dropping dead, who could reassure Colin that chickens wouldn't be next? Not to mention that the cost of eggs could increase, since people needed to get their protein somewhere if they couldn't have it in the form of a steak.

He'd used the goat butter of their own making to grease some of the eggs and preserved others in salt, to use in the winter. It was his first year doing this, and while Taron didn't make any comments, Colin knew he was proud.

One piece of civilisation that Taron kept up with was the radio. Not the kind of radio that played the latest hits and revelled in gossip about celebrities, but the kind that kept them up to date with news of weather, and in touch with the group of preppers Taron was acquainted with. The fact he'd never told Colin which guy he'd had radio sex with was still a thorn in Colin's side, but he'd find out sooner or later. Most of the time, the radio frequency stayed silent with breaks for regular updates in case of storms or the like, so it came as a surprise when it suddenly made noise while Colin was busy cleaning the plates.

"Taron? Colin? Over." The voice belonged to Gus, a guy who liked to keep everyone informed, which made him useful even if he sometimes peddled too many conspiracy theories. Colin always got a bit giddy knowing that Taron had introduced him to the others with pride. As his partner, no less.

He wiped his hands on the apron and picked up the mic. "This is Colin. What's up?"

"Colin, don't wanna be scaremongering, but I'm pretty sure this is it. Shit's hit the fan."

Colin rolled his eyes. "Like that time you said there was an EMP coming because the locust were acting weird?"

Gus exhaled, making the connection crackle. "One can never be too careful. But that's beside the point. I am serious right now. They were just talking on the news about it. The quarantine center in Dallas is full."

Colin frowned, but his heart was already beating faster. "The quarantine center? What are you talking about?"

"You two haven't been out of the woods for the past week, have you?"

A horrible, twisting sensation curled over Colin's insides, and he sat down on the nearby chair. "No."

"Good, stay where you are. Have the radio on twenty-four-seven. The cattle disease seems to have passed to humans. The government's just admitted to covering that up in the last two weeks. They advise staying indoors until they declare it's safe. Over a thousand people have already died, it's mental out here."

Colin swallowed hard, and he hovered his hand over the console. "Thanks, Gus. We'll report to you at the usual time. I'll let Taron know."

They said their goodbyes, and Colin walked to the door on strangely heavy legs. They had been preparing, but deep down he never really believed their efforts could prove life-saving.

The infection in Dallas could still be contained, but the transmission to human hosts did not bode well.

He walked down the porch and toward Taron, who looked over his shoulder, standing straight when he spotted Colin's expression. <What is it?>

Colin spread his arms and combed back his hair, not sure how to communicate what he'd just found out. "It's not Yellowstone."

Taron frowned with the question in his eyes, and Colin let his hands drop. "People are dying from that cow disease. Something's happening. Maybe we should... bug-in."

Taron nodded and leaned down to give Colin a kiss. There was no 'I told you so' or excitement in him, just cold determination.

<I'll get the animals inside.>

Colin squeezed Taron's hands and looked into his eyes. "I'll take the food downstairs."

They took a moment just looking at one another, and the exchange brought Colin peace. He didn't need to be afraid. Taron had been right all along—Colin was safer here than he would have been anywhere in the world.

They both were.

The end

THANK YOU

Thank you for reading *Wrong Way Home*. If you enjoyed your time with our story, we would really appreciate it if you took a few minutes to leave a review on your favorite platform. It is especially important for us as self-publishing authors, who don't have the backing of an established press.

Not to mention we simply love hearing from readers! :)

Kat&Agnes AKA K.A. Merikan
kamerikan@gmail.com
http://kamerikan.com

MORE CRIMINAL DELIGHTS

Thank you for reading a CRIMINAL DELIGHTS novel.

For more deliciously dark tales, visit:
http://criminaldelights.com

Each novel can be read as a standalone and contains a dark
M/M romance.

BOOKS IN THE SERIES:

K.A. Merikan
Wrong Way Home
Alex Jane
Devil Next Door
Katze Snow and Tiegan Clyne
Only the Devil Knows
L. A. Witt
Blood & Bitcoin
GB Gordon
Match Grade

Tal Bauer
Splintered
Michael Mandrake
Love Kills
Leona Windwalker
Beloved Possession
Sean Azinsalt
It's in My Blood
J.M. Dabney
By Way of Pain
Dora Esquivel
Hunters and Killers
M.D. Gregory
Sinner's Ransom
Michelle Frost
Cold Light
Abigail Kade
To Have and to Hold
Rorie Kage
His Final Curtain
Emma Jaye
Sweating Lies (Lies #1)
Emma Jaye
Splitting Lies (Lies #2)

CRIMINAL DELIGHTS NEWSLETTER

IF YOU'RE INTERESTED IN NEWS ABOUT THIS
SERIES, CONSIDER SUBSCRIBING TO OUR
NEWSLETTER

http://criminaldelights.com/newsletter/

HIS FAVORITE COLOR IS BLOOD

– WHEN LIFE GIVES YOU BLOOD, MAKE MAYHEM. –

Grim. Assassin. Leather-clad sex god. Has the most unusual taste in men.

Misha. Mutilated. Afraid. Will never trust again.

Grim is a bloodthirsty killer, and he owns it. Gay in a world of outlaw bikers, he firmly stands his ground if anyone dares to cross him. He takes pleasure in showing homophobes their place and fucking his way through a life of carnage.

But there is a part of him always aching for something he cannot get. When by chance he saves the most perfect guy he's ever met, he is not about to let him go. Even if it means he needs to smother his broken bird.

When a masked, bloodstained man rescues Misha from captivity, he doesn't know if he should thank the menacing stranger or stab him and run. Grim is not the kind of man who takes no for an answer, and Misha might now be in more danger than when he was trapped as a sex slave.

Misha cannot deny though that Grim is as alluring as he is frightening, and once Misha realizes what power his body holds over Grim, he understands that taming the beast of a man could be within his reach. But any possibility of a future together is like a house of cards when Zero, the sadistic crime lord who destroyed Misha's life, sets out to get him back.

Will the ruthless biker assassin at Misha's side be enough to conquer the monsters from his past?

Themes: Outlaw motorcycle club, organized crime, assassin, chase, disability (amputee), devotee, revenge, redemption, kidnapping, road trip, fear, hurt/comfort

Genre: M/M dark erotic romance, thriller

Length: ~110,000 words (standalone novel)

WARNING: This book contains adult content that might be considered taboo. Strong language, violence and torture. Reader discretion advised.

Get on AMAZON.

AUTHOR'S PATREON

Have you enjoyed reading our books? Want more? Look no further! We now have a PATREON account.

https://www.patreon.com/kamerikan

As a patron, you will have access to flash fiction with characters from our books, early cover reveals, illustrations, crossover fiction, Alternative Universe fiction, swag, cut scenes, posts about our writing process, polls, and lots of other goodies.

We have started the account to support our more niche projects, and if that's what you're into, your help to bring these weird and wonderful stories to life would be appreciated. In return, you'll get lots of perks and fun content.

Win-win!

ABOUT THE AUTHOR

K.A. Merikan are a team of writers who try not to suck at adulting, with some success. Always eager to explore the murky waters of the weird and wonderful, K.A. Merikan don't follow fixed formulas and want each of their books to be a surprise for those who choose to hop on for the ride.

K.A. Merikan have a few sweeter M/M romances as well, but they specialize in the dark, dirty, and dangerous side of M/M, full of bikers, bad boys, mafiosi, and scorching hot romance.

FUN FACTS!
- We're Polish
- We're neither sisters nor a couple
- Kat's fingers are two times longer than Agnes's.

e-mail: **kamerikan@gmail.com**

More information about ongoing projects, works in progress and publishing at:
K.A. Merikan's author page: http://kamerikan.com
Patreon: https://www.patreon.com/kamerikan

 facebook.com/KAMerikan

 twitter.com/KA_Merikan

pinterest.com/KAMerikan